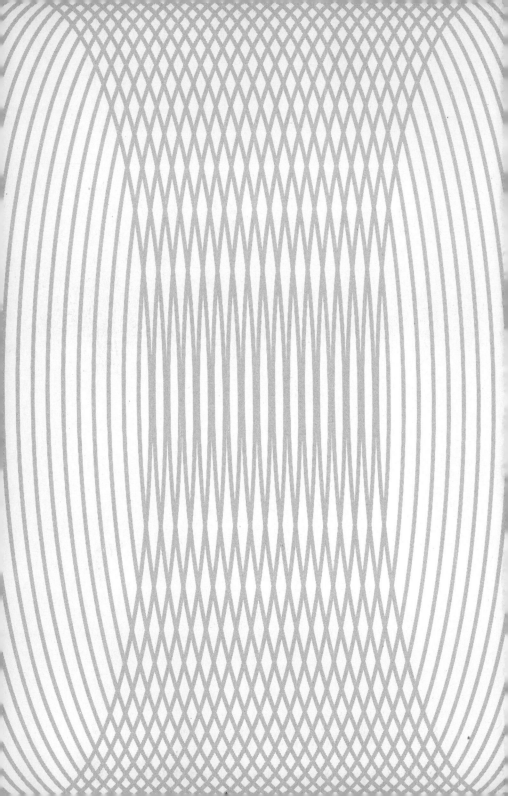

THOMAS TAYLOR

SCHOLASTIC INC.
New York

Text copyright © 2013 by Thomas Taylor

First published in the United Kingdom in 2012
by Chicken House, 2 Palmer Street, Frome, Somerset BA11 1DS.
www.doublecluck.com

Library of Congress Cataloging-in-Publication Data

Taylor, Thomas, 1973–

Haunters / Thomas Taylor. — 1st American ed.

p. cm.

Summary: Three boys, separated by generations, are linked in their ability to time-travel using their
dreams to appear, ghostlike, wherever and whenever they choose, but when Eddie, the first
dreamwalker, is targeted by Adam, a dream-terrorist, novice dreamwalker David must stop him.

ISBN 978-0-545-49644-5

[1. Time travel — Fiction. 2. Adventure and adventurers — Fiction. 3. Secret societies — Fiction.
4. Ghosts — Fiction. 5. Dreams — Fiction.] I. Title.

PZ7.T21865 Hau 2013
[Fic] — dc23

2012024406

10 9 8 7 6 5 4 3 2 1   13 14 15 16 17

Printed in the U.S.A.   23

First American edition, June 2013
The text type was set in Caslon.
Book design by Christopher Stengel

For Penny and Tim

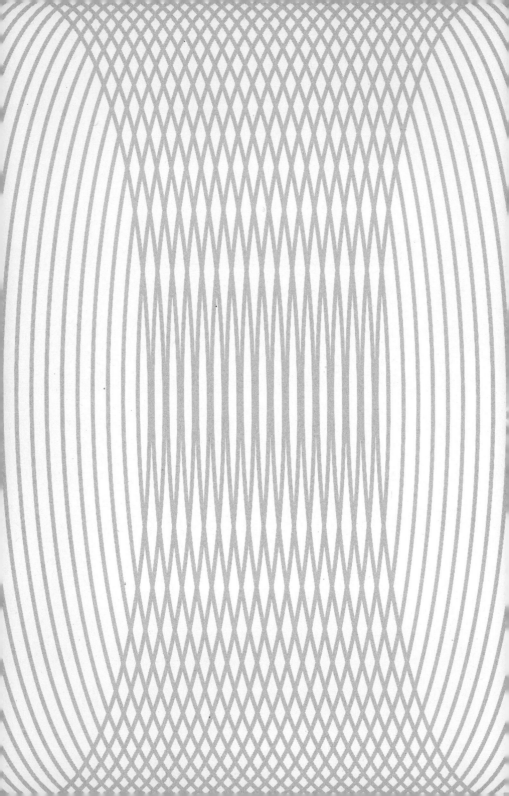

THE DREAMWALKER'S CODE

1. *Be seen, but not noticed.*

2. *Talk, but don't tell.*

3. *Leave no stone turned.*

CHAPTER · 1
UNSLEEP

David crouched on the roof of his best friend's house as the flames that consumed it leaped into the night sky. He couldn't even remember how he'd got there, let alone work out why. But as another chunk of roof collapsed in an eruption of fire and sparks, there was really only one question worth asking: Was Eddie still inside?

And unfortunately, there was only one way to find out.

Scampering up to the chimney stack, David peered through the heat and smoke. The roof at the far side of the house was a great gaping hole with fire towering out of it. He'd never get in that way. So how? *Think!*

Then, as he blinked in the glare, he realized he wasn't alone. A slim figure was calmly watching him from the far edge of the roof, even as flames flickered around him.

"Eddie?" David shouted. "Eddie, is that you?"

A bank of smoke rolled past, obscuring his view. When it cleared, David could see that the figure was a boy of about his own age. But it wasn't Eddie, it was . . .

David stared in astonishment. He was looking at *himself*. Even the clothes were his own.

He rubbed his eyes — this was no time to be seeing things. But then, as he looked again, the details began to change, melting away as more smoke drifted by, and the figure revealed itself to be a stranger after all: a tall, dark-haired boy in his late teens.

"Who are you?" David yelled. "Where's Eddie?"

The boy laughed, throwing his head back.

"You're too late!" The boy's voice was full of triumph. "If you're here for Eddie, Davy boy, then you're far too late."

"What do you mean?" David couldn't be sure he'd heard right; the fire was creating a wind of its own that roared in his ears. *"Who are you?"*

But the boy just laughed again. Then he turned and leaped straight off the roof.

David skidded to the edge and looked over. The garden, four stories below, was outlined in firelight. There should have been a broken body down there now — no one could survive a fall like that — but there was nothing. He looked out into the night at the houses beyond the garden, but all he could see was the silhouette of a black cat running along the far roofline. That was when he noticed that Eddie's place wasn't the only one burning.

Smudges of amber punctuated the horizon in every direction, picking out the dark shapes of chimney stacks and church towers right across the London roofscape. It looked as if the whole city was ablaze.

And the noise was terrible. Beyond the roar immediately around him, there was a tangle of sirens and crashes, and even sounds that could have been the drone of planes and the *stut-stut* of anti-aircraft guns, if David hadn't known better.

A neighboring building suddenly collapsed, snapping him into action. Forget the sightseeing, forget the strange boy — he

had to find Eddie. Impossible to get in through the roof, so . . .
a window?

As he slid his way toward the dormer window farthest from
the fire, David had a brief, dizzying glimpse of the street far
below and what might have been firemen. But he was moving
fast now and couldn't be sure. With a single fluid motion he
found himself crouching in an attic bedroom. Only it wasn't
Eddie's.

"Eddie!" David shouted. "Eddie, where are you?"

No reply, just the steady rumble of the fire. He had to
go farther into the house. He ran out onto the landing and
looked down.

The stairs were burning. A large piece of plaster had fallen
from the ceiling, covering the top flight. Everything above that
was blazing, but, though it was hard to be sure through the
glare, it looked as if the landing outside Eddie's room was still
intact. And Eddie's door was closed. But what did that mean?

Farther down, there was only a raging inferno. The whole
house had to be just minutes away from collapse.

"*Eddie!*"

Still nothing.

David hesitated then. He was taking an insane risk coming
this far into the house. Surely Eddie must have escaped by now.
And if he hadn't, if the fire had already got him . . . *No!* The
thought that Eddie might be dead made David sick inside.
Somehow he just knew he was still alive, that in some strange
way saving Eddie was precisely the reason he was here, no matter how weird that sounded. He looked down again and noticed
that the chunk of plaster on the stairs was propped against the

banister, leaving a protected space beneath it just big enough to crawl down.

David swore. "You're going to owe me for this big-time, Eddie," he said, bracing himself.

With a shout he ducked under the plaster and slid down to the next floor. It was hot there, hotter than anything he'd ever experienced. Without thinking, he burst free and ran for the door, his eyes firmly shut, desperately willing himself into the safety of Eddie's room. So desperately, in fact, that he forgot the door was closed. How odd, then, that he should suddenly find himself staggering to a halt inside Eddie's room anyway, the door still shut behind him.

"Eddie!"

"David?" croaked a voice from the darkness. "David, is that you?"

David squinted. The details of Eddie's room were hard to see, though light beyond the window picked out the brass of his old-fashioned bedstead. The room wasn't on fire, but the heat was crushing and the smoky air so oppressive that David was amazed he could still breathe.

There was a movement from the floor near the window. David saw his friend, slumped over, wearing a coat and clutching a satchel.

"Eddie! Why are you still here? And who was that on the roof? No, tell me later — we've got to get out, and I mean *now*! The building's about to come down."

In reply, Eddie lifted a battered notebook. Despite the gloom, David saw the words *Can't get out* written large across the page, surrounded by a riot of scribbles and crossings-out. Then Eddie burst into a round of choking coughs.

"I'll break the window! You need air!" David said, but Eddie waved the notebook at him again in sudden alarm.

Can't break window — air feeds fire!

"Eddie, this is no time for writing!" David shook his head in disbelief, even though he knew Eddie was right about the air. Eddie was always right about things like that. "Get up! There's a safe way to the roof, but it won't last."

"Yes, but David, you're . . ."

Eddie broke into another dry coughing fit as he struggled up. He seemed to be seriously ill. David couldn't understand it — why *was* Eddie in such a bad way when he himself was more or less fine? For a moment he felt that there was something he should have noticed — a feeling he often had with Eddie — but it was gone before he could fix his mind on it. Besides, Eddie had been breathing in smoke for much longer than him. No wonder he could hardly talk. David ran to the door, and Eddie stumbled behind him.

"David . . ." said Eddie, trying to point at something else he'd written, but David interrupted him.

"Later. When we open this door the fire will come into the room, okay? Keep low and follow me, but be quick!"

David grabbed the doorknob.

It wouldn't turn.

His fingers slipped around it without any grip whatsoever.

But hadn't he just come through here? He let go and swore, but before he could try again, Eddie had reached out a weak hand and opened the door.

"It's because you aren't —" Eddie began, but stopped as a wall of heat burst in, causing him to cry out in pain.

"That way!" shouted David over the roar, and he pointed to the gap under the fallen plaster. *"Go!"*

Eddie cried out again and jumped forward, scrabbling up the stairs in a desperate tangle of arms and legs. David was close behind.

The house gave a sudden groan, and a large chunk of ceiling came crashing down into the stairwell behind them. Eddie dragged himself out onto the top landing, sobbing with pain. His hair and coat were smoldering, and his glasses were cracked and smudged with blood and soot. He still had his notebook rolled tightly in one hand.

"In there!" said David, pointing to the attic bedroom.

The house groaned again and shifted as the lower walls began to crumble. Inside the attic room, Eddie slumped to the floor once more. The window was firmly closed.

"But I just came through here!" cried David. "How can it be closed?" He grabbed the latch, but as with the doorknob below, he just couldn't turn it.

"Stop pretending!" Eddie gave a desperate shout. "I know this is what you wanted. You're playing with me . . . waiting to watch me die."

"What?"

"I hate you!" cried Eddie. "You've killed me!"

"But . . ." David was shouting himself now. ". . . I'm trying to save your life, you idiot! *Both* our lives."

"You knew this would happen . . . somehow. You got me back here to burn!" Eddie raised himself off the ground in fury and waved the crushed notebook in his fist. "I thought I could trust you. But Kat warned me — she knew. She said you'd want to make me like you in the end. Why didn't I listen? You're a . . . a *monster* . . ." But the coughing stopped him there.

"Eddie, shut up! Look around you — the window . . . We've got to *get out now!*"

But in reply Eddie snatched up a narrow beam of smoldering wood that had fallen from the ceiling.

"Get away from me!"

David's mouth gaped in astonishment as Eddie swung this crude weapon around at him. He fell back, dizzy, and heard the window shatter.

With a tremendous pulse of heat, the fire surged into the room.

Eddie threw himself at the window. He grabbed the sill and dragged himself through it, ignoring the shards of glass. As David struggled to his feet, Eddie turned in the window and looked right into his eyes.

"I hate you! I never want to see you again!"

Then he was gone.

David stood there in shock. What was Eddie talking about?

There came a dreadful sound from the stairs behind him — the noise of tons of masonry on the move.

David got to his feet, hardly noticing that the floorboards beneath him were shrinking fast. The fire in the room beneath licked up between them, turning the air to light. Time seemed to slow as the groaning of the walls increased.

He had to get out. He tried to run, but his feet felt like lead.

The house gave a shudder and then the floor gave way completely. David just had time to cry out as he was sucked down into the raging heart of the fire.

CHAPTER · 2
THE HEADACHES ARE
THE WORST PART

David sat up with a cry and threw back the sweaty bedclothes. His heart was racing. That dream again. But — no, not exactly the same dream. A sudden spasm of pain through his temples made him cry out once more. He looked at his phone on the bedside shelf. It was 5:02 A.M.

"Oh, great!" There was no way he'd get back to sleep now.

David swung his feet onto the ground and massaged the sides of his head. He'd had a nightmare. He hadn't had one of those for ages, not since . . . well, not for ages. But did it mean something that his Eddie dream had been involved? Nightmares happened if you ate too much cheese, didn't they? David didn't even like cheese.

"Could've done without all that, Eddie."

David stood up and felt his head throb again. A nightmare and a headache too. What a way to start the day. It was cold in his room — the heating hadn't switched on yet — so he grabbed a blanket, wrapped himself in it, and stepped out onto the dark landing. He stood, listening. Had he really cried out loud? Had anyone heard him?

There was a *click* from the door across the landing. David saw the glitter from dozens of stickers catch the dim streetlight as his little sister's door opened a crack.

"Whatcha doin'?"

"Nothing, Phil — taking a pee. Go back to sleep."

Philippa peeped around the door as if she was talking to a friend who might become an enemy at any moment. She guarded her room like a fortress.

"She'll know if you've been in the kitchen," she said.

"I'm not going to the kitchen. Go back to bed!"

Philippa's door closed.

David waited for a moment and heard the faint rustle of his sister's enormous duvet, then silence. There was no sign that his mum had heard anything, so he had that at least to be thankful for as he crept downstairs to the kitchen.

The floor was icy cold. David poured out a glass of orange juice and sat on a high stool, lifting his bare feet into the blanket. One of his mother's tattered old books was on the bar, but he pushed it aside without interest. He sat there for ages, trying not to look at the clock.

David had been dreaming about Eddie for well over a year now, but nothing like this had ever happened. It was weird. No, what was really weird was having these bizarre dreams in the first place. David didn't think dreams meant anything, but sometimes he couldn't help wondering. Surely it wasn't normal to meet a complete stranger in a dream and then go on meeting him almost every night, until it actually felt like he'd become a close friend. Okay, some kids had imaginary friends, but since he'd just turned fourteen surely he was far too old for all that.

No, it was only a dream, and now it had turned into a nightmare. And who was that other boy, the one with the wicked laugh who had seemed to just vanish into nothing? The whole thing had been different this time. Perhaps that meant the dream was finished for good. David hoped so, until he realized that would mean never seeing Eddie again. Then he didn't know what to think.

"Stupid dream," he muttered, sipping the chilled juice from his glass. His headache was still bad but seemed to be clearing. "Stupid Eddie."

"I thought so," came a sudden, hissy voice from the kitchen door, and Philippa walked in. She was wearing her purple bathrobe and an irritatingly smug expression. "Give me some too."

"Some what?"

"Cake."

"I'm not eating anything, Phil. I just can't sleep, that's all. Go back to bed."

"Because of Dad?" said Philippa. She hopped up onto the stool next to David and gave him a look. David found his sister's looks difficult to return — she always seemed to know more about how he was feeling than she should.

"No. It's got nothing to do with Dad," David said. "I had a bad dream, that's all."

"Was it *the* dream?" said Philippa. "Why didn't you say? That's got *everything* to do with Dad. It started when he died."

David sighed. Why had he ever told Philippa about Eddie? She never forgot the slightest detail and was forever coming up with theories about him. She was the kind of person who believed that dreams were full of symbols and hidden meanings.

"Was it different this time, then?" said Philippa as she jumped down to fetch the cake tin. David could tell there was no way she was going to bed now.

"Look, Phizzy, just leave it. I don't want to talk about it. Okay?"

"He was my dad as well," said Philippa, digging straight into the whole cake with a tablespoon. "If you're getting something about him, I want to know it too."

"What do you mean, 'getting something'? Don't start all that again."

"David, dreams can tell us about how we really feel. You never cried enough when Dad died, so the sadness is coming out another way. It's obvious," Philippa said, showering her brother with crumbs in the middle of the last word.

David couldn't help smiling. Phizzy was the most irritating person on the planet, but she was still his own little sister — noisy, yes, and always smelling of sugar, but somehow he didn't mind her talking to him as much as he made out. And she was the strongest link he had left with his father. *Their* father.

"Phil, you haven't told anyone about my dream, have you? It's just that, well, they're saying things at school again. About me."

"David, I'll never tell anyone. Never!" Philippa said, and in such a way that David had to believe her. She was looking at him with her biggest eyes. "It's a special thing, too special to be told. It's our secret. I mean, a *real* secret. Eddie is your dream friend."

David winced. He'd been close to changing his mind about the cake, but hearing Eddie's name spoken out loud and in such a childish way made him cringe with embarrassment.

"Just don't tell anyone, yeah? Don't talk about it."

"I won't," said Philippa. "Not even to Mum."

"Especially not to Mum!!"

"Though she'd understand, Davy," said Philippa, examining her sticky spoon. "She'd love to hear that something's still happening with Dad. She might be happier if —"

"Happier?" David almost laughed. "If you tell her any of this, you'll just set her off again."

Philippa narrowed her eyes at him, the spoon stuck firmly in her mouth.

"At least Mum showed her feelings," she mumbled, "unlike my idiot, tough-guy brother."

"Just keep it to yourself, okay?" David snapped.

"But why not tell her?" said Philippa, waving the spoon. "You aren't the only one who misses Dad, you know."

David slammed the lid back onto the cake tin.

"There're nearly two hours to go before you have to get up, Phil. So why don't you take that cake to bed and read one of your stupid books?"

To his surprise, Philippa seemed to like the idea.

"I can always blame you when Mum finds the pan empty," she said, and she hopped down from the stool, grabbed David's glass of juice, and drank it all in one gulp.

"G'night," she said. "Or good morning."

"Whatever."

David watched his sister cross the still-dark kitchen to the door. She had a teddy bear tucked firmly under one arm. David recognized it as one his dad had once given him, but that was a long, long time ago. As he expected, his sister turned at the doorway in order to get the last word in.

"Davy?"

"What?" said David with a tired voice.

"These weird dreams you've been having? Have you tried asking *Eddie* about them?"

"Oh, go away, Phizzy!"

Five minutes later David crept back to his room and got dressed. There was no point in hanging around the house until school, so he decided to go out on his bike to blast away his sore head for good. At this time in the morning the roads would still be pretty clear and the air fresh.

He wasn't supposed to go out on his own in the dark, but there was no way he was going to be kept locked up any longer, especially since these days his mother probably wouldn't notice anyway. And wasn't the *teen* in *fourteen* supposed to mean something? He did take his phone, though. Just in case Mum got up earlier than expected.

It was freezing outside and gray-blue, with the dawn barely begun in the eastern sky — a typical autumn morning in suburban London. There weren't many people about, and those he saw were wrapped up in their own business, getting into cars or walking to catch trains. David didn't pay them much attention as he shot out into the street on his bike and raced down the road.

Phil and her stupid theories! She really did think Eddie was some kind of dream symbol of their father, despite the fact that their dad had been a healthy soldier named Richard, not a sickly bespectacled boy named Eddie. And Dad had had light, near-blond hair, whereas Eddie's, like David's, was dark brown.

Altogether, if Eddie resembled anyone, it was David himself. But it wasn't like looking in a mirror or anything. David was slim like Eddie, but also wiry and strong. And Eddie had an old-fashioned way of dressing that must cause him a lot of trouble at school. Except that Eddie didn't seem to go to school. And then there was all the writing . . .

David stopped the bike with a squeal of brakes. He was doing it again, thinking about Eddie like he was a real person. But Eddie didn't exist — he was just a figure from a dream, a made-up boy. Yes, the dreams were very vivid, and yes, when he had them he never realized that he was only dreaming. But now, wide awake and standing in the middle of the road as the rush-hour traffic was about to start, David told himself once again to get a grip.

He kicked up the pedal and raced off again. A van pulled out behind him. He cycled hard for a while and felt the last of his headache clear. Then he became aware that the van was just rolling along behind him even though there was plenty of room to pass. He looked back.

The van sped up immediately. The windows were dark, but David knew that anyone inside would be getting a clear view of him as the van eased past. It turned left and vanished from sight. David cycled on, but when he turned the corner himself he saw that the van was just rolling along again, exactly as if it were waiting for him. So David changed direction. He rattled down a flight of concrete steps, dodged the dumpsters down a back alley, and then zigzagged his way around some posts and back out onto a road. In no time he was jumping onto the sidewalk of his own street.

And the van was parked right outside his house.

David rode his bike down the covered passage to the yard and then dumped it in the shed. When he let himself in, his fingers fumbled with the keys. Stupid Eddie! Stupid dream! And now he was getting paranoid.

He flopped into an armchair and nervously sat out the rest of the time until school, trying to concentrate on the television.

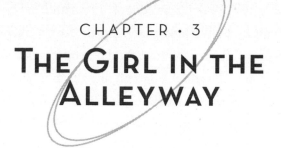

CHAPTER · 3
THE GIRL IN THE ALLEYWAY

On his way to school, David kept a wary eye out for the van with tinted windows. He didn't see it, but at the same time, he couldn't shake off the feeling that he was being watched. He cycled slowly, allowing Philippa to keep up. He'd been worried that she would want to talk about Eddie again, but instead she just gave him knowing looks whenever she caught his eye. He was relieved when they separated at the bike sheds and Philippa ran off to her friends. She was lucky, David thought, as he walked into the building alone.

His first class was physics, which was almost enough to bring back the headache. The teacher droned at the front of the class and pointed to a diagram of something to do with space and time, while David struggled to keep his eyes open.

"Didn't get enough sleep?" said a low voice behind him. David ignored it.

"Dreaming up some new stories about your dad?" said someone else.

David tensed.

"What was he last time?" whispered the first voice again. "Soldier, wasn't it? Or astronaut?"

All around people snickered.

David wasn't popular at school. He could never work out why. Perhaps he should have made more effort at the beginning, but it was probably too late now. And maybe it was his own fault for talking too much about a dad no one at school had ever actually seen, not even the teachers. It hadn't taken some of the pushier kids long to decide he was just dreaming it all up. Either that or hiding the fact that his dad was in prison or something.

There had been real sympathy, though, when news spread that David's soldier dad had been killed on some far-off battlefield. The head teacher had talked about it in front of the whole school, and even the kids who thought David was a joke looked at him with awe for a few weeks. But then someone noticed that he never talked about his father anymore — that he hardly talked at all, in fact. Suspicion returned, and it wasn't long before everything was back as it had been before. Unable to explain how empty his life had become, David found another way to express himself. There were fights, and because David was stronger than he looked, he often won, triggering the perverse logic of all teachers that the winner of a playground scrap is always to blame.

"Astronaut?" hissed someone else. "Nah, you've got to be real to be an astronaut."

David struggled to control his rage. He closed his eyes and tried to concentrate on the teacher's voice.

"David Utherwise! David!"

David jerked his head up and blinked in surprise. The whole class had turned to look at him. One of the school secretaries was standing in the doorway, clearly annoyed.

"David, could you please report to Mrs. Fernley's office," she said, in a way that suggested she'd already said it several times.

The class started jeering, though they did that with everyone when they were called out. But the kids sitting behind him made here-we-go-again noises until the teacher started shouting at them.

David made his way to the door. He couldn't think of any reason why the headmistress would want to see him.

"Have I done something wrong?" he asked the secretary as they walked down the corridor.

"Not this time," she said, raising an eyebrow at him. "There are some people here to pick you up, that's all."

"Pick me up? But . . . where am I going?"

"Well, surely *you* know," said the secretary.

David stared at the woman. There was nothing planned that he knew about, and his mum hadn't left him one of her notes, he was sure of that.

"What kind of car did they come in?"

"They haven't come in a car," said the secretary. "It's an ambulance."

"Not a van, then?" said David after a moment, but the secretary ignored him.

They arrived at the office and David was shown in. Mrs. Fernley was sitting at her desk, and as soon as David saw her gray face, he knew that something was very wrong. For some reason the blinds were closed, leaving the room in semidarkness.

"David, there you are," said the headmistress, her voice shaky. "Your doctor has come in person. Why didn't you go to your hospital appointment today?"

David wanted to say, *Because I didn't have one to go to*, but instead he looked at the woman who was sitting opposite Mrs. Fernley. Her face made David think of sharks, and her simple, chic suit had an unfriendly hint of uniform about it. Then he noticed there was someone else in the room. Standing in the shadows of the darkest corner was a teenage girl. She had white-blonde hair, and from her outfit she appeared to be a nurse, though in the gloom it was hard to be sure. The hairs stiffened on the back of David's neck — it was hard to be sure there was anyone there at all.

"Now, David," said the shark-faced woman, "if you're ready, we'll be going. We've taken an ambulance off normal duties to collect you."

David blinked at her. Then he looked at Mrs. Fernley. "Old Sternley" ruled the school by force of presence alone — she was the kind of principal who could quiet an unruly class simply by entering the room. Yet here she was sitting meekly behind her desk, fiddling with her pen, her head bowed. David was shocked.

"I've just been on the phone with your mother, David," Mrs. Fernley said eventually, her eyes never leaving the girl in the shadows. "She's waiting for you at the hospital."

"You've spoken to my mum?" said David in surprise.

Mrs. Fernley gave a startled nod.

"Yes, so let's not waste any more time, shall we?" said the shark-faced doctor with a sickly smile, and her chair scraped the floor as she stood.

"But I don't have an appointment at the hospital." David stepped back. "Mrs. Fernley, I'm not even ill."

At this, Mrs. Fernley seemed taken by a sudden doubt. She knitted her brow at David as if seeing him for the first time, and for a moment her normal expression of imperious authority returned — something David had never thought he'd be happy to see. She turned back to the doctor as if she was going to question her, but before she could speak, the nurse in the shadows stepped forward. She moved so smoothly it was almost as if she wasn't touching the floor, and she looked at the teacher with furious intensity, her eyes as bright as pins. Mrs. Fernley drew in a sharp breath.

"Everything is fine," the nurse said in a voice like frozen honey. "We are here to take David, that's all. Everything is fine."

Her voice was so persuasive that even David felt everything would be okay if he just went with them, no questions asked. As if sensing this, the doctor put her hand on his shoulder.

It was only as David found himself being propelled to the door that his alarm returned.

"But, Mrs. Fernley," he blurted out, "I don't know who these people are!"

Mrs. Fernley didn't even look his way as she stammered out a reply.

"Try not to forget your hospital appointments in the future, David. Your health is important."

Then David was out in the corridor, being swept along. The woman gripped him under the arm, so far up that he found it impossible to turn and confront her. And perhaps he really *did* have an appointment today — it wouldn't be the first time he'd got something like that wrong. He managed to take his phone from his pocket and began to key in a number.

"What are you doing?" snapped the doctor. Then, in a softer tone, she added, "We don't have much time, David. You can call your friends later."

"I'm ringing home," said David. No way was he leaving school with this woman without hearing from Mum first.

The woman didn't reply, but marched him through the main doors and out to the parking lot, where an ambulance waited. David stopped, planting his feet firmly as he waited for an answer. The doors of the ambulance opened, and a young male paramedic, who could hardly be older than the nurse, leaned out.

At last, his mum picked up the phone.

"Oh, hi, David," she said. "How's school?"

"Mum, do I have an appointment at the hospital today?" David asked, one eye on the paramedic. David saw him smirk as he pressed a button on a console.

There was no reply.

The line was dead.

"It must be interference from the ambulance," said the doctor. "Get in."

But David didn't move. The paramedic stared straight back at him with bright cold eyes, and David found he couldn't look away. He'd seen that devilish smile before. It was the boy he'd seen on the roof of Eddie's house.

He was staring at the strange boy from his dream!

The boy laughed at the look on David's face, and then in a

rush of movement he lunged at him, snatching up a syringe with his other hand.

David reacted instinctively. Before he knew what was happening, he'd used his foot to thrust himself back from the ambulance, knocking the doctor to the ground behind him. The paramedic's grasping fingers missed by a whisker.

"Grab him!"

David leaped up, leaving the doctor winded on the ground, and ran for the school perimeter. He could already hear someone running behind him as he grabbed the bricks and hauled himself easily over the top. He dropped lightly to his feet on the other side and sprinted down the path, ducking quickly into a narrow passage between two houses. He wedged himself behind the trash cans and tried not to move, though his heart was pounding. After just a moment's silence, there was a blur of movement at the end of the passage, and the nurse flashed past, moving faster than he'd have thought possible. He drew his head back, not daring to breathe. It was a full minute before he peered out again.

No one.

David released the air from his straining lungs, but almost immediately he caught movement in the corner of his eye.

Someone was down in the shadows at the other end of the passage, a slim silhouette. She had tangled hair, though the rest of her features were lost in shadow. She was beckoning to him.

"This way, David!"

David kept still and low. Who was she? How did she know his name?

The girl crept forward a little.

"Quickly! If you stay there they'll find you."

"Who . . . who are you?" David called, as loudly as he dared. But the girl didn't reply. She simply beckoned to him again, then shot back down the passage. In a second she'd disappeared out the other side.

Whoever this new girl was, she wasn't the freaky blonde nurse, and right then that was enough for David. He ran down the passage to try and catch another glimpse of her.

Stepping out into the street, David paused on the pavement. There was no one there, not even anywhere to hide. The girl had vanished so completely that once again he found himself questioning what he'd actually seen. Then, far, far down the road, the same tangle-haired head popped out from behind the trunk of a large tree and beckoned to him again.

David stared. How could she have got *that* far in just a few seconds? But he didn't know what else to do, so he sprinted toward her.

David didn't see the van until it had almost knocked him down. It screeched out of a side road and pulled up inches from his nose. The door slid open, and two pairs of black-gloved hands reached out and seized him. He opened his mouth to shout but a piece of damp cloth was clamped over his face. The cloth was soaked in something that filled his nostrils and instantly clouded his mind. He saw dark shapes. He focused briefly on the face of a man in a black visor.

Then the world went out like a light.

CHAPTER · 4
JUST A DREAM

It was a long time before David could be certain about anything again. He had a vague memory of being jostled about and moved between vehicles, and he was pretty sure that he'd been close to an aircraft of some sort. But it was only now, alone in a strange place, that he was fully aware of his surroundings.

He was sitting at an aluminum table in a large room with walls of rough-hewn rock. All around him, wooden crates were heaped up in the shadows. One of them was open, and from a mass of packing straw, something stiff rose into the air. It was a human arm. It took David a panicky moment to realize that the arm was made of stone, and that the crate must contain a statue.

The only light source was a rectangular ceiling lamp hanging above his head, which lit a glass of water and some dry-looking sandwiches that were curling on a small tray on the table. He glanced at the time but saw only a bare patch of wrist. They had taken his watch. He didn't even bother to look for his phone.

On one wall, the rock was so highly polished it was like a mirror. David looked at himself in this for a moment, and saw the fear in his own gray eyes beneath his roughed-up hair.

For a second he wondered if he was dreaming again — it certainly felt like he was in a nightmare — but the ache in his head and his thirst were real enough. So he drank the water, feeling faintly reassured by the slice of lemon in it, but pushed away the sandwiches. He glared defiantly at the black mirror, now certain that someone was watching him from behind it. Shortly after that a door opened.

A man walked into the room. He was tall and bearlike, with a crown of silvered black curls and deep-set eyes. He wore a coarse black coat with its lapels turned up, and looked like some crazy mix between a rock star and a dock worker. Perhaps he was fifty years old, David couldn't be sure. He crossed the room in a few strides and then sat with a grunt opposite David, almost knocking the table over.

The big man nodded slowly. David stared back at him and tried not to show how frightened he was. When the man finally spoke, he had what might have been a French accent.

"So, tell me, Mr. Utherwise, have you ever seen a ghost?"

David, who had been prepared to give nothing away, was so taken aback by this strange question that he blurted out an answer.

"No!"

The big man grunted again, as if he'd been expecting this.

"Incorrect," he said. "Be careful how you answer our questions. We always know when you lie."

"But I never have seen a ghost," said David. "And it's a stupid question."

The man's face hardened.

"It will go easier for you if you are truthful with me now, Mr. Utherwise, rather than forcing us to twist the truth out of you later. Just tell me when you were first approached, and we'll take it from there."

"Approached?" said David. "Who do you think I am? I'm only fourteen."

"Which is kind of the point," said the big man, his face hardening even further.

"I'm not scared of you," David cried out, trying unsuccessfully to stop his voice from going too high. "Who are you, anyway? What am I doing here . . . ?"

The big man brought his fist down onto the table with a loud *crash*, making the empty water glass jump.

"I ask the questions!" he shouted in a bellow that matched his enormous frame. Then he passed his hand through his hair, making a visible effort to calm down.

"If I had my way, you would not be here at all. But since it has been decided to give you a second chance, I suggest you cooperate fully. You might even be allowed to go home one day. So, I repeat the question: When did the Haunting make its approach?"

It was at this point that the door burst open and two more people came into the room. One of them came forward into the light: a thin, elderly man with a scruffy jacket and overgrown eyebrows. He had a bundle of loose papers and books in both arms, a row of cheap ballpoint pens in his jacket pocket, and a half-eaten apple in one hand. He looked so harmless and comical that David was surprised to see him confront the big man at the table with real anger.

"Why have you started without me?" demanded the newcomer. "No one asked my permission to cross-question the boy. I told you this was delicate." After this he switched to French, and a brief argument broke out between him and the big man.

Eventually, the big man stood and left the room, but the way he glared at David told him that he wouldn't be going far away. For now, though, David was just pleased to see the back of him.

The man in the tattered jacket sat down at the table where the big man had been, put his apple in his pocket, and began shuffling his papers, looking at David with a mixture of wonder and concern on his face. Several of his books slid to the floor, and David immediately felt less threatened. The other newcomer came forward and picked up the books but kept in the shadows.

"David Utherwise!" said the old man suddenly. "It's a great pleasure to have you here. I'm so sorry about all this and about . . . well, about what has just happened to you. Roman is under a lot of pressure at the moment, as are we all, but . . . well, we'll get to that soon enough. For now, though, let me introduce myself. My name is Professor Feldrake, and I think it's fair to say that you and I were never supposed to meet."

David watched the professor fuss with his papers. He wanted to protest that there'd been a misunderstanding, but this Professor Feldrake knew his name, so it really was him they were after. But why? Eventually the old man seemed satisfied with his clutter and files. He pulled a pair of antique spectacles over his ears and then sat smiling through them at David. One of his pens, a blue one, was leaking. Finally he spoke again.

"Yes, I really am sorry for all the trouble you've had, David, and for bringing you here like this, but despite how it must seem, you are among friends now. I'm afraid things have just got very dangerous for you outside this place."

"Just tell me where I am and what you want," said David, trying not to be too alarmed by the professor's words. "What is this place?"

"This place is called Unsleep House — the very heart of the Dreamwalker Project. You are currently in Switzerland, near Geneva."

"Un . . . Unsleep House?"

"That's right, though I don't expect the name will mean anything to you right now. As for what we want, well, you need our protection, but at the same time we need *your* help with, er, a little problem we've been having."

David felt his suspicion returning. Was this some sort of trick? Get the thug to rough him up a bit, then send in the nutty professor to be confusing and make him talk? And how could he be in Switzerland? It seemed impossible. He was supposed to have a double period of geography this afternoon, then meet Philippa to cycle home. But was it still the afternoon? Was it even the same day? There were no windows in this dark, stony chamber. Whatever was happening, David decided it would be best to say as little as possible, but unfortunately the professor's next question was so surprising that once again he couldn't help giving an answer.

"David, we know what you dreamed about last night, what you often dream about. Why do you dream about Eddie, do you think?"

David stared at the old man in astonishment.

"But how can you . . . ? Who . . . ?" He jumped to his feet. "There's only one person who knows about that! If you've hurt my sister . . ." he cried, bunching his fists.

Professor Feldrake held up his arms. "Whoa, David! It's okay, really. I know it's a shock, but I promise there's nothing bad happening here. We haven't gone anywhere near your sister, and don't intend to. However, we are very interested in your dream. Could you tell me about it? Please?"

David hesitated. Then he sat down again.

"It's just a dream I have."

"Yes?"

"There's a boy I meet in the dream — Eddie. We just talk and, you know, hang out in his room or mess about on the roof. What do you want me to say? It's just a stupid dream. And you seem to know all about it anyway."

"I know a little, yes. And would you say Eddie is your friend? I mean, putting the dream thing aside for the moment, you and Eddie get on very well, don't you? You trust each other, know each other's habits. Perhaps you're even best friends?"

David glared at the old man. The answer to this question was yes, but at the same time he couldn't forget Eddie's last words to him. You're not best friends with someone if they say they hate you and never want to see you again.

"Putting aside the fact that this conversation is completely crazy, yeah," David said. "You could say we were good friends."

"Were? Ah, yes, of course. Last night your dream was different, wasn't it? Dramatically different."

Professor Feldrake began rummaging through his papers and books, and even the apple made a brief reappearance. Eventually, after much flapping and muttering, he produced a battered old black-and-white photograph and slid it across the table. David picked it up and saw the intelligent but troubled face of a gaunt-looking, bespectacled boy, dressed in a tank top and tie. He went very still.

It was Eddie.

"He's real?" said David after a moment, though somehow he wasn't entirely surprised. After all, his dreams about Eddie had always seemed as real as the day. "I suppose I . . . I must have seen his picture somewhere. Perhaps in a book or . . . I don't know, somewhere."

"Perhaps," said the professor. "It's possible. This is a photograph of a young man called Edmund — Eddie to you — taken in 1940, a year after the start of the Second World War. He was just fourteen years old at the time, like you are now. He lost his father too, in the first months of fighting, though his mother kept it from him for years. Shortly after this photo was taken, the Blitz on London became intense, and in December 1940 Eddie's house was destroyed by an incendiary bomb. Eddie was in an air-raid shelter at the time, but it was still a lucky escape, and afterward he was sent to relatives in the country for the remainder of the war. Does any of this mean anything to you?"

"Why should it? That's all history. What's it got to do with me?"

"Well, this boy's name was Utherwise, like yours, David — Edmund Utherwise. He was your grandfather," said the professor.

"My *what*?"

The professor said nothing, but looked expectant.

David stared back. Then he shrugged. "I don't know a lot about my family," he said. "At least, not my dad's side. But I've never met any of my grandparents, and I'm sure I haven't seen any pictures of my grandfather, so why would I be dreaming about him?"

"To answer that I'd better tell you what became of him," said the professor, who began rummaging again. "But first, what about this man? Do you recognize him?"

David was given a second photo, this time a high-quality color image showing an elderly man with a thin beard who was sitting in a book-lined study, scratching the ear of a Siamese cat. Behind him a great many photographs covered a wall, and there was a neat pile of well-used notebooks at his elbow.

David shook his head as he dropped the photo back on the desk. He was feeling suspicious again and began to wonder how far he'd get if he knocked the professor down and ran for the door. But then he twigged what he was being shown. He looked again at the photos, comparing them. There was something similar about the eyes, the line of the mouth, and the long nose, something that suddenly reminded him faintly of his own reflection.

And he'd have known those notebooks anywhere.

"That's right," said the professor, "they are one and the same. This second photograph also shows your grandfather, Edmund Utherwise — *Sir* Edmund, actually — at the fine old age of eighty-five. He died a few months later."

David began to have a creepy feeling about where all this might be going. This man — Eddie, or whoever he really was — had died quite recently, then.

"So? It's not my fault if my own family never made contact with me. Why should I feel bad about not knowing my grandfather? I didn't even see him at —" David stopped himself. He didn't want to mention his dad's funeral here.

"There's no need to feel bad," said the professor. "I believe you when you say you've never heard of Sir Edmund and his work, but it's time for you to know. The fact is, your grandfather was one of the most accomplished scientists of the twentieth century, but his discovery is so extraordinary that he — and it — are also closely guarded secrets. You see, Edmund Utherwise devoted his life to a practical theory of ghosts."

"Ghosts?" said David, unimpressed. "I don't believe in ghosts."

"Most people don't," said the professor, "and this has undoubtedly helped us keep our secret. But believe me, his discoveries are quite real. The people who tried to kidnap you this morning, the fake doctor and the ambulance crew, they certainly have no trouble believing it. I'm afraid you're caught up in dangerous events now. Whatever you think about how you came to be here, please believe me when I say that *we* aren't the ones who mean you harm. We saved your life this morning."

"But what has all this got to do with me?" said David.

"Well, Edmund Utherwise began his research into the paranormal — into ghosts, that is — after strange experiences he had during childhood. Something happened to him as a boy that left him with an obsession with the spirit world. You see, Sir Edmund believed that he'd been haunted by a ghost."

The professor removed his glasses and gave David a very earnest look.

"And that ghost is you, David."

CHAPTER · 5
A PRACTICAL THEORY OF GHOSTS

David stared. Was this scruffy old man really telling him that he'd had a dream about the past and somehow actually gone there? Become, in fact, part of history? Being kidnapped was bad enough, but being held by a madman was far worse. David jumped to his feet and yelled at the professor.

"You're crazy! You have no right to lock people up and tell them stupid stories. Why should I believe anything you tell me? I just had a bad dream, that's all. It was *just a dream*!"

"There is no such thing as 'just a dream' for people like you and me, David," said a female voice, and David remembered that there was someone else in the room. "What the professor has told you is true," she went on, with what sounded like a German accent. A girl stepped forward out of the shadows.

She was about the same age as David, or perhaps slightly older, and was wearing some kind of black jumpsuit. Above her green eyes and pretty smile, she had a mass of loose brown curls. David was instantly sure he'd seen her somewhere before, and he sat back heavily into his chair when he got it. It was the girl who had called to him in the passageway outside his school. The girl who'd seemed to vanish into thin air. She smiled at him again and held out her hand.

"My name is Petra. I'm a dreamwalker, like you."

"A *dreamwalker*?" David took the slim hand and somehow remembered to shake it. "But what . . . ?"

"What is a dreamwalker?" Petra's eyes danced with amusement. "Well, you know what a *sleep*walker is, don't you? Someone who walks while they are sleeping? Well, I do the same thing while I dream. And so do you."

David stared at the girl, then at the old man, then back at the girl again. They were obviously quite serious about what they were saying.

"But . . . what does that actually mean?"

"It's not as complicated as it might sound," said the professor, in a teacher's manner that clearly came naturally to him. "What do you think a dream is, David?"

"Er . . . I suppose I always thought dreams were just a jumble of stuff from the day. You know, memories and sights and sounds, all muddled together."

"Well, that'll do for a start," said the professor. "On the surface a dream is just that — a mixed-up collection of recent experiences. But doesn't that sound rather boring? I mean, have you never wondered why our dreams are so much more interesting and odd than our actual daily lives? What about those things that *don't* come from your recent experience — the strange people and places that can suddenly pop into your dreams from out of nowhere? Have you never wondered about them?"

"No," said David, "not until now, anyway. Although . . . yes, I did sometimes wonder about my Eddie dreams. They always seemed so real."

"Ah!" said the professor. "Good." He removed his glasses and began cleaning them on his tie. "You see, there's more to what we see in our sleep than just recent experiences being played back in our heads. In a sense a dream is also a *window* for the mind, allowing us fragmentary glimpses of the waking world beyond our skulls. At least, that's the case for most people. For you, though, the effect is stronger — much, much stronger. For you and Petra and others with your gift, that window is more like a doorway, a doorway that allows your mind to leave your sleeping body altogether. We call this dreamwalking."

"Oka-a-a-y." David folded his arms and scanned their faces for some sign that they were making a fool of him.

"All right," said the professor with a chuckle, "we can go into the theory later. In practical terms, what it all comes down to is this: If *I* dream about Stonehenge or the Eiffel Tower or Mount Rushmore, it's all just in my head, okay? But if *you* dream about these places . . ."

David glanced over at Petra. She was watching him as closely as the professor was.

"You're saying I can actually go there?" David said. "But that's crazy."

"It may sound crazy to you now, but that's exactly what I'm saying," said the professor. "At least, your *mind* can actually go there. Your body stays exactly where you left it, fast asleep. Now, earlier Roman asked if you'd ever seen a ghost. So . . . have you ever wondered what ghosts are?"

"Not really. I just thought they were meant to be the spirits of dead people."

"I don't know anything about the dead," said the professor, "but I can tell you that some ghosts at least belong to the living.

You see, that's how you appear when you dreamwalk. Like a ghost."

"But . . ." David shut his eyes for a moment as he tried to make sense of what he was hearing. ". . . my Eddie dream — you said I was back in the year 1940."

"Yes!" The professor's face lit up, like a kid who'd just been reminded it was his birthday. "And that's the real wonder of dreamwalking. Don't you see? It's not just that you can go any*where* you want, it's also any*when*. Freed from the body, your dreamwalking mind can ignore the laws of nature, David, even time itself."

"You're . . . time-travelers?" said David, amazed as the thought finally hit him.

"No," said the professor, the look on his face becoming suddenly wistful. "*You* are. I can only dream."

Petra shifted uncomfortably in her seat. "All this talk! Professor, wouldn't it be easier to just show him?"

"I've already made arrangements for that," the professor replied. "David, you're going to need to accept all this as quickly as possible if you're going to be any use to us. So, what do you think? You've been dreamwalking accidentally for about a year now, but are you ready to do it deliberately? Are you ready to free your mind, to become — in a sense — your own ghost?"

David didn't know what to say, but if these two were playing some trick on him, they were very good actors. And suppose it was true? What the professor had said about Eddie certainly sounded right. The dream-Eddie had always seemed the scientist type — constantly asking questions and never just accepting the answers, writing everything down in those notebooks of his.

His own grandfather! Besides, no matter what was coming next, no matter how incredible it all sounded, there was no way he was going to look bad by showing fear. And he couldn't help liking the way Petra was looking at him.

He nodded. "You said I can be useful in some way. How?"

"Come with me," said the professor, standing, "and I'll show you."

CHAPTER · 6
THE MAP OF TIME AND PLACE

David was led out of the stone chamber and into a wide corridor of metal and glass. People bustled down it purposefully, carrying folders or box files, and one man was pushing a cart loaded with enormous, crumbling leather-bound books, which seemed entirely out of place in the strange modern surroundings. David wanted to ask about this but stopped at the sight of two teenagers running down the corridor. Even the most officious-looking adults stepped aside to let them pass. Both were wearing the same kind of black suit as Petra. But though it appeared featureless from the front, on the back, where the wearer couldn't see it, was a bizarre logo: a sleeping face, with a third, open eye in its forehead.

"What's the outfit for?" David whispered to Petra.

"The science guys call this a 'zero-retention suit,'" Petra said, making a face as she spoke. Then she nodded to the professor, who had walked ahead to talk into a mobile phone. "They love to give things stupid names. What they mean is it's completely plain so that your dreaming mind retains no memory of it. That way, you can easily mask it when you're dreamwalking."

David said nothing, but Petra must have seen the confusion on his face, because she flashed him one of her brilliant smiles.

"Ah, don't worry — it will all be clear soon. And don't be too impressed by any of the science guys, not even the professor. *We* are the important ones here — no one over eighteen can dreamwalk reliably. The adult mind is just too rigid. The science guys would be nothing without us."

The corridor ended in a wide, circular cavern with further metal corridors radiating out of it, some descending steeply while others rose and disappeared into the rocky ceiling. Everything was lit artificially — David couldn't see a single window or skylight. He felt completely disorientated as the professor led him up a spiral staircase and into yet another corridor. Here they headed toward a wide doorway that was lit with a rich golden glow.

The professor hung up and slipped his phone into his jacket. "Tell me," he said to David, "are your eyes sensitive to bright or flickering light?"

David wasn't sure what was expected of him, so he just shrugged.

"Take one of these anyway," the professor said, removing several pairs of sunglasses from his pocket. He held them out to David like a conjuror about to perform a trick. David took the coolest-looking pair, glancing at the light ahead and wondering what on earth he was about to see.

They came out onto a gallery halfway up a vast cavern that rose above them like the inside of an aircraft hangar. The professor produced a big pair of tortoiseshell sunglasses and forced them over his normal spectacles. He walked to the rail and pointed over the edge with a dramatic gesture. David put his sunglasses on and edged forward. When he saw what was there his mouth fell open.

Below them was a wide, hectic workspace, filled with people and oversized computer monitors. There was a strong smell of hot plastic and fresh coffee, and from somewhere in the haze far above David heard the unsteady hum of straining air-conditioning units. Throughout the cavern, men and women sat or stood squinting into the screens, discussing what they saw or bustling about over bundled cables to compare notes on clip pads and pocket displays. The atmosphere was not only energetic, it was slightly panicky, and David couldn't tell if the waves of heat that rose from the room below were from the computers or the heads of the scientists themselves.

At the far end, the wall was made entirely of darkened glass, and David could see nothing through it. The gallery where he was standing ran right around the chamber, following an irregular circle along what was clearly a natural rock wall. There were glass-fronted offices all along it, dug back into the stone.

But it was the thing in the center of the room that made David stare.

Floating in space above a circular dais was a huge sphere of colored light. Its surface was a rainbow mass of swirling shapes, and yet David could clearly see more colors and living swirls right down into the very heart of it. His eyes just couldn't decide whether to focus on its surface or its interior. He couldn't begin to comprehend what he was looking at, but despite this — or perhaps because of it — it was by far the most beautiful thing he'd ever seen. It lit the cavern like a captive sun.

"Amazing!" he said.

"Welcome to the Map Room of the Dreamwalker Project." The professor grinned from behind his retro shades. "When we get to my office, I'll tell you what this means and precisely what we do here, but right now I want you to look at this. What do you think that pretty holographic sphere is showing?"

David looked again at the ball of wondrous light. A hologram? Glancing down, he saw that a group of six people were standing below it, pointing to a small jagged black mark amid the tumbling colored swirls and talking over each other in strained voices. He tried again to focus on the sphere, but it just seemed to be a mass of shifting colored smudges. Breathtaking and fizzing with energy, but meaningless.

"I suppose you want me to believe that this thing shows people's dreams," said David slowly. "Is that what they're all looking at?"

"Not quite," said the professor. "That sphere is the Metascape Map, a four-dimensional hologram charting all possible places and all possible times. You don't need to worry about that right now; all you need to know is that we can use this Map to locate and follow people like you — dreamwalkers, that is. This is how I know about your dream, David. We've been using this Map to protect you, but also to protect a very special young man who was your own age in the year 1940."

"Eddie?"

"Eddie. But while we can bring *you* here safely with us, I'm afraid Eddie isn't so fortunate. In fact, right now there's nothing we can do to help him at all. You see, Edmund Utherwise has disappeared, and we need your help to find him again. Because if we don't, if our enemies find him first —"

The old man seemed suddenly unable to speak, his face becoming grim behind his dark glasses.

"Enemies?" said David. "Wait. In my dream there was a boy on Eddie's roof. I'd never seen him there before, but —"

"Last time you dreamed about Eddie," Petra said, coming to stand beside David, her own eyes protected by a stylish pair of dark glasses, "there was another dreamwalker there. And if the professor can't find words to describe him I certainly can!"

"All right, Petra, all right." The professor stared out at the hologram. "David, the boy you saw was Adam Lang. He is the strongest and most capable dreamwalker we have ever known, and something of a hero to us here at Unsleep House, but —"

"Hero?" Petra spat the word out. "He's nothing more than a traitor and a murderer!"

The professor held up his hand. "Okay, Petra! David, I'm sorry to say that about a week ago Adam Lang decided to turn his back on his friends and his years of good service here. He has gone over to join our enemies."

"The Haunting." Petra spoke the word as though it tasted foul on her tongue.

"Haunting . . . what?" said David. "And why's this Adam after Eddie? What's Eddie done to him?"

"Well, it's not what Eddie has done, it's what Eddie will do when he grows up that Adam's really after. As I told you, Eddie devoted his life to trying to understand the ghostly visits you made to him as a child, and eventually, as an adult, he succeeded. He is the one who unraveled the secrets of dreamwalking in the first place, David, the man who set up the Dreamwalker Project, who built all this."

The professor swept his arm around the vast chamber of light and science.

"But there are other dreamwalkers out there. Some have been banded together in a group known as the Haunting. For them, the ability to dreamwalk is nothing less than the power to change history. They certainly think nothing of destroying lives in order to get what they want. That's why we've had to keep Eddie such a closely guarded secret, and you too, David. But Adam knows everything. We trusted him with everything!"

By now the professor was gripping the rail so tightly his knuckles were showing white.

"And now he's decided to give his new masters what they've wanted for years — the utter destruction of Unsleep House, the only thing that stands in their way — by arranging the early death of Eddie Utherwise."

"So last night, when I saw Adam on Eddie's roof — ?"

"Last night was Adam's first attempt," Petra said. "Originally Eddie was never at home during the air raid that destroyed his house; he was in a shelter when it happened. But Adam changed that part of his history — he *made* Eddie go home. And because he was from the future, Adam knew precisely the moment the bombs would fall."

"*Made* him go there?" David shook his head as he tried to take in what he was hearing. "But Eddie's smart — why would he do something so stupid?"

"Because of you," said Professor Feldrake. "Don't forget, you were his inspiration — you're Eddie's ghost. All Adam had to do was disguise himself as you and tell Eddie to go home, and Eddie obeyed. Eddie was fascinated by the mystery of his ghostly visitor, obsessed by it — he would have walked into an erupting volcano if someone promised him answers."

"Then we have to warn him!" David was almost shouting now. "I have to do this dreamwalk thing — go back and tell Eddie someone's after him!"

"Unfortunately, it's not that simple." The professor's lips tightened. Then he pointed at the Metascape Map, to where the jagged black line marred the rainbow brilliance of the sphere. "See that? It's a change in the time line — the mark of history being altered. You may have saved Eddie from the fire, but afterward he ran away, potentially deviating completely from the original path of his life. What happens to him next hangs in the balance, but the longer he strays from his original history in the year 1940, the greater the danger to us here in the present. Which is why it's so disastrous that we have no idea where he's gone. But that's where you come in."

"Me? What makes you think I can help?"

"You're his best friend, aren't you?" Petra turned her sunglass-covered eyes directly onto him. "Of course you can help."

"But that's crazy! I just had some stupid dreams. How can I possibly know where he's gone?"

"Maybe you don't right now, but you'll probably find that you do when you've given it some thought," said the professor. "Because while Eddie may have seemed a little odd to you, he wasn't just some awkward loner. He was entirely friendless. Edmund Utherwise had a fragile psychology, little understood at the time, and spent his whole disturbed childhood locked away by an overprotective mother. No matter how strange the circumstances of your friendship may seem to be, David, you're the only one who knows the fourteen-year-old Eddie personally. You really are our best hope of finding him now."

David said nothing. There was no mistaking the desperate hope in the old man's voice or the trust in Petra's smile. But he was bound to disappoint them. How on earth could he know where Eddie would have gone? They'd clearly picked the wrong person to help them, after all. It was just a matter of time before they realized it.

"Don't worry." The professor slapped him on the back, apparently mistaking his silence for simple nervousness. "You'll get at least one training run, and help from some of our best dreamwalkers. You won't be going back to 1940 alone. But first there's something more you need to see."

The old man put his arm on David's shoulder and led him along the gallery. David didn't resist. He just gazed deep into the crackling, scintillating sphere of the Metascape Map and tried to imagine where on earth Eddie could have got to.

CHAPTER · 7
LONDON, DECEMBER 17, 1940, 12:10 A.M.

Eddie was hiding.

It was dark where he was, and cold, but he knew that cold was good for burns. He pushed his cheek harder against the icy bricks and pulled his hair to try and focus his thoughts. But he couldn't, not with the sounds of the fire that had just destroyed his home still roaring outside.

You nearly died, whispered the voice of Eddie's doubt in his head. *You were supposed to die* . . .

Eddie shook his head into the bricks, but the voice went on.

Why else would David make you go home during an air raid? And why did he come back, if not to watch you burn? Kat was right . . .

"No," Eddie said aloud. "He helped me. He got me out."

YOU broke the window. You helped YOURSELF. Kat was right . . .

Eddie quickly patted down his coat, which was still smoldering in places, and for one awful moment he thought he'd lost his notebook. But no, there it was, still rolled up in his pocket. He took it out, reassured by the soft paper cover. Squatting down against the wall in a chink of light, he opened the book to a new page. He took out his pencil and started to write.

Q. What do I do now?

No confusing answers inside his head. The question was out now, on paper, ready to be dealt with in proper order in a place the voice couldn't reach. He drew a circle around it. Eddie knew that every question was only the start, but this was as good a start as any. After all, what *was* he going to do now? There was no other choice but to keep writing.

A. Get warm — It's <u>freezing</u>. But...
Q. Am I seriously hurt? Am I still in danger?
Because...
<u>*DAVID*</u>
Q. What do I do about David?

Eddie broke out into a sudden fit of coughing, pain shooting through his lungs with each convulsion. After a moment it passed, but when he put the pencil on the paper again he ignored the question about David and went back up to draw a ring around *Am I seriously hurt?* Then he drew a line off to one side. This had to be dealt with first because everything else depended on whether or not he should see a doctor, especially since blood was smudging the paper as he wrote. But Eddie really didn't want to see a doctor.

He took himself on a quick mental tour of his aches, asking his body for answers. As they came to him he wrote furiously, willing the answers to be good news:

Pain: right ankle — hurts to walk, but nothing broken.

Pain: chest. I breathed in smoke. Lots of smoke.
Hurts to breathe.
Pain: hands and face. Burns. Water good for
burns . . .

Eddie stopped writing. He could actually hear running water. He was under a flight of stone steps by the back basement door of a house at the end of his street, and a thin stream of water was pouring down from the brick arch at the entrance. He tucked the book and pencil under his arm and cupped his hands in the water. It had to be from the hoses of the firefighters — Eddie could still hear the clamor they made as they fought the flames. This reminder of the fire almost made him panic, but the water was so cold when he splashed it over his face that it shocked his mind back into focus. With his wet hand he explored his face lightly, then took up the pencil once more.

. . . burns not serious. Just painful.
Pain: hands — bleeding. Sharp?

Something hard was embedded in the heel of his right hand. He fumbled for it and gasped as he tugged out a sliver of glass. He closed his eyes tightly and shoved his bleeding hand back into the trickle of icy water until it went numb.

Only a fool would make friends with a ghost. Look how much he's hurt you.

Eddie shook his head and dived back into the security of the page. On the list, he circled *Pain: chest,* drew a line away to the side, and crossed out the others. Of all his injuries, this was the only one that really worried him. He would have to take that into account when he decided what to do next, and as if to underline that, another coughing fit engulfed him.

When it had passed, Eddie snatched up his pencil and wrote the first thing that came to him.

Mother?

The word triggered vivid visions of home. He recalled it so vividly that he could almost smell it. How could he even begin to accept that it was gone, confined to the past by a brief moment of destruction? In his mind's eye he saw his room, his books arranged in their proper order, the brown pattern of the wallpaper. He remembered his mother's sad smile as she watched him from the door. He remembered how he sometimes found her crying . . .

Then Eddie saw that he'd written *Father?* without thinking.

He stared at the word for a moment before crossing it out in a smudge of blood and ink. He hated not being able to answer a question, to not even be able to begin answering it. He drew his pencil line away.

Q. What will Mother do?

The answer to this was so obvious that Eddie didn't even write it down. She'd do what she had been threatening to do for months and send Eddie away from the bombing, to live with his aunt in the country. Now that their home was gone, Eddie's mother would surely come too, but even this couldn't make the prospect of his aunt's house appealing, with its stuffy rooms and ticking clocks. Eddie found he'd almost crushed the end of the pencil between his teeth as he thought of her. His aunt was the rich one in the family, and therefore powerful. She also made no secret of the fact that she thought there was something wrong with Eddie.

Doctors. My aunt will make me see doctors.

Eddie drew hard lines through *aunt* that were almost as black as the mark he'd made scribbling out *Father*.

Mother will be safe in the country, but I cannot go.

Then he drew a ring around this and took a line back up to an earlier question:

What should I do about David?

He chewed on his pencil a moment, and then drew fierce lines through most of what he'd written. He circled *David* and then connected it with a new word.

Kat.

Thinking of Kat made Eddie smile, despite the burns on his face. Kat was the one who had warned him to be careful of David. Eddie hadn't listened to her — he'd been too busy probing the mystery of his ghostly visitor — but Kat had cared enough to say something, and now she'd been proved right, hadn't she? Being right was what mattered most to Eddie, and no voice in his head could ever contradict that. He watched his pencil make lazy, affectionate circles around Kat's name. She was a good friend. His mother always said he should be cautious about having friends, that they wouldn't understand him, but Kat didn't seem to have any trouble. He'd kept their friendship secret, though, just in case.

Eddie wrote his own name next to Kat's and connected them with a single neat line. Then he completed the triangle by connecting his name to David's too. At what he judged to be the exact center of this triangle, Eddie drew a fat question mark and started a new line from it that went over to the next page. But what he would write there he had no idea. Not until he'd talked to Kat some more.

And now Eddie realized he'd answered his very first question. What he should do now was go to Kat's place. She would help him work out the rest.

He closed his book, rolled it carefully, and slipped it back into his pocket. He picked up his satchel. Inside he felt the reassuring bulk of a dozen new notebooks, enough to tackle the problems of his world well into the future. Next to them, he knew, were a bunch of pencils in a rubber band, a sharpening knife, a flashlight, glue, stamps and string, and a dozen other things he'd need. He pulled the satchel over his shoulder tight and safe.

Eddie slipped out into the smoke and dark to find Kat.

CHAPTER 8

THE MUSEUM OF THINGS THAT WEREN'T

Professor Feldrake's office was off the gallery and just above the wall of dark glass David had noticed earlier. It gave a clear view down into the Map Room below and had the word DIRECTOR on a sign at the door.

Except for the green of a very elderly computer screen on the professor's desk, the office was lit only by the shifting light of the hologram outside. The room was a chaotic jumble of files, books, and even flaking scrolls. The walls were almost entirely covered by shelves, which sagged with leather spines, framed photos, and myriad antique objects from all ages of human history. There were so many teetering stacks of printouts on the floor that there was barely space to walk.

"The professor still believes in paper," Petra whispered to David.

It looked for a moment as if the old man was going to ask the girl to leave, but he eventually waved for them both to enter. At the far end of the room a pair of ornate wooden doors — entirely out of place in the modern architecture — stood closed. The professor took an enormous ring of elaborate metal keys from his desk and began sorting through them.

"There's something I still don't get about all this," said David, looking around at this Aladdin's cave of an office and watching the shifting light of the hologram pick out the strange shapes within. "If what you've told me is true — this whole time-jumping, dreamwalker thing — why don't people know about it? I mean, it's amazing! Why keep it secret?"

"Well, think about it for a moment," said the professor, holding each key up to the golden light to inspect it. "We're talking time-travel here, but not in the way most people expect. It's not as if we can sell tickets, is it? Just a few very gifted people can go, and only teenagers at that. We're running the most extraordinary intelligence agency the world has ever known, but no one's exactly given us permission to do that. Nations guard their history as fiercely as they guard their borders. They wouldn't take kindly to a bunch of kids running through their precious past, believe me."

"But why not? What are they scared of?"

"The truth!" said Petra, doing a surprisingly good impression of the professor.

"Yes," said Professor Feldrake, waggling a long iron key at Petra like an admonishing finger, "the truth. No laughing matter, young lady."

Then he turned to David, clearly sensing the chance to give another lecture.

"So much of what people think they know about history is mere conjecture, David — guesswork based on scraps of evidence, more myth than reality. Do you think people are ready to hear the full truth about Jesus, for example? Or Mohammed or the Buddha? I mean *everything* about them? Or what about the great events that shaped national identities — the American War of Independence or the French Revolution or the Space

Race? The truth behind these things is usually rather less comforting than the stories we tell ourselves about them. No, it's better for all if the Dreamwalker Project stays firmly under wraps."

"So what's the point of it, then?" David picked up a fossil ammonite from the professor's desk and turned it around in his hands. "Why send dreamwalkers into the past at all if you won't tell anyone what they see?"

"I didn't say we don't use the information we gather," Professor Feldrake replied, rattling the key into a buckled iron box lock on the great doors. "We just have to be careful how we release it, that's all. But this isn't the reason I brought you here, David."

And he turned the key with the centuries-old sound of tumbling cogs.

The doors fell open, carrying into the office a cold breeze, laced with a powerful smell that David knew somehow but couldn't identify. Darkness waited beyond, a darkness that even the light of the hologram couldn't reach. David took an instinctive step back.

"Professor, who is Adam working for now? What is the Haunting?"

"Ah, what indeed?" said Professor Feldrake with a mischievous glance over his shoulder. Then, without warning, he stepped into the darkness beyond the doorway and vanished from view. For a time his footsteps floated back with a surprising echo, then there was silence.

David turned to look at Petra.

"I think he's expecting you to follow," she said.

David worked hard not to gulp. Only a short while ago he'd told Roman that he didn't believe in ghosts, yet staring into the dark ahead it took a great effort of will to force his legs forward. But he was very aware that Petra was watching him, and he tried to rationalize his fear away as he edged across the doorway. The dark closed around him.

"Professor?" His voice trembled.

No reply.

He went farther still.

Light burst out right in front of him. A spectral figure leaped from the dark, its arms raised, its twisted face an unholy shade of livid blue.

A ghost!

David cried out in terror and stumbled back, tripping over his own feet.

The specter loomed over him.

Then he heard a loud *click*.

Banks of neon light erupted into life all around. They revealed a vaulted rock chamber even vaster than the one that contained the Metascape Map. It shocked David with its sudden size. And the ghost was still there! But as David lay where he'd fallen, he saw that the ghostly figure was flat now and surrounded by a very unscary crumbling gilt frame. It was nothing more than a life-sized painting, standing in what appeared to be some kind of enormous museum gallery.

"That wasn't funny!" David's heart was still pounding as he shouted. Petra came over and helped him up, not quite managing to hide her grin. The professor, who was standing by a bank of switches, raised his hands in apology.

"I'm sorry, I'm sorry," he said. "But I do that with all our new people. The power of fear can never be overstated. You've just learned an important lesson, David, and been given the answer to your question. Fear is a powerful motivator. The Haunting uses it to gain power over their victims. When those victims live in the past, this gives the Haunting power over history too. Control history, and you control the world."

As the last of the strips flickered on, David could finally take in the full scope of what he was seeing. He soon forgot his anger. Behind the ghost painting was a cave of treasures.

Row after row of shelves, tables, and display stands reached up over three floors, right to the ceiling. Almost every available surface and cabinet was crammed with objects, paintings, statues, books — innumerable artifacts from every strand of world history. Chinese dragons were pushed up against Egyptian sarcophagi, beside stacks of books and medieval carvings. A giant stone statue of a woman with snakes in her hair and wild, terrifying eyes towered in the center of the room, and David remembered the ancient Greek story of the Gorgon. The cabinets nearer to him were heaped with glittering objects and antique machines of bewildering and outlandish types. All around stood wooden crates like the ones he'd seen earlier, some half empty, some closed and stacked high.

And now David recognized the smell. It was the whiff of age and ancient things, the accumulated odor of history.

"Ghosts have been seen in every age of man," said Professor Feldrake, walking over to stand with David before the painting. "El Greco, the man who painted this, certainly saw one. And more recently, since the invention of the camera, there have been photographs." And he pointed across to a nearby display.

David moved closer — it was full of photos of wispy forms, man-shaped lights in the dark, silhouettes in burning windows. Some of them were even familiar to David as famous images of ghosts.

"Time to start believing in them," said the professor. "The Haunting is aptly named."

"The Haunting is behind all this? They're the ghosts people see?"

"*Dreamwalkers* are ghosts," the professor corrected. "Ours are seen too, and people have been accidentally dreamwalking for thousands of years, entirely unaware of the effect they've been having. But the Haunting is different. Their dream-walkers — 'haunters,' we call them — deliberately set out to scare."

David turned away from the disturbing pictures, too creeped out to say anything. He looked back up at the giant statue of the Gorgon. Its hair was a writhing mass of serpents, and its face set with a petrifying expression. It was no less scary than the photos, but as David turned to look elsewhere, his eyes snapped back to it.

"That's . . . that's *you!*" he said, turning to Petra.

Petra's eyes flashed back at him, her tangled hair suddenly reminiscent of snakes. Then the defiance vanished from her expression and she looked down with shame. Shame, and something even worse.

"Everyone makes mistakes," she mumbled.

"It's not just ghosts," said Professor Feldrake, quickly taking David's elbow and leading him away. "Haunters pass themselves off as other supernatural beings too: angels, nature spirits, monsters out of legend — anything they can be sure will terrify or impress. They understand the value of myth only too well."

"But why do they do it?"

"Money, power, the sheer thrill of it . . ." The professor ticked them off on his fingers, a look of disgust on his face. "Imagine someone had missed out on a huge inheritance because their ancestor had been the *second*-born son. How much would they pay to send a ghost back in time to try and cause the will to be changed? Or even terrorize the first-born into an early grave? To persuade him to buy a ticket for the *Titanic*, say, or haunt him into signing up for the trenches in the First World War — things that were never part of his original history. People will do almost anything to rid themselves of a ghost. The Haunting has grown rich and powerful by terrorizing the past, David, and we have never been busier trying to stop them. Cleaning up the mess they make has filled this chamber — everything you see here was created directly out of the Haunting's interference with history. We'll even raid normal museums ourselves, if it means putting the historical record straight."

They came to a halt beside the glass of a softly lit display case. Inside, beside a small painted portrait of a woman, a crumbling book was open at a finely detailed chalk drawing. It depicted a panel or tray of switches beneath a box. The inside of the box contained a complex diagram heavily adorned with notes. Judging by the yellowing of the paper the book was obviously very old, yet the drawing bore an uncanny resemblance to something David saw every day of his life.

"No way!" He turned to look at the professor. "A computer?"

"Yes, indeed. Drawn in the sixteenth century by Leonardo da Vinci. Obviously it wouldn't have worked — he'd never have got the parts — but the *idea* is centuries ahead of its time. This drawing could have upturned years of human history if we hadn't been able to get it hidden until the present time."

"The Haunting did this too? But . . . what's this got to do with scaring people?"

"Fear is just the beginning. Do you know the saying, 'knowledge is power'? Well, in the past, knowledge of the future is not only powerful, it is beyond price. It can dazzle kings, buy the service of emperors, and certainly bewitch brilliant men like da Vinci. In exchange for the information shown in this drawing, da Vinci painted a small canvas and had it hidden away. It must have seemed a tiny price to pay the haunter who visited him, but a newly discovered painting by Leonardo da Vinci would be worth billions in today's art market. Imagine it — another Mona Lisa!"

Professor Feldrake tapped the glass above the small painting of a woman's head that hung beside the book in the display case.

"Fortunately, we got hold of that too. If only we were always this successful."

David stared at the painting for a moment, then walked on in a daze, his eyes roving over more objects. He read their labels as he passed: THE BAGHDAD BATTERY, an electrical apparatus from the ancient world; THE ANTIKETHERA DEVICE, a navigational computer from Ancient Greece; THE COVENTRY CANNON, a machine that appeared at first glance to be a musical instrument but which turned out to be nothing less than a steam-powered machine gun from medieval England. David shook his head in disbelief. It didn't take much imagination to see that an unscrupulous time-traveler could use history as a gold mine.

"Now do you see how vulnerable historical figures can be to a rogue dreamwalker?" the professor said, coming to stand beside David.

"Fear gets their attention, then secrets of the future buy their devotion. It's a potent combination, and one the Haunting are masters at using. Adam will be using it now, David — he'll be using every trick in the Haunting's book to find and eliminate Eddie."

CHAPTER 9

LONDON, DECEMBER 17, 1940, 8:01 A.M.

Morning brought light to a wounded London. The docks, which had been hit hard in the night raid, were chaotic but busy. Those whose livelihoods depended on the river toiled alongside firemen and soldiers to clear the ruin. Pumps were worked at full capacity, bringing the waters of the Thames to bear on stubborn flames as a thick atmosphere of smoke and winter dampness crept between the warehouses. Blast-twisted cranes leaned in from above like dead trees in a mist.

A man named Charlie Grinn looked out through the grubby window of Spurlington's Shipping Agency and wondered why his men weren't back yet. Grinn was a dangerous man to disappoint — just ask the late Mr. Spurlington — but he didn't like being without his bodyguards, not when you couldn't see more than a dozen paces down the foggy quayside.

"Anything could step out of that," he murmured to himself, angrily taking a swig of whiskey from one of Mr. Spurlington's finest cut-crystal tumblers. "Bleedin' coppers everywhere."

Grinn never stayed in any one place for long, but thanks to the Luftwaffe the docks were so dangerous at night that a wanted man with a gambler's heart could forget the police for a while. Grinn would be spending the next few days at the Agency offices, and if the lads were doing their jobs properly, they'd be out and about, making sure the place was secure.

Secure — that was a joke. The building next door had been secure until a bomb had landed on it. Grinn smiled to himself, smoothing his thin mustache as he thought how terrified his men would be at having to stay there. But they'd never dare defy him, not Charlie Grinn — not the most ruthless manhunter in London, Blitz or no Blitz, never a question asked and the body disposed of for free. He took another swig and looked over at the dartboard they'd fixed up.

"Time for a quick game," said Grinn, but as he began turning from the window, he stopped and looked back. Had he just seen someone out there in the smoke and mist, someone watching the office? One of his men? Or had it just been a cat? He narrowed his eyes, but there was no one there now, just the faint impression of people working far down the quayside.

"Bah. I'll be seein' things next."

Grinn walked away from the window — and froze. In the glass pane of the front door, behind the reversed letters of the name Spurlington, was the dark and unmistakable shape of a person, standing just outside. Grinn's hand went straight to his pocket. His fingers quickly found the bone handle of his switchblade, rejected it, then pulled out his revolver.

"What do you want?" he called.

No reply.

Grinn took a fortifying swig and put the whiskey glass down, cursing his men for being late. He strode to the door and yanked it open.

"We're closed," he said to the person standing there, the gun almost concealed behind his back. "Sling yer 'ook!"

"Actually," said the figure in the shade of the doorway, "you'll be open for me."

Grinn found himself staring into the shadow beneath a dark hat, at the face of a remarkably good-looking young man. He was wearing a suit fit for royalty, though he could hardly be out of his teens. Grinn liked a good suit himself, but this boy wore his like an insult, and Grinn felt suddenly small and insignificant, which was certainly not something he was used to. The stranger raised his hat slightly and locked his coal-bright eyes onto Grinn's.

"My name is Adam. I'm looking for Charles Bartholomew Grinn. And I've found him, haven't I?"

"No, he . . . he ain't 'ere," said Grinn, unexpectedly flustered by the intensity of the young man's gaze. He suddenly wished he hadn't drunk so much. Then it occurred to him that this wasn't the cleverest answer he could give, so he spoke again.

"I mean, I don't know anyone of that name."

"Don't mess me about, Grinn," said the visitor. "I have a job for you, that's all."

"Job? What job?"

"There's someone I want you to find. A boy. Shouldn't be difficult, just a little boy. And when you've got him . . . well, I'm sure a man with your reputation will know what to do." And Adam's handsome face split into a demonic smile as he drew his finger across his throat.

Grinn backed away, shaking his head. There was something about this Adam that wasn't right at all, something that seemed completely out of place in the world of hard men and easy murder Grinn was used to — something wholly unnatural. He tried to shut the door, but his arm wouldn't obey.

"This is me being nice, Grinn," Adam said, anger rising in his voice. "Or would you prefer me to get nasty?"

Grinn swallowed, hard. Adam's voice, which had had honey in it just a moment before, now hammered through his head with unconcealed menace, while his eyes narrowed to two points of fathomless black, drawing Grinn's in deeper and deeper . . .

"I . . . I can't help yer." Grinn's own voice was almost a squeak now. "Get lost!"

And he slammed the door, though it took an enormous effort of will to do so.

"Bloody snoop." Grinn shook his head to clear the confusion that had come over his mind. What was it about that boy's eyes? He shuddered and took a deep breath, then another. He went back to his glass, refilled it, and drank it dry. When he finally dared look back at the door, the dark shape had gone.

He picked up his darts, testing the weight of one to stop his hand shaking. He turned to the board and eyed the triple twenty. But he couldn't concentrate. It felt as though those black eyes were still on him. He blinked, and then sighted his dart again.

Those eyes.

As Grinn looked, it suddenly seemed as if the visitor's face was indeed staring right back at him from the bull's-eye. He gave a strangled gasp and let the dart go. It flew wide and bounced off the metal lines.

Grinn's mouth dropped open in terror.

The face of the strange boy really was emerging from the middle of the dartboard.

Grinn staggered back and sent his whiskey bottle crashing to the floor. The boy named Adam was now standing in the room — Grinn had just seen him step through twelve inches of solid brick! He reached for his gun.

"Get back! Blimey, what *are* you?"

"In a hurry, Grinn, that's what I am. And in no mood to play 'chase me' with you."

Grinn was once again transfixed by the two points of darkness in the very centers of the boy's eyes. His heart pounded in his chest. There was a roaring in his ears, and what little willpower the whiskey had left him began to crumble as the uncanny visitor came closer.

"Get back!" Grinn cried again, and he fired his gun while he still could.

The shot boomed in the office, followed by two more as Grinn panicked. The bullets spattered plaster from the wall right behind their target, but Adam was entirely unaffected. Instead he stepped forward again and into a shaft of the weak sunlight that was beginning to filter through the morning mist.

At the touch of the sun, the boy's body changed. It took on a ghostly quality as the tones of his clothes and skin took on an eerie bluish light. Grinn dropped his gun in disbelief. His knees gave way, and he tumbled to the ground beside his weapon. He stared up in shock as the ghostly figure came to stand above him. Then Adam spoke again.

"You are right to fear me, Charlie Grinn."

Grinn couldn't speak, his lips drawn back from his teeth in a grimace of pure terror. Cold tears ran down his cheeks.

"But I want more than your fear," Adam went on. "They say that no one knows the back streets of London like you do. I require your services, and I'm fully prepared to pay. I know about you, Grinn — I know you're a betting man. I even know you're going to the races today. So you listen carefully to what I say now. Go to the races as if nothing happened here. When you see a horse called Angel Voice, put all your money on it. Do you hear? *All* your money. You'll make a packet."

"Angel . . . Angel Voice?" Grinn managed not to choke on the words.

Adam nodded, pouring his gaze down at him. Grinn felt as if his mind was being ransacked for some sign that he would do as he'd been told. Then the young man's eyes released him and he slumped to the floor like a discarded puppet, not daring to look up.

"Put your money on the horse, Charlie Grinn," said Adam's voice, but it sounded different now — distant, and growing farther away. "I will visit you again very soon."

Then there was silence.

Grinn lay still for a long time before he could raise his head again.

The boy named Adam was gone, leaving nothing but a sense of gaping emptiness in the room.

CHAPTER · 10
THE MAP AND MISTY

David was silent as Professor Feldrake led him and Petra out of the extraordinary museum and locked the doors. They followed the old man onto the gallery and down a spiral staircase to the Map Room. As they walked out amid the flickering screens and the tense people who sat in front of them, dozens of pairs of eyes darted his way, and some people called his name in greeting. Everyone seemed to know who he was; everyone seemed to expect something of him. Above them all, the brilliant sphere of the Metascape Map crackled, bathing everything in its syrupy light.

The professor drew David across to the circular desk beneath the hologram and spoke briefly to a Japanese-looking man in a patterned shirt who sat there wearing a pair of wide-lens goggles.

"David, this is Jiro," said the professor. "He's our chief talent spotter, and also the lead programmer of the Map. Whenever someone out there in the world accidentally drifts out of their dreams and starts dreamwalking, it's Jiro here who spots them. That's how we first became aware of you."

"Hello, David," said Jiro, turning to the boy. The lenses in his goggles were concave and either violet or gold, David couldn't be sure. They made him think of dragonfly eyes. Jiro seemed suddenly to remember he was still wearing them. He shoved them up onto his forehead and gave David a small sitting bow.

"I remember the day exactly. You made an interesting shape on the scopes, young man."

"Hello," said David. "You saw me on that?" he added, pointing up at the blazing sphere. "How can you see *anything* on that?"

"With these," said Jiro, tapping the goggles, "and with a lot of experience. But I can only see you there when you dreamwalk — I couldn't track you there now. And of course, I couldn't do much without Misty."

"Misty? Who's Misty?"

"I am," said a voice out of nowhere. *"And I'm pleased to meet you, David."*

"Misty is our computer," said Professor Feldrake. "The Metascape-Interactive Space-Time Computer System, or MISTICS. We'd be a bit lost without her."

"Feel free to ask me anything you want, David. I like being useful," said Misty. *"Is there anything you would like to ask me now?"*

David felt a pleasant tingle at the nape of his neck when Misty spoke. Her voice was high and enchanting, calling to mind a beautiful young woman, and yet there was also something fake about it. As if it was *too* perfect.

"Um . . . yes," said David. He felt foolish talking to someone he couldn't see, but he really wanted to hear that voice again. "What's that?" He pointed up to where a patch of the Metascape hologram was highlighted with an open blue cube.

"That is dreamwalker number seven," said Misty. *"His name is Théo. He is fifteen years old and was born in Paris. I like him."*

Petra made a face.

David looked again at the cube. There was a patch of shifting color inside, but without the cube around it he'd never have picked it out from the rainbow chaos of the hologram.

"I'm glad to hear that, Misty," said Professor Feldrake. "But what's Théo still doing there? I thought he was supposed to have come back by now. Or has he found some sign of Eddie?"

"No," said Jiro, "but we picked up a haunter nearby, and since Théo was already in the same geo-temporal locality we diverted him to investigate."

"And? Where was the haunter exactly?"

"London docks, the morning of December seventeenth, 1940. For a moment Misty thought she detected Adam's psychic pattern, but whoever it was, he was gone before we could get a proper fix. Théo's just checking out the area."

The sight of a dreamwalker being monitored on the holographic map reminded David of something that had been nagging at the back of his mind since his conversation in the professor's office.

"Why am I only just hearing about all this?" he said. "I mean, if what you say is true, I've been dreamwalking for over a year now, and you could even see me on this thing. So why didn't you come and pick me up before?"

The professor glanced at Jiro, who returned the look. Jiro pulled his goggles down again and turned his attention back to the hologram. The pause before the professor's answer was just long enough to make David wonder how much was still being kept from him.

"David, you're a special case. Normally we would have contacted you immediately, but your dreamwalk is just too important. So it was decided to, er, cover you up. To keep you safe."

"Important how? Why am I special?"

"Well," said the professor, "it's Eddie, really — he's the special one. We couldn't risk doing anything to disturb your friendship with him. Don't forget, your dreamwalks with Edmund Utherwise are the inspiration behind all his work. Without them he probably wouldn't have discovered dream-walking at all."

David felt a touch of jealousy at "he's the special one" and was surprised that such an ordinary emotion could find its way into such an extraordinary day.

"And anyway, your father wouldn't allow it," said Jiro, his goggled eyes still fixed on Théo's cube.

"My father!" cried David. "You met my dad?"

Jiro looked uncomfortable and rolled back around to the other side of his desk. It was the professor who spoke next, and David could tell he was choosing his words carefully.

"Well, of course we had to check with your father. We aren't kidnappers, David, I've already told you that. When we first detected you, your father didn't want you to come here; he wanted you to live an ordinary life. We respected his decision. Actually, it made keeping you under wraps much easier."

David said nothing. He could tell the professor was still keeping something from him, but it didn't feel like the moment to confront him about it. Besides, if the professor was lying, maybe David would be better off trying to find out why some other way. Maybe Petra would help.

"So you've been watching over me ever since?" said David, trying to change the subject.

"You bet!" Jiro scooted back around on his chair. "Regular dreamwalker surveillance: at home, at school, in your dreams . . . you've been Petra's pet project since we first identified you. She's been your own spectral bodyguard."

David looked at Petra and felt a blush coming on. How closely had she been watching him?

"Right now, though, David," said Professor Feldrake, "I propose to send you on a test run with Dishita, one of our most accomplished dreamwalkers. She can show you what all this means in action and answer any more questions you may have."

"I'm going too," said Petra, with her hands on her hips and her feet firmly planted. "It's my job to watch him, not Dishita's." And the way she said it made it clear that the professor would have a hard time stopping her.

"Oh, very well," said the professor. "Let's go through to the Somnarium and get on with this. Time is short." But as they turned to leave, a shrill alarm broke out on the console in front of Jiro.

"What's that?" The professor doubled back. "Is Théo all right?"

"We've picked up a new haunter in his location — same date and time," said Jiro, his fingers darting across a touch screen, shutting off the alarm. "Wait . . . there's something else."

Jiro took hold of two large dials, one in each hand, and began to turn them both. Above him the colored swirls of the hologram danced crazily about before settling back to the same lazy tumble. Only this time the cube around Théo's location was in the exact center of the sphere. Close by it was another cube, this one colored a vivid red. As they watched, a second red cube formed itself, farther from Théo than the first but slowly closing on his position.

"Two haunters!" cried Professor Feldrake. "Misty, is one of them Adam?"

I'm trying to isolate their patterns now, Professor, but I need more time for a positive identification of either —

"Then just get Théo out of there," the professor interrupted. "We can't take any risks."

"No," boomed a voice from somewhere in the Map Room, and the man named Roman pushed his way toward them. "Misty, tell Théo to stand his ground."

"Commander, can't you see he's outnumbered?" the professor said. "He shouldn't be there on his own."

"Dishita is on her way, and Petra is already here," Roman replied, indicating to Petra to run. "It will be three against two. A victory for us, I think."

Petra was just jumping forward when the professor shouted, "Stay where you are!" in such an unexpected tone of command that Petra skidded to a halt.

"I am director here, Roman. We get Théo out. Now."

"Under crisis security protocols — *Director* — I too have the right to direct dreamwalkers." Roman walked up to the professor, dwarfing the old man with his bulk. "This isn't some archaeological mystery for your little history club, Feldrake. Right now we take every chance we can against the Haunting."

Above the two men, the second red cube was still closing on Théo's blue. The whole room had fallen silent, except for the insistent fizzing of the Map.

"Misty, go and see Théo," said the professor at length, still facing Roman, though clearly annoyed that he had to tilt his head so far back to look him in the eye. "Put him on direct."

"Yes, Professor," said Misty, then her voice was replaced by that of a teenage boy with a strong French accent. "Théo here. I have company. What shall I do?"

"Is it Adam?" Roman demanded before the professor could speak.

"No," said Théo. "No, it is a girl. I am inside a bombed-out warehouse. She is in the shadows outside. Just standing there."

"Théo, there is a second haunter there," the professor said. "Getting closer. Can you see who it is?"

"Are you sure, Professor?" said the voice of Théo. "There is only me and the girl."

"It must be Adam." Petra couldn't stop herself from speaking any longer. "Professor, let me go and help Théo."

"No, Petra! Théo, I want you to get back now. No heroics."

"But, it is all fine here," Théo replied. "And I have not yet learned anything of use."

"Get a better view," Roman said. "If you see Adam, attack him on sight."

"I am moving closer to the girl," Théo continued, whispering now. "I don't think she's seen me . . . it is very dark in here, but . . . wait! There is something else, something moving . . . it might have been a cat, but . . ."

Just then the alarm broke out again, high and urgent.

"Haunters!" Jiro cried. "Two more of them, coming through from the eighteenth century!"

All eyes turned upward in time to see further red cubes materialize in the Metascape Map. Now there were four reds, all closing fast on the one blue.

"It's a trap!" the professor cried. "Théo, get out of there!"

"The girl is moving," came the voice of Théo. "It's too dark in here . . . what's that?"

"Théo, you have to wake up," the professor shouted, his fists clenched. "Wake up!"

Before everyone's eyes, the four haunter cubes converged in a sudden rush, overstamping the blue one with angry red. Théo's cube winked out.

"Théo?" Petra called out into the silence that followed.

Nothing.

Then Jiro let out a long sigh.

"It's okay," he said, jabbing his finger at a little screen. "A green light from the Somnarium — Théo's just waking up. He always was fast, that one."

A rumble of voices and a hiss of released breath ran around the room.

"Oh, thank heavens!" The professor sat down heavily in a chair next to Jiro's. "I'm too old for all this."

Roman gave him a meaningful scowl and stalked off.

"Are we still taking David in after that?" Petra asked, and David was touched by the protective way she stood beside him.

"We don't have any choice," said Professor Feldrake. "But please take him somewhere far, far away. He's not ready for London 1940 yet — it's just too dangerous."

Once the professor had got his breath back and straightened his spectacles, he took David through a gliding door in the glass wall at the end of the Map Room. Beyond was a long chamber. The only light came from blue strip bulbs recessed into the rock, so that the space was bathed in a very soft glow. There were beds along each side of the room, about twenty in all, and beside each bed there was a small workstation with dimly lit screens and touch pads. David looked back through the tinted glass. He saw the faint bustle of the Map Room, but no sound carried through to him. The room was absolutely silent and the air smelled of lavender.

On one of the beds, a boy was sitting up, a lopsided grin on his face. He glanced over at the newcomers and gave the thumbs-up sign. Petra did the same, flashing him her most dazzling smile.

"Who's that?" David needed to know.

"That's Théo," she replied, still looking at the boy.

David stared at him too, trying to imagine what he'd just experienced, until the professor touched him on the arm.

"This is Dishita," he said. "She's now our most senior dreamwalker."

David found himself face to face with a serious-looking girl with tied-back hair, who the professor explained was from Delhi. She looked back at David like he was from Nowhere.

"So, you're him, are you?" she said, shaking his hand.

David was a bit disconcerted by this, so he just said, "Hullo."

"Go easy, Dishita," said the professor. "I'd like you to take David on a dreamwalk — one of the routine safe spots, mind — and answer any questions he may have. Petra will go with you."

"Is this the start of his training, Professor?" Dishita said. "Because this hardly seems the time to be holding some newbie's hand."

"We'll have to suspend the training program in his case." The professor sounded as though he was saying something he'd already said a dozen times before and didn't want to say again. "Just give him a taster, Dishita. He needs to be up to speed on all this as soon as possible, because I'm putting him into active service today."

Dishita might have rolled her eyes, but in the dim light it wasn't easy to see behind her glasses.

Three people came into the room then and David couldn't decide if they were nurses or technicians. They moved over to sit at three of the workstations. Petra and Dishita walked over to two of them and the professor motioned David to the third.

He sat down on the bed.

"Are we supposed to go to sleep now? Because I can tell you that my head's buzzing with all you've told me today. It'll take me hours to get to sleep."

"Don't worry about that," said Professor Feldrake. "We can't join you on a dreamwalk, not with all our technology, but I'm sure even Petra will agree that we can help you get there. These machines will send you off and adjust your brain waves to mimic deep REM sleep. They will also help you concentrate."

David was suddenly nervous. Adjustment of brain waves didn't sound like something he wanted to go through.

"Does it hurt?" he said, as the nurse laid him back on the bed. She placed some kind of soft mask over his face and temples and adjusted it to a snug fit.

"No, no," said the professor. "Just relax."

"But how long will it take?"

The nurse pressed a button.

David fell asleep.

CHAPTER 11

LONDON, DECEMBER 17, 1940, 11:45 A.M.

Charlie Grinn was not accustomed to being stared at. When people did watch him too closely, bad things usually happened to them soon afterward. But for once, Grinn hung back, nervously stroking his moustache. Over in the race enclosure, in a particularly dark corner, someone he didn't want to see again stood like a disembodied shadow. It was the boy named Adam.

Grinn turned to a big, flat-nosed man beside him.

"See that creepy kid, Tater?" Grinn said, indicating the dark figure with his head. "Get rid of him."

The big man grunted and waddled off toward Adam, his arms swinging at his side like a wrestler's. Relieved, Grinn turned away, his second minder following close behind. It'd be interesting to see how someone as unimaginative as Tater would be affected by Adam and his trick with the blue light. Grinn cursed himself for falling for it that morning and was just grateful that none of his men had been there to see it. It was a good trick, though, however it was done. Still, it would be better to just get rid of this Adam for good, and a taste of Tater's fist should see to that. Grinn turned his thoughts back to the horses. He'd bet three times already, losing more money than he liked to think about each time, and he could really do with a change of luck. The name Angel Voice danced in his mind.

Grinn had checked on the horse Adam had mentioned as soon as he'd got to the race track, but it was hardly a dead cert. In fact, those in the know reckoned the animal was little more than dog food waiting to be canned. Anyone betting on Angel Voice would certainly make a small fortune if the wretched creature won, but no one would be stupid enough to put any real money on a nag like that.

Grinn watched the horses for the next race being paraded nearby, Angel Voice among them. If only there was some way of knowing in advance which of the animals would win, he thought, and he fingered the handle of the switchblade in his coat pocket. Could he get close enough to cut the favorite? No, too many people.

His minder tapped him on the shoulder. Tater had returned. And it was obvious he was badly shaken.

"What is it?" Grinn snapped. "Is he gone? Come on, what do I pay you for, you lugging great galoot?"

The man couldn't speak for a moment. His teeth were chattering, and Grinn just knew it wasn't from the cold.

"Looks like he's seen a ghost, boss," laughed the other minder, but his smile faded when Grinn didn't return it.

"He just said two words, guv . . ." Tater muttered eventually. "Something about an Angel Voice."

Grinn looked back into the enclosure. The boy named Adam was nowhere to be seen.

Charlie Grinn gave Tater a dark look, then made his way to place his bets. He put a hefty sum on the favorite, a horse named Bulgar. He really needed a win to improve his mood, and Bulgar should deliver. But, since Grinn was also a chancer at heart, he also put a few shillings on Angel Voice, just in case.

The race began. Bulgar burst from the starter's hurdle like an unstoppable force, but then stumbled early on and couldn't catch up. To Grinn's mounting astonishment and against all expectation, Angel Voice steadily worked his way to the lead. With spectators shouting in frustration and fury around him, Grinn watched Angel Voice lope across the finishing line, winning the race by a nose. Bulgar came last, losing him a solid fiver. But at that moment, Grinn didn't care. That "just in case" bet more than canceled out his loss.

Grinn stroked his neat whiskers. Perhaps it would be worth having another chat with this Adam after all, weird eyes and creepy tricks of the light notwithstanding.

As Tater went to collect his boss's surprise winnings, Grinn shoved his way through the crowds to the enclosure, scanning the faces for the strange boy. He didn't have to look for long.

"Congratulations, Mr. Grinn."

Adam was where he'd been before, lurking in a gloomy corner. Grinn looked him over again, carefully avoiding his eyes. He took in the suit, the stylish hat, the long ivory-capped cane. There was money there, Grinn could see — lots of money. It was time Grinn took charge of this situation.

"Right, how did you know? About the horse. Or was it just luck?"

"Oh, I know all sorts of things, Mr. Grinn — many, many useful things."

"Including race winners *before* the race? Do I look like a mug? Give it to me straight, now — what do you want, and what will you pay?"

"I told you. There's a boy I want you to find. His name is Edmund Utherwise. He went missing last night, and now he's hiding in the city somewhere. And when you find him and make him disappear, I'll repay you with wealth more fabulous than you can even imagine."

"Like I said, do I look like a mug?" Grinn was determined to stand his ground this time, even though his two bodyguards had slunk back behind him. "You're going to have to do better than guess a race winner if you want to deal with me."

"Ah, but Mr. Grinn . . ." Adam's devilish grin danced across his face. ". . . if you find this boy, I'll tell you the surefire winners of a hundred races like this. You'll be a millionaire by summer."

"Oh, I get it." Grinn's lip curled. "I pay for your bets and then give you half. Well, listen up, you little —"

Grinn felt sweat break out on his forehead as Adam relit his dark gaze to its fullest intensity. The boy threw out his arm so that his hand left the shade of the enclosure and entered the winter sunlight. Instantly it turned an eerie blue. Then, slowly, one long bony finger extended and pointed straight at Grinn's face.

"I don't have time for this! You have one last chance, Charlie Grinn. The next race will be won by Trojan Mate. Put all your money — and I mean *everything in your pockets* — on Trojan Mate! If the horse wins, you will find me at sunset, in front of

Saint Paul's Cathedral. If the horse loses, you can forget we ever met. Now go!"

Grinn stumbled back as if he'd been pushed. He could hear Tater gasping like a frightened child just behind him. Adam drew back his hand, which was once again enveloped in darkness.

"See you this evening, Grinn," came Adam's voice, though already Grinn had trouble seeing him in the shadows. "Come alone."

Grinn found himself nodding, even as he realized that the corner of the enclosure he was nodding at was completely empty.

CHAPTER · 12
LEAVE NO STONE TURNED

David was dreaming.

In his dream, he was standing on a mountain road, without any recollection of how he'd got there.

It was daytime, but the sky was gray and the wind fresh. Ahead was a view down a steep slope to a valley divided up into neat fields. Behind him, the road rose up to a solitary house — a château of some kind. In all directions the horizon towered with snowy mountain peaks that brought to mind every picture David had ever seen of the mighty Swiss Alps.

"When you've quite finished gawping . . ." said a precise voice. Glancing back, David was mildly surprised to see Dishita looking at him. Petra was standing at her side.

"I'm dreaming!" said David, and Petra laughed. Dishita looked unimpressed.

"Let's not waste any time, shall we?" she said. "David, the reason the professor is not here to explain further is because he can't follow us now. In fact, to the best of our knowledge there are only a few hundred people in the world with the ability to communicate like this, though not all of them have been activated."

"Activated?" said David. "What does that mean?"

"It means made aware," said Petra. "The first step in making a controlled dreamwalk is becoming aware that you are dreaming. The machines in the Somnarium help you do that. Now you are in control of your dream. Soon you will learn to do it on your own."

"That's right," snapped Dishita, who clearly didn't like being interrupted. "Most of the people we activate are then offered a place on the Dreamwalker Project. At present our youngest dreamwalker is ten years old, and the oldest is eighteen. The ability to project consciousness diminishes at the end of adolescence."

"Science-guy speak," whispered Petra. "Dishita wants to be one of them one day."

David looked around. The wind chilled his cheek and moved the branches of the trees. Overhead, where the clouds gathered, a large bird was circling. It all seemed so real. Could it really be just a dream? After a moment he became aware of the two girls waiting for him.

"So, where is this?" he asked. "And what do we do now?"

"Well, we could have a picnic," said Dishita sarcastically. "That château over there is Unsleep House. The places you have already been shown, the Map Room and everything, are in the rock beneath it. But this mountainside is just a neutral point, somewhere for us to meet in dreamspace. We haven't come here to admire the Swiss countryside. As it sounds like this will be the only training run you're going to get, we should go somewhere — we should dreamwalk." And when David didn't answer she narrowed her eyes and added with a nod, "Perhaps through that door?"

David turned and was surprised to see a blue door standing in the middle of the road. There was nothing to hold up the frame, and he had the eerie feeling that he could walk all around it if he wished.

"Oh. Did I make that?" he asked.

"No," said Dishita, "this is my dream, not yours. We can't wait all day for you. Now, what would you like to see? Where in time would you like to go?"

David's mind went blank. What a question! Petra came to his rescue.

"I know something you might like," she said, and the door swung open. David looked through, his eyes growing wide in wonder.

Beyond the doorway he saw the light of a different day, where the sands of some far-off place shimmered in the heat of a desert sun. He caught a sudden rush of hot rocky air and sensed a mixture of smells that clearly didn't belong to a Swiss mountainside. It was like staring into another world.

"Is that . . . the *past*?" he said.

Dishita ignored this question. She walked briskly to the door and stepped through, beckoning to the others to follow. The light reflecting from her hair altered immediately and she already seemed to be an unimaginable distance away. David looked at Petra.

"What will I see?" he said.

"Don't worry about it," said Petra, her ready smile twitching with amusement. "It's going to be amazing, David. It's always amazing." And with that she took his hand and pulled him through the door.

David was standing with the two girls in the shadow of a broken stone wall. Beside him, between outcrops of rock, were the remains of some rough stone buildings, tumbled down and decaying in the sandy earth and casting long shadows with the sun low in the sky. They were on the slopes above another valley, only this time it was broad and arid, studded with shrubs and strange grasses. He stared in disbelief, shocked to find himself somewhere else entirely.

He moved his feet on the gravel experimentally, but didn't hear the crunch of small stones he was expecting.

"Try and pick one up," said Dishita.

David stooped and scrabbled for a stone, but he couldn't even move one, let alone take hold of it. He stood bolt upright again.

David's mind fought with the situation. However, even as he struggled with the reality of sudden relocation, he also couldn't help wondering why he had been brought here. He looked over at his two companions, standing beside him in the shadow of the broken wall. Then he looked down at himself and saw that he was still holding Petra's hand. He let go and patted himself down.

"But . . . but this is my body. I'm really here!"

"No, David," said Dishita. "That is your dreamself, your specter. It's the form your mind takes now that it has left your body. The only form it knows."

"You mean, my spirit? My *soul*?"

"We don't like to use the word *soul*," said Dishita, and something in her voice suggested she was uncomfortable using it even now. "We usually just refer to our dreamselves as ghosts.

As you are about to find out, in this state you have some very ghostly properties."

"What do you mean?"

"Watch closely," said Dishita, and she stepped out of the shadow of the wall and into the direct sunlight. Her whole form grew instantly faint, and she was suffused with a smoky glow.

"Come into the light," she called.

David did so. He raised his hands and looked at them closely, fascinated, but still shocked, by the strange bluish light that seemed to boil inside them with the sun's touch. And he could see right through them to Petra, who hadn't left the shade. She smiled back at him but appeared entirely normal.

"The first thing you must learn about your dreamself is to keep its ghostly nature hidden," Dishita explained. "Keep to the shadows, David — don't go into the light. We can only risk being outdoors in overcast weather. In direct sunlight . . . well, you can see for yourself. You must never let anyone see you like this."

David stepped back into the shade and became normal-looking again.

"Okay," he said, "okay. To keep dreamwalking a secret, you mean?"

"To stop people from freaking out," said Petra. "How would you feel if you saw a ghost?"

"Right. Got it. But . . . but there's no one here now."

"No, but there soon will be," said Petra, pointing off to the horizon.

David looked into the distance and saw a long line of

movement along the valley floor, shimmering in the heat. Sunlight flashed from a thousand faraway reflections.

"What's that?" he asked.

"It's an army," said Petra. "And look, there's the other one," she added, pointing in the opposite direction. Sure enough, a similar line of moving figures could be seen rippling in the sweltering air. It looked as though they would meet just below the point where the three companions were standing.

"This is amazing!" said David, still struggling to accept what his senses were showing him. "It all seems so real."

"It is real," said Dishita. "Or rather, it *was*. This is no longer a dream, David; this is the year 1028 BC, and we are in the ancient Middle East. Don't ask me why — this was Petra's idea. For some reason she thinks you want to see an act of mindless violence."

"He's a boy, isn't he?" snapped Petra. "I thought he'd like a battle. Besides, he has a personal connection with this one, actually."

David wondered what that could possibly mean. Was Petra teasing him? The three of them stood for a while in silence as the warriors of the two armies drew closer.

"But what will they think?" David said eventually, pointing at the approaching men. "They're about to see three ghosts standing in the desert."

"They won't see any ghosts because we are going to be very careful," said Dishita, sounding more and more like a teacher. "We mustn't do anything to draw attention to ourselves or risk altering the course of history. If someone in this time caught sight of you fading away or drifting through a wall — oh, yes, we can do that too — they would probably be terrified. Who knows how they might react? What if they changed their behavior entirely? What if someone who was supposed to live to be a hundred saw your ghost and ran and tripped and broke their neck? Something like that could cause incalculable changes to the time line, resulting in an entirely different present. We must do everything we can to blend in, to avoid . . ."

Petra gave an enormous and exaggerated yawn. Dishita stopped speaking and glared at her.

When David looked at Petra again, she was no longer dressed in the featureless black jumpsuit, but instead wore a loose white tunic, tied around the waist, and a pair of golden sandals. There were almond-shaped leaves in her hair.

"Wow!" said David with wide eyes. "A disguise?"

"We do that if we think we might be seen," said Dishita. "But right now Petra is just showing off. We are going to hide, so there's no need to dream up a costume."

Petra gave Dishita a bored look. She kicked out with her feet and rose gracefully into the air, sailing across the ruins and coming to rest on a small broken wall, slightly higher up the rocky outcrop but still in the shade.

"The view's better from up here," she called.

David stared, his mouth wide open. He felt as if he'd just seen an angel fly. And since he found it hard to take his eyes off Petra, he didn't notice that Dishita had grabbed him until he was high off the ground himself. She carried him through the air at the end of her arm and set him down behind Petra's wall.

David was speechless.

"Petra, we should get back," Dishita said. "I think David's had enough surprises for one day."

"Wait a bit," said Petra. "He needs to see this first."

The two armies were now close enough for details of their armor to be seen — bronze helmets, breastplates, and bands of metal around ankles and wrists. Most of the warriors carried spears and shields, although many had bows. Fluttering above both armies were long pennants and painted figures on poles.

The strange sound of ancient horns filled the air and the two great bodies of men came to a sudden halt, one to the dream-walkers' left and the other to their right. Even at a distance, David felt both sides radiating animosity at each other. Looking again at the weapons, David suddenly needed to ask another question. It was the kind of thing Eddie would ask if he were here, and David was proud to have thought of it himself.

"What . . . what would happen if someone fired an arrow in my direction? I mean, if I'm a ghost, would it just go straight through me?"

"Yes," said Dishita. "It would move through the air as if you were not there, and you would suffer no physical harm. Your mind might not like it, though, if it's not prepared. It might even be enough to break your dreamwalk. You don't want to wake up suddenly, believe me. The headaches can be terrible."

David said nothing, but he remembered his dream about trying to save Eddie from the fire and how he felt when he woke up.

There came another great blast of horns and trumpets from the army on David's right, and the warriors gave a thunderous cheer and began beating their shields with their spears. The noise was tremendous, but the warriors of the opposing army remained still and silent. David looked back at the cheering men and saw something moving head and shoulders above the rest. The front rank split apart, and a warrior stepped forward.

He was enormous. David had never seen anyone so massive in his life — he must have been nearly nine feet tall. He had a great shaggy black beard and carried a shield and a giant spear that appeared to be solid bronze. The huge warrior strode right up the opposing army, let out a booming shout of defiance, and bashed the spear against his shield with a sound like a cathedral bell. He towered over his enemies, who shrank back. David found room in his overloaded mind to feel sorry for them. How could they ever hope to fight a monster like that?

The giant man then turned his back on his enemies and strode with arrogant slowness back to stand before his own men. His army was jeering, and although David couldn't understand a word they shouted, he knew they were mocking their enemies. He turned to Petra.

"So who are they?" he said. "And who is that huge man?"

"Can't you guess?" said Petra. "This is a famous historical event, though some believe it's just a myth. That is the army of the Philistines, and that huge man is their champion. He has just challenged the other army to send out a champion of their own so that the battle can be decided in single combat."

"So who are *they*?" asked David, pointing at the silent men on the other side. "And who could possibly fight that giant man?"

"Those are the Israelites, David," said Petra. "And you know who will step forward to fight, even if you haven't yet remembered."

David looked over at the Israelites and felt his memory stirring. Then he looked back at the giant man facing them. A giant.

"Is that . . . is that *Goliath*?" said David, feeling foolish even as he asked. Petra smiled.

"Then that must mean . . ." But David was too amazed to finish his sentence. Instead he turned back to the Israelites. There came an answering fanfare from somewhere behind them, and their front rank parted. A young boy stepped out.

"Yes, David, that is your namesake," said Dishita. "The boy David, future king of Israel. The boy who slew a giant." And she glanced at Petra with the first smile David had seen on her face.

Petra looked very pleased with herself.

CHAPTER · 13
THE CANE
AND THE SPEAR

As the three dreamwalkers watched from their hiding place, the boy who would one day be king walked forward with uncertain steps, before coming to a halt some twenty paces from the giant.

The Philistine warriors were by now roaring with laughter and hurling insults at the Israelites and their tiny champion. This other David, who was wearing nothing more than a simple white tunic and sandals, very much like Petra's, was armed only with a sling that dangled from one hand. With the other he was fingering a small bag of stones. There was real reluctance about the way he stood there alone, exposed to both great danger and ridicule, but there was also defiance in the way he held his head. David felt instinctive sympathy toward him.

Goliath, who had been roaring with laughter with his men, suddenly held up his spear, and his army fell silent. Then he spoke.

These were the first clearly spoken words that David had heard in this ancient time, but if he'd hoped dreamwalking would somehow allow him to understand, he was disappointed. The words were rough in the mouth of the giant, and clearly hostile, but he could tell nothing more. There came a moment of silence, and then it was the boy's turn to speak.

The young Israelite's voice was extremely small compared to Goliath's, but the words were clear and sounded brave. The Philistines roared back with derision, banged their shields, and threw back their heads in laughter.

Then something strange happened. Off to the side of the army, in the shade of some further ruins, a new figure emerged. David was astonished to see what appeared to be a man in a black city suit stroll out from behind a crooked tree. He even wore a trilby hat and carried a cane! David blinked in surprise . . . and then saw that he had been entirely mistaken. The man was just another soldier, dressed in the same light armor and carrying not a cane, but a spear.

The newcomer took up a position near his comrades, but while the great mass of fighters was focused on the two champions, this new man was looking elsewhere. He had a low helmet that almost covered his eyes, but David could have sworn he was staring straight up at the three dreamwalkers.

"A trick of the light?" David murmured aloud.

"What's that?" said Dishita.

"Well, for a moment I thought I saw . . ." But David wasn't sure what he'd seen, if anything, and neither of the girls seemed to have noticed this odd figure. He was about to say something more when the battle began.

Goliath stepped forward and started to circle his young opponent with a stooped, menacing movement. He stalked to the left and then doubled back, his shield and spear raised threateningly. David the Israelite hurriedly put a stone in his sling and began to twirl it. The laughter of the Philistine army grew so great that Goliath decided to change his approach. He turned to his men and gave an exaggerated shrug.

His audience cheered.

Then he thrust his great spear into the ground, leaned his shield against it, and hung his helmet on top. Goliath turned back to face the boy with his hands on his hips. The Philistines hooted with pleasure while the Israelites looked on in silence.

Then David raised his arm, gave his little sling a couple of final whirls and released the stone. It zipped across the space between him and Goliath and struck the mighty warrior on the forehead. Goliath instantly raised his hand to his head. The Philistines laughed hysterically.

David Utherwise looked back at the strange new warrior in the ruins and saw that he'd begun to move. He was now running straight toward them, and at great speed.

"What's that man doing?" he asked, and the two girls turned to look.

"That's strange," said Petra. "This has never happened before." Then she added, "Oh, no . . ."

"Adam!" cried Dishita. "He's here!" And she rushed forward to meet the approaching warrior.

"No!" cried Petra.

The warrior leaped straight up the rocky slope — an impossible feat for a normal person — and hefted his spear in his right hand, clearly preparing to throw it. As he left the shade he became instantly translucent and spectral in the sunlight.

"Wait, Adam!" cried Dishita. "It's me! We must talk."

Adam pulled back his arm and flung his spear. It sped straight through the air and slammed into Dishita.

The girl disappeared instantly.

David stared, dumbfounded, into the space where she had been and then looked again at the warrior. Somehow the spear was back in his hand.

"We go!" cried Petra. *"Now!"* and David felt himself being pulled from behind. The world tipped, the shaft of a spear passed inches in front of his nose, and suddenly he found himself looking out into the desert from the other side of an open door.

He saw the terrible Goliath framed in the doorway. He saw the blood pouring from his head. He saw the mighty giant begin to fall.

The door slammed shut, and everything went black.

David woke to a great commotion of sound. He reached up and pulled the mask from his eyes, and felt a throb in his head as the light of the Somnarium reached him. He sat up despite the ache and looked over to Dishita's bed. Half a dozen people in white coats were standing over her, with a cart of high-tech equipment stationed on the side. The professor was there too, and Petra leaped from her bed and rushed over to join them.

David swung his legs over and stood up with an immense effort. He stumbled to Dishita's bed.

"What happened?" he asked.

The scientists ignored him, but the professor looked up, his face ashen. He seemed to have forgotten all about David for a moment.

"Dishita has suffered psychosomatic shock," he said.

"There's a possibility of personality damage. We have to get her to the hospital — this could be very serious, I'm afraid."

"Nonsense," said Petra, who appeared at David's side. "Dishita is strong."

As if to prove that statement, there came a low murmur from the bed, followed by a few faint words in Hindi. Dishita sat up and said, "Don't fuss, I'm fine."

David could see that she was far from fine. Her forehead was covered in sweat and she was sickly pale. But the atmosphere in the room grew less urgent, and several of the white coats stepped back, removing the instrument cart. Dishita was helped onto a stretcher and wheeled out of the Somnarium, still protesting.

"Adam was there," said David. He suddenly felt very tired and irritable, despite having apparently just slept. "He attacked us . . ."

"I know, I know," said Professor Feldrake. "But we didn't pick him up on the Map until it was too late. I shouldn't have let you dreamwalk so long — Adam's always been difficult to detect, and there was always the risk the Haunting would detect you first. But I never expected him to act that fast."

"Of course you didn't," said a voice, and everyone turned to find Roman standing in the doorway of the Somnarium. "But you should have done. Adam knows all our training sites. Naturally he would have the Haunting monitoring them. I hope you are not going to tell me you didn't plan for this possibility, Professor."

The professor sat on one of the beds and started cleaning his glasses on his tie. He seemed very old and frail.

"And I also hope you are not going to tell me that this chance to hit back at Adam was wasted," Roman went on, turning his fierce eyes on Petra. "You fought him, yes? Adam was destroyed?"

Petra looked annoyed and flustered.

"It was all too fast. I had to get David clear . . ."

"Get David clear," Roman repeated, incredulous. "Get David clear? David is nothing! You let Adam get away just to bring this useless boy home safely?"

"Commander, you know Petra stands no chance against Adam on her own," said Professor Feldrake. "He's the strongest dreamwalker we have ever known. We were caught off guard, that's all."

"Caught off guard? We are fighting for our survival against a rogue dreamwalker who wants to turn history on its head, and you were *caught off guard*?" Roman shook his head. "And now we have lost Dishita. Something is going to have to change here, Professor. This isn't a research program anymore. How long before you realize that we are at war?"

The professor said nothing.

"I have a report to file," Roman said, his voice a low growl. "Our political masters are expecting results. They will not be expecting this." And with that he left the room.

"We've lost Dishita?" David cried. "What happened back there? What did Adam do to her?"

"They call it a mind pulse," said Petra, still staring angrily at the place where Roman had been. "Free from the body, the mind is very powerful. If you concentrate hard enough you can even make an attack — an attack of pure mental energy. Adam was always very good at it. Adam was always good at everything. Poor Dishita. She's good at it too, but she would never have believed Adam could attack her like that. She won't let him do it again."

"We've lost so many dreamwalkers in the last few days," added the professor. "But we haven't lost Dishita. She was lucky this time."

"Was it really luck?" David was struck by a sudden realization. "Or was it just that Adam was after someone else?"

Both the old man and the girl looked at him.

"Me. It was me he really wanted to hit, wasn't it?"

The professor got slowly to his feet.

"I told you earlier that you are our best chance of finding Eddie. And don't forget, you have already saved him once from Adam. The Haunting can't tolerate you helping us, David — you are probably now our only chance to defeat them. They will go to any lengths to eliminate you. Adam will kill you if he can."

"You're our David," said Petra. "But he's their Goliath."

CHAPTER · 14
LONDON, DECEMBER 17, 1940, 4:57 P.M.

By the time Eddie reached Kat's place, he was exhausted. It had taken him the best part of a day to get there. Night was falling fast, but seeing the cheap Victorian elegance of the boarded-up and crumbling façade, he knew he'd got it right.

He'd never actually been to the old theater before, but Kat talked about it all the time. As a servant she had a tiny room on the top floor of Eddie's house, but her brother lived rough and had taken over the attic of this abandoned theater about a year ago. Eddie couldn't imagine living like that, but Kat made it sound like a magical place. She'd never told Eddie the address, but he'd pieced it together anyway with the help of an old city map and the scraps she'd let slip. Now that map was pasted into one of his notebooks, covered in workings-out.

She won't want you here, nagged the voice of Eddie's doubt. *She might not even be there.*

Eddie shook his head. With the house destroyed, where else would she be?

"At least I never told David about this place," he muttered under his breath. "At least *he* won't find me here." But speaking made him cough so violently he nearly lost his glasses.

Eddie's chest felt as though the fire that had almost killed him the night before was still raging inside it somewhere. He thrust his hands into his pockets and grasped the rolled-up notebook. Reassured, he stumbled down the alleyway beside the theater, picking his way over the split boards and air-raid rubble that had been heaped there, until he came to the side door.

It was boarded shut. And not in the loose way he'd expected — someone had been here recently and done the job properly. He couldn't budge a single plank.

The cold deepened. It'd been chilly all day, but the temperature was plummeting as night drew on, and Eddie could feel it gnawing at his ribs. He gave the boarded-up door a furious kick, then slid down beside it.

You shouldn't have come. Now the cold will get you instead of the fire.

Eddie grabbed his hair and pulled. Wasn't there something else Kat had said about the theater? Hadn't she mentioned another way in?

Yes! A rope. She'd said there was a rope hanging from a broken iron ladder.

Eddie got to his feet and strained to look down to the end of the passage. It was almost too dark to see anything, but there was a little light left in the sky. Eddie pressed the side of his head tight against the brick wall and looked up diagonally, so that anything fixed to it might show up silhouetted against the dusk. And there it was.

It was a narrow ladder, cemented into the wall. The bottom third of it was missing, but something was tied to the lowest rung. Eddie clambered deeper into the passage until he was directly beneath the ladder, and sure enough, tucked behind a rusty gutter pipe, he found the knotted end of a rope.

He seized the frozen rope as high as he could and croaked with pain as he pulled himself up. Even with gloves on, the pressure on his scorched palms was almost unbearable. He managed to get his feet onto the lowest knot to relieve his hands, but then his ankle ached unbearably as he put his weight on it. He hung there for a moment, his body trembling and his mind threatening to float away.

You're too weak. You'll never make it.

He squeezed his eyes shut. He couldn't give up, not now. There were just too many unanswered questions. Somehow he heaved himself up again to the next knot, and then again and again. Just as his arms threatened to give out and his chest felt like it was going to explode, his hands found the bottom of the ladder.

From there the climb was easier, though by the time he reached the roof and pulled himself over onto the slate tiles, Eddie was shattered, and his breath rattled in his throat. He lay there gasping. His burned coat was falling apart, and though there was only a light wind on the roof, it chilled him to the core. It would be suicide to rest now. He rose slowly to his feet.

It was entirely dark by then, air-raid dark. With the blackout in force, it occurred to Eddie's drifting mind that London was vanishing into a twilight more complete than anything it had known since the Romans had begun to build there. Even the sounds of a modern city seemed to melt away with the last of the day. For a moment he could have been in another time altogether, a traveler into the past. It was an idea that had always excited him.

He dragged himself a little way up the sloping roof and pulled off his satchel. The feel of the notebooks inside was like the reassuring hand of an old friend, and he almost took them out. But his books were useless to him if he couldn't see to write. He scrabbled in the bottom of the bag, pulled out his flashlight, and pushed the switch.

Nothing happened. It was broken.

Eddie clutched the bag tightly and pulled his hair.

It was then that he heard a sound.

He held his breath and listened. Was that a voice? His mind began to swim, but then the sound came again. Yes, someone was talking close by. And was that a faint crackling, popping sound, like burning pine? In his fevered mind's eye Eddie saw himself writing *fire?* on a crisp new page, and *burns!*, but then crossing out *burns!* and writing a list of altogether more comforting words:

> Light. Warmth. Safety.
> Kat.

He crept toward the sound, not even bothering to test his weight on the rickety tiles, until he reached the summit of the roof. Peering over the top he saw a ragged hole in the other side. It was lit from within by a flickering orange light.

For a moment terror paralyzed Eddie as his mind flashed back to the fire that had so nearly killed him the night before. But then he noticed something else. Was his nose playing tricks on him or was that the scent of toast in the air? He crept nearer and looked into the hole.

There was Kat, sitting some way back beside a glorious fire and holding a rough slice of bread above the flames with a long metal stick. Beside her was a very blond boy in a cap, who must be her older brother. Eddie watched them for a moment through the sheet of smoke that poured through the hole and out into the cold night.

He'd found Kat.

Without another thought he swung his legs over the side of the hole and dropped through.

His arrival had an electrifying effect on the two people by the fire. Kat leaped up instantly and gave a short scream, dropping the toast, while her wide-eyed brother grabbed a copper kettle and held it out as if it were the most intimidating weapon you could wish for. The girl recovered first.

"Eddie?" Kat shouted. "Eddie! You could've given us a heart attack! What're you doing here?"

"Eddie?" said the boy, lowering the kettle. "What, the geezer you work for?"

"Not him, his family," said Kat. "He's all right. But, Eddie, what happened to you?" she added, as Eddie struggled to his feet, revealing the black and bloodied state he was in.

"No! You weren't in the house?"

Eddie nodded, hanging back and staring at Kat's brother. He clutched the notebook in his pocket. He wished the boy would go away and leave him alone with Kat.

"Eddie, say something," Kat said. "Don't clam up on me now. What were you doing at the house? Didn't you hear the sirens?"

"It's gone," Eddie said, tilting his head so that Kat's brother vanished from view behind the metal rim of his spectacles. "The house. All gone."

"I know it's gone, dun' I?" said Kat, looking away. "I lived there too."

Eddie took the rolled-up book from his pocket and began flicking through it.

"Eddie . . ." said Kat.

"What's he doing?" said Kat's brother, whispering.

"Eddie," Kat said, "this is my brother, Tomkin. Put the book away now and come and sit by the fire."

Eddie was uncertain for a moment, but the promise of warmth was too much. He limped over and slumped down by the fire opposite the others. But now that he could no longer avoid Tomkin, he found he couldn't look at anything else.

"Oi, quit starin' or your eyes'll pop out!" Tomkin snapped.

"It's all right, Tom," Kat said. "He doesn't know you, that's all."

"Neither do I know him. What's he want here, anyway?"

"Eddie," said Kat, "why were you at home during the raid?"

Eddie finally tore his eyes off Tomkin and looked down into the pages in front of him. He turned them fast until he reached one that was near the start of the book. Then he held it up. Amid a storm of scribbling and crossing-out, one question stood out clearly, surrounded by a heavy ink ring:

What is David, really?

"Eddie, what do you mean?" Kat looked wary.

"He said he'd tell me. Last night," Eddie replied. "He promised me."

"Who did? David?"

Eddie looked down again and said nothing. He knew Kat wouldn't want to hear that he'd listened to David, but he could tell she was trying to catch his eye.

"Eddie, why are you here? What about Mrs. Utherwise? Why aren't you safe with your ma?"

In reply Eddie flipped the pages again and then held up the bloodstained, sooty double page where he'd worked out his reasoning for not going to his aunt's house.

"He's a bleedin' fruitcake," Tomkin muttered to his sister. "Shame he's not the eating variety."

"It's just his way of doing things, Tom. Eddie, you shouldn't be here. You're hurt, and your mother must be going mad. You can stay here tonight, but —"

"What?" cried Tomkin. "No, he can't!"

"Tom, it's freezing outside."

"Yeah, but I don't want some nutter staring at me while I sleep."

"He's not a nutter. He's the smartest person I've ever met."

"Oh, is he?" said Tomkin, looking at Eddie through narrowed eyes. "And I'm just your dumb brother, I suppose."

"Shut up, Tom. And stop waving that kettle at him. Make yourself useful and get a brew on."

Tomkin went farther into the attic and began filling the kettle with rainwater, still glaring at Eddie. Eddie glanced back at him fearfully, then turned his gaze to the flames.

The fire was built on a buckled metal plate propped on four short towers of bricks. Eddie stared at it. He turned its shape around in his mind until he'd worked out what it was, then he wrote *thunder sheet* in his book. He'd read that such things were used for sound effects in plays, but this one would never thunder again — fire had seen to that.

"Eddie?" said Kat. "I asked you just now if it was David who told you to go back to the house during the air raid. Look at me, Eddie. Was it David?"

Eddie nodded, but he didn't look up.

"I knew it!" cried Kat. "I told you, didn't I?"

"Who's this David?" said Tomkin, fixing the kettle over the fire and allowing it to splash a little water over Eddie. "Come on, Kat, what is all this?"

"You wouldn't believe it if I told you," Kat answered. She sat down by the fire and threw a chair leg onto it. Then she shook her head at Eddie.

Tomkin stuck his thumbs in his suspenders.

"Try me," he said.

Eddie jabbed his glasses into place with his thumb. Why wouldn't this hostile boy just go away?

"David," he said, straight at Tomkin, "is a ghost." Silence hung in the air, but then Eddie spoiled the effect by adding, "Possibly."

"Right," said Tomkin, the word stretching out with the boy's smile of disbelief.

"It's true," said Kat. "Eddie's house is haunted. *Was* haunted, that is — there's nothing left to haunt now. Anyhow, I know it's true. I seen it once, didn't I? Skulking in the shadows of Eddie's room. Horrible and lost-looking, it was, like it shouldn't 'ave been there." And she shivered.

Tomkin's eyes twinkled at his sister, and he started to laugh, but the looks the other two gave him stopped him short.

"Don't tell me you're serious," he said. "I thought you said he was clever. There ain't no such thing as ghosts."

"Not everything's in your papers, Tom," snapped Kat.

"No ghosts, that's for sure," Tomkin said, looking to one side. Eddie followed his gaze to the great piles of newspapers that stood around the attic at the fringes of the fire's glow, and he remembered Kat saying her brother sometimes worked as a paperboy. Beyond the papers, points of reflected light winked back from peeling, gold-leaf costume parts and vanished into the eyeholes of long-forgotten masks. The bizarre shadows they made danced unsettlingly with the firelight. There was surely no worse place to deny the existence of ghosts.

Eddie wrote something in his book, then handed it to Kat together with his pencil. Beneath the freshly written words *What is David really?* was nothing but empty paper.

"You think *I* know the answers?" Kat said. "Oh, no, Eddie, that's not why you came here, is it?"

Eddie stared at her through his cracked lenses and said nothing. He could hear Tomkin snickering, but he wasn't interested in that. If Kat had been right about David being dangerous, what else did she know?

"Eddie . . ." Kat began.

"Oh, come off it," said Tomkin then. "You're kidding, right? With all this ghost talk? I mean, come on! You're not saying there was a real bona fide phantom, are you?"

"Tell him, Eddie," said Kat.

Eddie pulled his hair a bit as he looked at Tomkin.

"I'll tell you what I know," he said eventually, and he quickly and precisely described the strange ghost boy who called himself David: the way he would suddenly appear, the strange way he was dressed, and the impression he left that he had no idea he was a ghost at all. He spoke in a dry, matter-of-fact way, like a scientist describing an unusual experiment, but it was clear that both Kat and Tomkin were affected by it. Kat pulled a large overcoat around herself and huddled nearer the fire. Tomkin tightened his scarf and did the same.

"That's a creepy tale you've got there," he said, when Eddie had reached the end, "but I'm not ready to believe it. It must have been one of your neighbors, some kind of joke maybe. You toffs go in for stuff like that, don't yer? Larking about. Or perhaps you were just dreaming — you said it only came at night, this ghost."

"I wasn't asleep," said Eddie. "He was really there. Yet . . . not there at the same time, though he appeared solid enough." He leaned toward Tomkin as if he was about to tell him a secret. "Once, when he wasn't looking, I touched him. My hand went straight through."

At that moment the kettle began to whistle and Tomkin jumped.

"Jeez, can't we talk about something else?" he said.

"You're the one who kept on about it." Kat punched her brother in the shoulder. "'Fraidy guts!"

"It's just a story." Tomkin punched back. "'Fraidy guts yourself."

"It's no story," said Eddie. "Kat, you told me once that a ghost is a dangerous friend. How did you know?"

"The dead must be jealous of the living," said Kat. "Stands to reason. I knew it'd try to kill you in the end. I told you."

She was still holding his notebook, and Eddie wondered why she wasn't writing anything down. Kat shook her head again.

"If you've come here for answers, I can't help you, Eddie. Just be pleased the ghost's gone, and go and find your ma."

"But there's more to know," Eddie said. "He talked as if he had a real life . . ."

"A restless spirit who doesn't even know it's passed on!" Tomkin declared, but his mocking, false-dramatic tone fell flat.

"Restless?" Kat shuddered. "You're welcome here, Eddie, but I hope to heaven your ghost doesn't follow you." She closed the notebook and handed it back. "Tomorrow, you're definitely going back to your ma."

Eddie took the book in silence.

"Yeah, come on, mate," said Tomkin, pouring hot water into the pot. The attic was filled with a comforting scent of tea that helped to take the chill from the atmosphere. "It's all in yer head. You said it tried to kill you, right, but how'd a ghost do that if your hand could go right through it?"

Eddie said nothing.

"Nah, seems to me like it had to be some kind of dream," said Tomkin. "I mean, if it can't touch you and you can't touch it, all you're left with is a fat lot of nothing, ain't yer?"

"But there are still questions . . ." Eddie said, worrying at the corner of his book.

"Questions!" Kat sounded exasperated. "They say curiosity killed the cat, don't they? I take that as a personal warning, and you should too. Just be glad it's gone."

She handed Eddie a woolen black overcoat. With so many homes lying in ruins, Eddie didn't need to ask where it had come from. He took his own frazzled coat off and pulled on the new one, turning the collar up against the cold behind him. He clutched a hot mug of tea in his hands. He'd always thought he could count on Kat, but he hadn't expected this. In the archway, after the fire, he'd tried so hard to work out the right decision that it was a shock to be told he'd got it completely wrong. It seemed that Kat didn't understand after all.

"Mother will leave town now," he said in a small voice. "She'll take the train to my aunt's house. She's probably already gone."

"Don't expect us to sub you for a ticket," said Tomkin, poking the fire.

"I have some money. I'll go tomorrow."

Kat gave a sigh of exasperation.

"I'm not throwing you out, Eddie," she said, "but surely you can see your place isn't here. Get out of the city and be safe. You're lucky."

Eddie didn't reply, he was already writing. If he had to work it all out by himself, he might as well make a start straightaway. And maybe it was more urgent than Kat realized, because no matter how he looked at it, he couldn't shake off the feeling that someone — or some*thing* — wished him harm.

CHAPTER 15

THE SHOWING GLASS

After the shock of his interrupted dreamwalk, David was led out of the Somnarium in silence and away from the nervous activity of the Map Room. The professor had ordered him to go and rest and had sent Petra to show him his room. But David's mind was racing now. The attack in the desert made him finally see the full implications of the Haunting's desire to kill Eddie. By the time they'd reached a door marked DREAMWALKERS' LODGE, he felt as if his stomach were full of ice.

"Wait! How can I rest? Adam is after Eddie . . . I have to get out there and stop him."

He backed away from the door and turned around, but Petra held on to him.

"Hey, calm down! You won't be able to help anyone if you panic."

"But you don't understand." David pushed her away. "Eddie's my granddad. If Adam kills him when he's still a boy, before he's even had any children, it's not just Unsleep House that won't exist now — my *dad* won't ever have been born. And where will that leave *me*? Where will that leave . . . oh, my God . . . Philippa!"

Petra grabbed David's wrists and forced him to look into her eyes.

"David, you've got to stay focused. Tell us where to find Eddie, and we can keep things the way they should be, the way they are now."

David looked at her, hardly seeing who it was. Until a few moments ago, his father had been just . . . *just!* . . . dead, but at least that meant he was beyond harm. After all, in the common-sense world, being dead already at least meant *new* stuff couldn't happen to you. But time-travel changed all that. In the world of dreamwalking, even the dead were in danger. It was a moment before David was aware that Petra was still talking to him.

"In your dreamwalks with Eddie, there must be something he said that can help us. Think, David. We could rescue Eddie now if you told us where to look."

"I don't know where he is. How would I? It was just a . . ." But David stopped himself. He'd wanted to say *just a dream*, but he would never again be able to think of dreaming in the same way.

Petra let go of him and gave him an encouraging smile.

"Hold out your hand."

David hesitated, then did as she asked.

"There," Petra said, folding his hand in both of hers. "Completely solid and real, isn't it? You're still here, aren't you? Well, that can only mean one thing — Adam hasn't reached Eddie yet. So relax, David — take the rest you need. And search your memory."

She released his hand and activated the door release to the Dreamwalkers' Lodge. The door slid open, and she stepped into a wide, floor-lit corridor. There were identical rows of sliding doors along both sides, stretching far down to double doors at the end. The look of the place was sophisticated and strangely complete after the bare rock and exposed cables of the rest of the base. It felt like looking into a rich man's spacecraft or a very futuristic hotel.

David hesitated on the threshold for a moment, then followed her inside. She was right. He himself was living proof that Eddie was still safe. And, yes, maybe a rest would help him remember something useful.

"You have a room along here," said Petra. "I'll show you. The doors down at the end there are for the Cave. A common room, I think you'd call it."

"The professor said you've been losing dreamwalkers," David said. "Was that Adam too?"

Petra nodded. They walked a little farther, and then she stopped before a closed door. Most of the doors had names on them, but not this one.

"Carlo's room," said Petra. "He ran into Adam a few days back. They say he'll be in a coma for years, or . . . well, he won't be back here, anyway. And Siri is still in the hospital. She doesn't speak, and they have already started emptying her room. And then there's . . ." She stopped when she saw the look on David's face.

"It would do no good to hide these things from you," Petra continued. "We have lost almost half our active dreamwalkers to Adam in the last week alone. This is why you need to stay focused, David. Adam is terribly dangerous."

They walked on in silence and eventually came to a room with David's name on it.

"Number five?" he said. "Is that me?"

"Yes, you're one of us now, part of the Dreamwalker Project. Five is your number. Mine is eleven. They're not ranks or anything, but that didn't stop Adam from insisting on being number one."

She glanced along the corridor toward another door, this one closed with security tape. According to the nameplate it was Adam Lang's room. David tried to imagine that tall figure walking around this place in a dreamwalker's black suit.

"How old is Adam?" he asked.

"Eighteen," said Petra. "Mr. Perfect is coming to the end of his career. That is probably what made him go and join the bad guys."

"But why, though?" said David. "What's really in it for him?"

"The Haunting will give him anything he desires — and I mean anything — if he can destroy us. Adam has been their worst enemy for years, but they'll happily forget all that if he shows them how to kill Eddie."

"But we can still stop them, right? I mean, surely there's someone here who can stand up to Adam."

Petra pushed back her hair and looked at David directly. "Someone has to," she said. "And I'm sure someone will."

David couldn't hold her gaze.

"Everyone says he's the most powerful dreamwalker ever," he said.

"He's the strongest we've known, yes, but now we have a new dreamwalker on our side, someone we haven't tested yet."

David looked at her, uncertain.

Petra gave a sigh of frustration, then pointed at a blue panel beside David's door.

"Put your hand on there."

David did so and felt something warm turn a complete circle inside the pad. The door slid open.

"They took your details as soon as they had you on the plane," said Petra, gesturing into the room. "Go on in; this is your new home."

David walked inside. The room was quite large and softly lit, but entirely characterless. There was a ready-made bed, a desk, and several empty bookshelves on the wall, but nothing homely about it at all. Over the bed was a prominent sign:

THE DREAMWALKER'S CODE

1. *BE SEEN, BUT NOT NOTICED.*
2. *TALK, BUT DON'T TELL.*
3. *LEAVE NO STONE TURNED.*

"Shouldn't that be 'leave no stone *unturned*'?" said David, but the look on Petra's face told him it shouldn't.

There was no window in the room, but one wall was made entirely of black glass, so highly polished that it was a clear mirror, floor to ceiling. Petra walked up to it and raised her hand. A video image appeared that took up most of the wall. The girl drew her fingers lightly through the air, shrinking the image size, then changed the channel several times with little flicks of her wrist.

"You'll get used to that soon," Petra said, yawning.

"So, what will Adam do now?" said David, sitting on the bed and rather hoping that Petra would do the same.

She gave him a faint smile.

"David, all you do is ask questions. But I want to go and lie down — Adam's not the only one who has been busy. Perhaps we can talk about this later? If you really can't wait, use the Showing Glass, but I think you should rest also."

David said nothing as Petra walked to the door. He felt a bit sorry for her — he knew he'd been firing off a lot of questions, but what did she expect? And there was one left that he just had to ask.

"Petra, did you ever meet my dad? I mean, did he ever come here?"

Petra paused at the door as it slid open.

"Your father? Well, David, if he was a visitor to this place I see no reason why someone like me would need to be told about it."

What kind of answer was that? Had Petra been told to keep something from him too? David suddenly remembered that he hadn't known her for more than a few hours, and he could see she was watching him closely from behind her unruly hair. He opened his mouth to speak, but she raised her finger to her lips.

"Use the Showing Glass, David — that's what it's for. Or you could always ask Misty." And with that she left.

David stared at the closed door. Petra had spoken the name of the computer with contempt in her voice but mischief in her eyes.

David lay back on the bed. He tried to get his head around the fact that he had gone from being an ordinary schoolboy to some kind of time-traveling ghost in a single day, but it still all seemed too bizarre. Surely all *this* was the dream, and he would wake up in a moment and find Mum knocking at his door, telling him he was late for school. He wondered about his mother for a moment, then sat up. She must have gone to the police hours ago. And what had she told Philippa? He remembered how she'd reacted when uniformed men had come to tell the family about his father's death. What would be going through her mind now? David's own mind began to race again, and he realized that he was nowhere near ready to rest.

He got up, stood before the black wall, and began waving his hands through the air as Petra had done, calling up panels and images on the mirror. After about five minutes of frustration, the basic commands became clear, and he felt ready to use the so-called Showing Glass. And somehow the machine recognized him, for his own name and photo appeared as the user, along with the words, *David Utherwise, dreamwalker number five. Access level: limited.*

David resented the word *limited*, but thinking how Roman had treated him he wasn't surprised. Swallowing his irritation, he typed out *ADAM LANG* and then waved *send*. An ID file appeared.

At the top left of the file was a photo. David had no difficulty recognizing the good-looking, black-haired boy who stared back at him, a shade of arrogance in his eyes and mouth. A true golden boy. David knew the type from school. And suddenly it all seemed so personal — this person really was out to get him and his whole family. David shuddered and scrolled down to read the file.

Adam Lang was from the United States, but he'd been with the Dreamwalker Project for over nine years. His profile gave few details of his personal life apart from an interest in something called Applied Psychic Field Theory. But there was a lot about his astonishing mental strength, including a chart showing Adam's Psychic Projection Quotient against that of other dreamwalkers. No one came close, not even Dishita. It was clear that the "science guys," as Petra called them, absolutely worshipped the great Adam Lang. David wiped the file away in disgust.

The next page was titled "Career History" and contained many sections that were blanked out. This must be what "Access level: limited" meant. Around these, though, David could still see that Adam's dreamwalking accomplishments were extraordinary, and no one, the file said, had done more to block the activities of the Haunting. When haunters tried to sell the Japanese the secret of the atom bomb in 1938, it had been Adam who'd personally devised the plan to stop them. And when haunters tried to engineer the early death of Howard Carter so that they could raid the tomb of Tutankhamen themselves in the present day, Adam dreamwalked for a record-breaking forty-two hours to ensure they failed. In fact, the list of secret honors Adam had been awarded filled a whole page of their own. David looked again at the smug face at the top of the file and wondered how much of Adam's current behavior was thanks to the excessive praise that had been heaped upon him in the past.

He cleared the screen and then typed in *the Haunting*.

"Hello again, David," said the voice of Misty. David jumped in his seat.

"Would you like me to help you? I like being helpful."

David hesitated a moment. Did this mean that Misty was everywhere in the base, listening? Could this be why Petra hadn't given him a straight answer about his father?

"Er, hi," he said. "I just wanted to know more about what I'm up against. Can you tell me about the Haunting, please?"

"I would be delighted to," said Misty, *"though they cover their traces so well that even I have limited knowledge of them. Is there anything specific you would like to know, David?"*

"Yeah. Who are they exactly?"

"The Haunting is a rival dreamwalking organization that seeks power over the present time through interference with the past. Whereas we study history in order to better understand the present, the Haunting terrorizes it in order to bring about a present more to their liking —"

"I know all that," David interrupted, "but *who* are they? Who's in charge? Who's going to be paying Adam his reward?"

"That information is officially unknown."

"And unofficially?"

"That information is unknown, David."

"But surely someone knows. Somebody has to be controlling the Haunting."

"My extended memory contains more information than the entire World Wide Web, David," said Misty, with a very definite hint of artificial hurt pride in her voice. *"Perhaps there's some other question you would like me to answer?"*

David stared at his own reflection in the black surface of the Showing Glass. It seemed incredible that the Dreamwalker Project, with all the resources it obviously commanded, not to mention the wonder of dreamwalking itself, couldn't identify the mastermind behind the organization trying to destroy it. Almost too incredible. But he wouldn't get far by annoying the Project's computer.

"Okay, Misty. Here's one. Is there no way to just stop Adam from dreamwalking? Some kind of gadget, or . . . you know, high-tech force field . . . thing?"

"Do you mean the Inhibitor, David?"

"Er . . . maybe. What is it?"

"A function of the Metascape Map. If we wish to prevent dream-walking at a given geo-temporal locale, we can disrupt the Psychic Field. It is in constant use at Unsleep House, preventing anyone from dreamwalking in at any time and date, and also preventing anyone from making an unscheduled dreamwalk out."

David ground his teeth. So there would be no chance of making a sneaky dreamwalk from his bed, then.

"But could it be used to stop Adam? To keep him away from Eddie, I mean."

"Only if we knew where Eddie was at every single point in his life. Now that he's run away, that's no longer the case. David, may I ask you a question now?"

David nodded, partly to test if Misty could see him as well as hear his voice.

"Where is Edmund Utherwise?"

"Misty, believe me, I wish I knew."

Everyone here seemed to think he had the answer to this question, and there were even people out there who wanted him dead as a result, but David really had no idea where Eddie might have gone. How on earth could he? However, even as he thought this, he experienced an unexpected twitch of memory, as if some recollection had just crossed his mind but was too fleeting and faint to grasp. Could it be that he knew something after all? He really needed time to think.

"Misty?"

"Yes, David?"

"You're a machine, right? A thinking machine?"

"I'm an artificial intellect, if that's what you mean," said Misty in a voice full of synthetic self-satisfaction. *"I am the first of my kind, and despite the lack of processing capacity made available to me —"*

"Okay, but does being a machine mean you can only tell the truth? I mean, can you lie?"

There was a brief pause.

"I wouldn't like to tell a lie, David. I really don't think I could."

Good.

"Misty, did my father ever come here?"

Another pause.

"I'm afraid I have to go now, David. I am required in the Map Room. I have enjoyed this little chat, and I hope we can do it again soon. Good-bye, David."

Silence.

"Misty?"

Silence.

David sighed. He shut down the Showing Glass and flopped onto the bed. Exhaustion had finally caught up with him, despite all the extraordinary things he had to think about. And now he had one more thing to think about too. It was becoming clear that his father *had* been here. But why? And why wouldn't anyone give him a straight answer? His thoughts began to melt together, and soon, despite his troubled mind, he drifted off to sleep.

CHAPTER 16

EDDIE'S GHOST

David slept for hours, and if he dreamed at all he didn't remember a thing. When he finally woke up he was ravenously hungry and remembered that he'd eaten nothing all day. He got out of bed and saw that it was nearly ten P.M. He decided to take a shower, but on his way to the small bathroom he spotted that the wardrobe was slightly open. He slid back the door and found six identical black outfits, the so-called zero-retention suits, each with the number five stitched in gold thread and the strange logo on the back.

Was he really ready to wear such a thing? As the son of a dead soldier, he hated the very idea of uniforms. But after his shower he put on one of the suits after all. As he admired himself in the mirror, he had to admit that the outfit looked cool.

Dreamwalker number five.

David was about to leave the room when something else caught his eye. On a bookshelf that he'd thought was empty, something slim was propped up in the corner. He could have sworn it hadn't been there before. He picked it up and felt his stomach contract when he saw what it was.

He was holding one of Eddie's notebooks.

David turned the book around and around in his hands, staring at it in amazement. He'd often seen these plain little books in the hands of the boy in his dream, but now he was actually holding one. And it was real — not some dreamed-up image, but a solid book of creases, yellowing paper, and rusty staples.

"Blast it, Eddie, where are you?" The feel of the book in his hands made David's long-lost grandfather seem suddenly very close, as if all he had to do was turn around to find Eddie standing there, squinting at him through his spectacles, ready with his pencil to scribble over yet another page. But Eddie wasn't close at all. As David flicked through the pages, the furious jottings and crossings-out flashing before his eyes, he caught a whiff of age from the paper. He realized for the first time the enormous truth of just how far away Eddie really was, locked into his own time and lost in what might as well be another world.

David stopped flicking at a page where a single question stood out in bold letters, heavily circled: *What is David?*

Every line that had been drawn away from this question led to a tangle of crossing-out.

David looked at this for a long time before he closed the book. All those times he'd seen Eddie with his nose in one of these books, he'd never realized that the subject of all that writing had been himself.

Instead of putting the book back on the shelf, he rolled it up and stuffed it in his pocket, just as Eddie used to do. He and Eddie both had questions, it seemed. David swore to himself there and then that before all this was over they would both find their answers.

David picked his way back through the maze of corridors to the canteen. He ordered an enormous meal and sat at a table on his own. People looked at him and sometimes whispered, and he could tell that he was being watched. Roman came in briefly and poured himself a small cup of coffee. He gave David a long, hard stare before stalking out. This didn't help David's appetite, and he left his meal half finished after that. He went back to the Lodge, feeling highly self-conscious and more than a little out of place.

Back in the corridor he decided not to return to his bedroom but instead to visit the place called the Cave that Petra had mentioned earlier. He pressed his hand against the panel, and the double doors slid open.

His first impression was of a large crazy-shaped space with no ceiling at all, just a high shadowed vault where two rock faces arched together. Seeing this, David finally understood that the whole complex must have been built within a natural split in the mountain, beneath the château he'd been shown in the dreamwalk. The thought made him giddy as he walked to the center of the room.

There were armchairs and sofas scattered in groups near a low-lit bar on one side of the cavern, while the rest of the space was divided into different areas, one clearly for gaming, another for dancing and music, and yet another housing a multimedia library with a giant screen. One wall was taken up by an enormous slab of yellow rock, which clearly didn't belong to the mountain. On the rock a spindly human form was painted in a strong line of vivid blue, surrounded by a halo of fuzzy dots. At the feet of the figure crept half-human, half-animal shapes in reds and browns.

Opposite this striking feature, an enormous window reached the whole height of the wall, sealing the cavern with a single sheet of glass. It was the first window David had seen since he'd arrived, and through it he could make out a black, jagged horizon beneath a twilit sky studded with stars.

He noticed Petra curled up in an armchair. She waved at him, and he walked over to find Dishita sitting there too, still looking frail. There was also a dark-haired boy who looked familiar. When David got closer he realized it was Théo, the boy he'd watched narrowly escaping the Haunting on the Metascape Map. None of them was wearing a black dreamwalker suit as David was now, and his heart sank as he realized he'd got it wrong again.

"Here's number five!" called Petra. "All dressed up and one of us at last."

"I don't feel it," said David, blushing. "I still can't believe I'm really here."

He sat down and was introduced to Théo as a waiter came over. It was as he ordered himself an icy drink that he remembered his mother.

"There's no phone in my room," he said to Petra. "I need to call home. My mum'll be going mad."

"Ah," said Petra, "you can only call out from the front desk, actually. If they let you."

"But she must be wondering where I am."

"She probably already knows," said Dishita. "Or rather, she thinks she does. They're bound to have told her something she'll accept. Unsleep House employs some very persuasive people. None more so than us dreamwalkers."

"What does that mean?" said David.

"Remember the château you saw on your dreamwalk earlier?" said Dishita. "My family thinks it's a top-flight science academy. And they were only too ready to believe it, especially with a dreamwalker telling it to them. A freed mind is so much stronger than a captive one, David, as you'll know when you can finally be bothered to take the training course."

"Other people think it's a hospital or a Swiss finishing school," said Petra, glaring at Dishita, "or whatever it needs to be. Your mother would have been told something entirely convincing, David; don't worry about it."

"It's easier for dreamwalkers who don't live at Unsleep House," said Théo, "the part-timers who work from home. It's only us misfits the Project keeps here, where we can look out for each other."

Théo put his hand on Petra's shoulder and gave a slight squeeze. For some reason she seemed grateful to him for what he'd just said.

David changed the subject.

"So this Unsleep House I keep hearing about, it's just the name of the château, then?"

"Yes," said Dishita, "though we rarely use the old place these days. It was a gift to your grandfather from the Swiss government."

"They gave Eddie a stately home? That's insane!"

"When the Dreamwalker Project took off, the United Nations wanted it based somewhere neutral." Dishita shrugged, as if what she was saying was entirely normal. "The Swiss were only too happy to have us. Sir Edmund renamed it, and it's been Unsleep House ever since."

"Eddie really is a big deal for you people, isn't he?" said David.

"Sir Edmund is *everything* to us," Dishita replied.

David looked again at his sophisticated surroundings, and tried to imagine what the shy, geeky boy from his dream would say if David told him he would one day turn out to be the founder of all this. Not to mention the discoverer of something as extraordinary as dreamwalking. His eye was drawn back to the strange rock painting of the spindly blue man.

"I see you're admiring the art," said Dishita with a chuckle. "And so you should. That is the oldest image of a dreamwalker yet discovered. Or rather, I should say, of a *haunter.*"

"How old exactly?"

"Oh, only about thirty thousand years."

"What?"

"It was found in a cave in southern France a few years ago. That particular shade of blue would have been very difficult for prehistoric man to create, so they must have really wanted to use it. The further back you try and dreamwalk the harder it is to do it accurately, but the Haunting are always pushing the limit. We managed to stop them that time, but the professor insisted on securing the evidence once the cave was discovered. They set it up here as a reminder of what we're up against."

"Talking of which," David said, "are you okay? I'm still not sure I understand what happened to you earlier, but it looked like it must have hurt."

Dishita seemed pleased David was asking, but it was clear she wasn't going to be fussed.

"It was nothing. Just an unpleasant surprise."

"That wasn't a normal spear, right?"

"No, there wasn't really a spear at all," she said. "When we make a mind attack like that, we often dream up something that fits the environment we're in to help us do it. But it's just pure mental energy. The spear was simply a way to project that energy."

"Yeah, but you vanished," said David.

"Like I said, it was a surprise. Knocked right out of my dreamwalk like some newbie. I'll get Adam for that."

"So is that what Adam wants to do to Eddie? Kill him with a mind attack?"

Théo let out a laugh, then tried to cover it up. He stood, said good night, and left the Cave.

"No," Dishita said, in a voice that suggested she'd just been asked something very stupid. "Even the strongest mind pulse has no effect on the physical world. It's a dreamwalker weapon only."

"So what's Adam planning, then? How dangerous can he be to Eddie if he can't even touch him?"

"Didn't you visit the museum earlier?" said Dishita. "He'll do what the Haunting always do — find someone in 1940 to terrify into helping him. And whomever he chooses, it won't be anyone Eddie will want to meet in a dark alley, that's for certain."

"You've stopped the Haunting before, though. So . . ."

"But with Adam it's different, David. He used to be one of us. He knows how we operate. He knows to keep moving so that we can't pinpoint him on the Metascape Map. He's got every advantage now, except one: He clearly doesn't know where Eddie's gone either. That's where you come in."

"I keep telling you people," David said, "I don't know where Eddie is."

"Are you sure?" Dishita narrowed her eyes at him. "Because if you did know, we could get Eddie to safety tonight, move him to some random place in 1940 Adam could never guess at. You could end all this very quickly."

David folded his arms, wishing more than ever that he did know something, if only to shut everyone up about it.

"I looked Adam up on the Showing Glass thing," said David, "but I couldn't get much sense of him as a person. Except for all this business about him being the best dreamwalker you've ever had."

"Ha!" Dishita looked unimpressed. "He'd love to hear you say that. He's good, yes, and his mind's very strong, but that doesn't mean the rest of us are losers. Adam's too arrogant and selfish to really be the best."

"David, can I ask you something?" said Petra.

David nodded, grateful to have questions going the other way for a change.

"What's Eddie actually like? As a teenager, I mean? We know he was good-looking and painfully shy, but what was he like to be with?"

David blinked. Didn't they know? And *good-looking? Eddie?* David realized both girls were watching him eagerly, and a flash of jealousy interfered with his fears for Eddie's safety once again. He tried to ignore it. Anyway, if you liked tall and thin with sad eyes and decades-old clothes, then okay, perhaps Eddie was good-looking. To David, though, he'd always seemed sickly — far too pale to be healthy. No doubt that was because of all the books and writing . . .

Dishita let out a gasp.

David followed her gaze and found that he'd absentmindedly taken Eddie's notebook from his pocket.

"That's one of Sir Edmund's notebooks! They're priceless! Where did you get it?"

"I found it in my room. And if you really want to know what Eddie was like, just look inside."

Dishita took the book as if it were a sacred text, allowing the pages to fall open, one after another.

"It's one of his early ones. So few of them survive . . ." Dishita trailed off. David guessed she was noticing that almost everything that had been written in the book had then been crossed out. She glanced up at David.

"That's what he was like," said David, pointing at the scribbles. "Lost. But desperate not to be."

Dishita sniffed and handed the book back.

"He was still very young. He hadn't made any of his breakthroughs yet. But believe me, Sir Edmund had a brilliant mind."

"Yes, but we're not looking for Sir Edmund," said Petra. "We're looking for the confused boy who will grow into him. Is that what you're trying to tell us, David?"

David wasn't sure he'd been trying to tell them anything, but he nodded anyway and tried to look smarter than he felt.

"You know, now that I think about it, Eddie was exactly the kind of person who *would* make friends with a ghost." David chuckled. "But I've been wondering about something. You say Eddie discovered dreamwalking as an adult, but when he was a boy was he a dreamwalker himself?"

"Yes," said Dishita, "we think so. Dreamwalking can be hereditary, you know. Sir Edmund remembered especially vivid dreams from his childhood that he later came to realize were probably dreamwalks. Don't forget, you yourself didn't realize you could dreamwalk until we told you, but there was no one to tell Eddie. By the time he'd worked it out by himself, his own abilities were long gone."

"And you were his inspiration, David," said Petra. "Eddie's ghost."

David grew thoughtful again. If dreamwalking was hereditary, and David had the gift, and his grandfather had had it too, then . . .

"Do you really have no idea where Eddie might have run to after the fire?" said Dishita, interrupting his thoughts. "Because they're going to ask you again. Roman is planning to interview you extensively, starting first thing in the morning. They're expecting some new information. It might get a bit heavy."

"Oh, great!" said David.

He wondered just how heavy Roman would get before he accepted that David had nothing at all to tell them.

"I wish I could have a rummage in Adam's room."

The two girls looked at him in surprise.

"What for?" said Dishita. "Security's been all over it since Adam disappeared. Roman searched it personally."

"I don't know," said David. "I just can't quite believe in Adam Lang. Everyone keeps telling me he was so powerful and amazing, but no one's *that* good. Maybe if I could get a better sense of him, I could think of some way to stop him. Everyone has a weak spot."

"Maybe," said Petra, "but there is no way to get into Adam's room without either his handprint or security clearance. And the door's taped up. I'd love to break in, but they would notice."

"Oh, the tape can be stuck back on," said Dishita quietly.

The conversation moved on after that, and Dishita became withdrawn and eventually stopped speaking entirely. It was long past midnight when they rose to go to bed. As they walked out into the corridor and said good night, Dishita broke in with an unexpected question.

"Do you really think it would be worthwhile looking in Adam's room?" she asked.

David shrugged. "I'd certainly like to know more about him. Especially since he seems determined to wipe out my whole family."

Dishita seemed to be caught in indecision, but after a moment she spoke.

"In that case, meet me in the corridor in two hours' time. I know how to get into Adam's room."

CHAPTER · 17
LONDON, DECEMBER 17, 1940, 6:45 P.M.

Charlie Grinn stood before the classical front of Saint Paul's Cathedral and waited. In the inside pocket of his trench coat he could feel the gloriously thick roll of notes that he'd won when the horse named Trojan Mate had come home first, much to everyone's surprise. Two unlikely wins in a row — neither of them the least bit predictable. Grinn loved gambling, but he loved winning more, and he was now faced with the promise of a fortune, all for the paltry price of the life of one insignificant boy.

But how could Adam possibly make good on his promise? How could anyone know the future? Then again, there was clearly something very peculiar about the strange boy in the improbably good suit. Only that morning Grinn had seen him apparently walk through a solid brick wall, and though common sense insisted it must have been some sort of trick, Grinn couldn't see how he'd possibly done it.

The gangster pulled his coat collar up around his ears. The sun was gone and it was bitterly cold. Was that a black cat he could see sauntering past him? With the blackout in force, the city nights were so dark it was hard to be sure of anything. Grinn's eyes darted around the plaza and he was relieved that he could still just about pick out the five men he'd scattered around as security against some sort of setup.

"Still don't trust me, I see," said a voice right behind him.

Grinn spun around to see the dark figure of Adam standing just a pace away.

"I told you to come alone."

"Why should I trust you?" Grinn stammered. "You're not normal, not . . . natural. How did you know about those races? Who *are* you?"

"I told you, my name is Adam. And didn't I explain that I have special knowledge of things? Come on, Grinn — clearly the horse won or you wouldn't be here now."

"Adam? Right," said Grinn, grateful that the young man's gaze was not boring into him as it had done earlier. He really didn't want to feel that sensation again.

"So, Mr. Adam, you said something about a boy."

"Yes. You are well known in this city as a man who can find people, Mr. Grinn, a man who can get things done. No one knows London's underworld as well as you. Come with me now, and I will give you your next target, and then — when you have killed the boy — we can go about making you rich."

With that, Adam moved away, covering a great distance with each enormous stride. Grinn was taken by surprise and almost had to run to keep up.

"You want me to do it now?" he said. "Good thing I always carry a knife, Mr. Adam, but what's the hurry?"

"Unfortunately, there is a slight complication," Adam replied over his shoulder. "The boy in question has gone into hiding. You may need your network of contacts to find him first."

"You don't know where he is?" Grinn said, without thinking. "But I thought you said you knew things."

Adam turned on Grinn, his eyes bright and terrible as two black suns. The gangster almost fell over with shock. The five bodyguards who were trailing them stopped too, but none dared approach.

"We can either work together, Mr. Grinn, or I can drop you now and find someone else. Which will it be?"

"All right, all right," said Grinn, holding his hands up. "You lead on, and when I know enough, I'll get the lads out hunting. We'll have this boy in a day or two, don't you doubt it, Mr. Adam."

"A wise decision. Now hurry! Like you, I can't stay anywhere for too long," Adam said as he strode off. Grinn jogged along behind him in silence.

After half an hour walking, they came to a part of the city that had been hit in the raid the night before, a residential area. Grinn felt a sense of satisfaction at the sight of so many rich people's houses in ruins and the thought of the treasures that lay in them, waiting to be looted. He'd have to get the lads busy here too.

They came to a street that was especially badly hit and stopped by what remained of one particular house. The smell of wet soot and burned belongings was bitter and strong.

Adam climbed the steps of the collapsed house and pointed down into the rubble of what must have once been a hallway.

"Who's got the light?" Grinn called out to the five men behind him. "Come on now, look sharp!"

Tater came forward and handed his boss a flashlight. Grinn flicked it on, turned the narrow wartime beam to the floor, and saw a shattered picture frame. He reached down and lifted a badly scorched photo from the wreckage. Despite the fire and water damage, he could clearly make out a thin boy with glasses and a studious look.

"This," said Adam, "is Edmund Utherwise. He is your target. Find him and snuff him out, and little Eddie boy will make your fortune. Are you man enough for the job, Mr. Grinn? I want it done. I want it seen to."

Charlie Grinn stared at the boy in the photo. There was a slight sense of unease in his mind — it was just a child, after all — but Grinn was long past having much of a conscience about these matters. He could no longer even count the number of people he'd killed, so what was one more life? Especially when people were dying all around him in night after night of air raids. *Business is business*, thought Grinn, as he put the picture in his pocket.

"I am, Mr. Adam — more than man enough. I'll get the boys on it straightaway. If this Eddie is still alive and still in the city, I'll find him. And then I'll introduce him to this." And with that he took the bone-handled knife from his pocket and flicked out the blade. The metal gleamed in the beam of the flashlight.

Adam let out a long sigh of satisfaction.

Then he spoke.

"Now, listen up, Grinn. It's true I don't know where little Eddie is hiding right now, but I may yet be able to lead you to him. It just so happens I know precisely where he will be at noon tomorrow."

CHAPTER · 18
THE FORESHADOW

Still dressed in the dreamwalker suit, David slid back his door and peered out. The corridor was very dimly lit now. He looked down toward Dishita's room and noticed the shadows move slightly. Dishita stepped forward into the low light and David went to meet her, his footsteps silent with the soft rubber of his boots. Within moments Petra had joined them, and they all crept over to Adam's door. Both David and Petra were looking at Dishita expectantly. The older girl gave each of them a small pocket flashlight.

"I suppose I should explain," she whispered, "but I won't. All you need to know is that our doors have an emergency release. The codes are simple, and Adam and I amused ourselves by breaking them one afternoon."

Dishita seemed embarrassed. She turned away and began peeling the adhesive tape off the door, sticking it across the wall for later. When she'd finished, she reached her fingers into a recess in the wall, and a small panel swung silently open. There was a keypad and a narrow screen on it.

"I didn't know about that," said Petra. "You mean Security can just get into our rooms?"

Dishita shrugged and started keying in digits. "I don't know the code for *your* room, Petra."

The door hissed open and Dishita slipped into the dark beyond, beckoning the others to follow. Once the door had been closed, Dishita switched on her flashlight. The others did the same.

David saw that Adam's room was identical to his own, except that someone had clearly lived there for a very long time. It was also obvious that the room had been thoroughly searched. There were clothes and personal stuff everywhere, and a mass of printouts teetered in the center of the desk, beside a laptop on standby. It looked as if someone had been working at the desk very recently, probably an investigator from Security. On one wall was an impressive collection of oriental swords, and on another — quite bizarrely — was a series of photographs of a sinister-looking black cat. Something about it seemed familiar.

"He's a cat lover?" David had hoped to learn all sorts of interesting things in his enemy's room, but an interest in small furry animals hadn't been one of them.

"Oh, that," said Dishita. "That's Adam's little trick. He's been perfecting it for years. Most dreamwalkers are restricted to their true dreamselves when they dreamwalk, but Adam can change himself entirely. The cat is his favorite. Nasty, sneaky creature. Like Adam himself."

"You remember he made himself look like you?" said Petra. "To lure Eddie home? Most of us would struggle to do something like that, but Adam was always proud of being a shape-shifter."

On the floor were two cardboard boxes, shoved to one side as if dismissed. David made a mental note of the cat thing and began to go through them.

"So, what are we looking for?" said Petra.

"Anything interesting," David replied, not really knowing himself. "Anything that tells us what Adam will do next, I suppose. And anything we can use to stop him."

"Don't you think we're working on that already?" Dishita aimed her flashlight at him, but David didn't answer. He still felt that all this was intensely personal, and he didn't trust the man named Roman to do a proper job.

Petra opened the wardrobe and climbed inside. Dishita went to the desk.

"David," she said, "look at this."

She was holding a large pile of printed papers. On top was a series of detailed maps showing bomb damage in London during the Blitz, giving precise times and locations.

"See what I mean?" she said. "Adam is very thorough."

"Okay, but we've already saved Eddie from that one. If you find a piece of paper marked *Plan B*, I'd like to see it."

David turned back to his cardboard box. It contained a surprising number of books, some of them pretty old, just carelessly tossed inside. And they all appeared to be about ghost sightings and haunted houses.

"Why would he have all these?"

Petra came out of the wardrobe.

"Ah, they're nothing," she said with a grin. "We all read those."

"But why?" said David.

"Why do you think? In case we're in them. You know, being spotted by Victorian chambermaids in the library at midnight, or floating down castle stairways. We try hard not to be noticed but it still happens. I was once seen rising up through a kitchen floor in Renaissance Venice. I've never heard so much screaming! It's probably in one of these books, actually . . ."

"We can't stay here long," Dishita snapped. "Petra, you can show off your scrapbook later."

Petra grinned at David and then began looking under the bed.

"I bet the best stuff's under here."

David looked around. Where else could they look? Then he remembered the Showing Glass.

"Can't we find out what he's been looking at on this?" he said, raising his hand to activate it.

"Don't!" cried Dishita, pulling his hand away. "If you switch it on, you'll alert Misty. We're not supposed to be here, remember? Besides, he would hardly keep anything secret on there."

David thought about this and was surprised that it reminded him of his mother, of all people. She owned a secondhand bookshop and café, and he was used to seeing tattered old books piled up at home, as well as hearing her low opinion of computers. He grinned when he thought what she'd say if she saw the Showing Glass or heard Misty. He had a sudden pang of homesickness and wondered again what his mum must really be thinking about his disappearance. David turned back to the books, something she had once said to him very clear in his mind.

"Talking of secrets," he said, "what's the best way to keep a secret in the Internet age?"

Dishita gave him an impatient look.

"No, seriously," he said. "How do you keep a secret from a computer hacker? Easy — you write it on a piece of paper."

David emptied the books out of the box and onto the bed. There were ten in all. Every title was on some ghostly theme, but one of them caught his eye: *Ghosts and Hauntings through the Ages*. At least, that was what it said on the dust wrapper. But the dust wrapper, as his mum would certainly have pointed out, was ever so slightly too big. He took it off to reveal the true title hidden on the book itself: *The Real Railway Children: The Story of London's Evacuees*.

"This one's got nothing to do with ghosts," said David. Petra and Dishita came over to look. "It is about Eddie's time, though. But why would Adam be reading about kids and trains?"

David thought of his mum again and balanced the book on his hand, spine down. It fell open at a place that had obviously been looked at a lot. David closed the book and then let it fall open again. The same thing happened.

The double page that lay open before him contained a single large black-and-white photo. It showed a railway station with swarms of children in coats, scarves, and caps, grouping up around a train shrouded in steam: evacuees from the Blitz, with boxed gas masks around their necks and blank faces that stared into an unknown future without their parents. It was like so many pictures David had seen in history lessons at school, but as he looked at it he had a sudden idea and began scanning the faces closely, wishing there was more light.

"Oh, give that to me," Dishita said. She snatched the book and lit it with a steady beam. After a moment she gasped and held the book out to David, tapping the photo with a long, red fingernail.

"Who is this, David?"

He looked into the photo, and his breath caught in his throat. Among the anxious faces and steam clouds was someone he knew.

It was Eddie.

He grabbed the book back.

"There's no date," he said. "So maybe . . ."

"Maybe nothing!" Dishita pointed again. "Look at him closely."

David peered into the photo and, despite the coarse grain, he could see that Eddie's hair was wild and his face marked with burns. The coat he was wearing looked far too big for him.

"In the original time line, Eddie and his mother left the city by train the day after their home was destroyed," said Dishita, speaking quickly. "They went from Paddington station. Obviously we've been back to watch that train — it was one of the first places we visited when your grandfather went missing — but Eddie wasn't there. The station was so crowded we had to give up, and anyway, history had changed, making the Archive unreliable. But this picture proves that he *did* go to the station at some point shortly after the fire. All we have to do is find out exactly where and when this photograph was taken, and we'll have him."

"But . . ." David blinked at Dishita. ". . . but how can Adam have this? I mean, how can Adam have seen Eddie in this picture *before* he'd done anything to change his history? It doesn't make sense."

"Oh, when will you take that training program, David? In the world of time-travel, common sense gets turned on its head. This photo is what we call a *foreshadow*. Sometimes, when someone in the present has *absolutely made up their mind* to change the past, tiny traces of the consequences of that change can already be detected in history, even before the change is made. This is one of the reasons we often get ahead of the Haunting. No wonder Adam tried to hide it. I just don't understand why Misty didn't pick up on it, because technically . . ."

But David had stopped listening.

In his head was a vision of Eddie, walking along the edge of a platform, lost and alone. In the shadows of a nearby railway arch Adam was watching. Beside him crouched the faceless figure of some heartless killer, willing to do Adam's bidding out of fear or greed. A train was approaching the platform. Eddie stopped to watch it pass, unaware of the movement behind him. All it would take was one quick shove . . .

David caught sight of his own reflection in the dark of Adam's Showing Glass. For a moment, as the flashlight beams moved, he saw himself fade away, just as he would surely do if Adam killed his grandfather. And now it seemed that Adam had succeeded where David had failed: He'd found Eddie. In the Showing Glass there was only blackness now.

David began to panic.

"Why are we still standing here?" he cried. "We've got to tell the professor!"

Petra put her hand out to him and was about to say something when the door flew open. Four security men barreled straight in, short batons in their hands. Behind them, filling the entrance, loomed the massive figure of Roman.

CHAPTER · 19
THE HOLE IN MISTY'S MEMORY

In a silk robe covered with swirly patterns, the professor looked even more out of place in the ultramodern surroundings than he normally did. He was clearly annoyed to have been woken and insisted on dealing with the "break-in," as Roman called it, in his own office. David, Petra, and Dishita waited beside his desk while the professor stood on the other side, grumbling as he tried to clear a space to sit. The four security men were at the door. Roman loomed over the professor and glared at him.

"This is a serious security breach, Professor," said Roman, clearly struggling to express his anger in English. "Hand them over to me. You have other dreamwalkers."

"Hardly, Commander," said Professor Feldrake. "With all those we've lost recently, do you really think I'm going to let you start locking up the few we have left, just because you failed to spot a loophole in our security? No. Please wait outside while I have a little chat with these young people."

"'Little chat'?" Roman spat the words out. "These 'young people' treat this place like a playground, while you arc the soft schoolmaster with your little chats and your piles of . . . rubbish," he added, waving at the scholarly chaos of the professor's office. He strode to the door, but then turned.

"This place needs a strong leader, Feldrake. If you want more time for your dusty old books and 'little chats,' it can easily be arranged." And with that he left in a bearlike huff, taking his guards with him.

"I'm afraid he's right," said the professor after the men had gone, "much as I hate to say it. The people who fund this place are getting scared, and may well take things out of my hands. As Head of Security, Roman would effectively be in charge of everything we do. Is that what you three want? Heaven knows there are enough soldiers about the place already. The research program is virtually dead as it is."

No one spoke.

"David, you've hardly been here twenty-four hours yet," said the professor in exasperation. "And Dishita, I'm surprised at you. Petra, less so."

"It was my idea," said David. "I just wanted to know more about Adam. And I have the right — he's trying to kill my whole family!"

"But you could have just asked," said the professor as he finally sat down. "It's late now, but come and see me in the morning, David, and I'll try to answer your questions. Now go to bed, all of you, while I think of something to tell Roman."

"But I found this," said David, taking from his pocket the book he'd found in Adam's room. He handed it over and explained about the dust wrapper. The professor sat down again and looked at the book with interest, then let it fall open. David pointed at the photo.

The professor's eyebrows jumped.

He pressed the book open with a large fossil ammonite and jabbed a button on his desk. In a moment Roman was back in the room.

"Did you know about this?" said the professor.

"That book was impounded by Security," snapped Roman, eyeing the discarded dust jacket. "Of course I knew about it. I went through Adam Lang's room personally. This is just one of those ghost books the children waste their time on. Nothing."

"Oh, it's much more than nothing," said Professor Feldrake, removing the fossil and handing the book to Roman, a mixture of triumph and alarm on his face. "I think these 'children' have just found what we've all been hunting for. And in a 'dusty old book' too."

Roman grabbed the book, clearly prepared to dismiss it. But then he stopped and stared. Eventually he looked at David, the set of his face completely transformed as if a great weight of stress had just been lifted off it.

"Misty."

"Yes, Commander?" said the honeyed voice of the computer.

"Analyze." And Roman held the book up into the air, flat open, gripped with one enormous hand. There was a brief pulse of light from the ceiling.

"This photograph is not in the Archive."

"What!" cried the professor. "But how can that be?"

"It was removed eighteen months ago as part of routine memory optimization."

"Who signed for it?" The professor spoke as if he knew the answer already.

"It was dreamwalker number one: Adam Lang."

The professor slumped back into his chair.

"Eighteen months!" he said, shaking his head. "He's been plotting against us *that* long?"

"Misty," said Dishita, "search outside sources. The photograph shows platform one at Paddington station sometime in December 1940."

"Connecting to World Wide Web . . . Please wait . . . I have it. This photograph was taken on the eighteenth of December, probably with a Leica III due to the photographer's preference . . ."

"Stop!" Roman bellowed. "What time *exactly*? Analyze!"

"That information is not available," said Misty after a moment. *"I couldn't tell you, Commander, even if you asked me nicely."*

But before Roman could reply, Dishita spoke again. "I'm sorry, Misty. Please estimate the time of taking from available data."

"Given that the building has a glass roof," Misty replied in a vaguely hurt tone, *"the angle of visible shadow at the time of year suggests that this photograph was taken between eleven thirty and noon. I hope you'll agree that this analysis is useful."*

"Thank you, Misty," said Dishita. "And it would be even more useful to know if Adam's been active since he attacked me in the desert. Has there been any sign of him, or any haunter, in London at the time and place this picture was taken?" When this question was met with silence, Dishita added, "Please, Misty."

"As you know, Dishita, I often detect Adam's presence in London, but unless more processing capacity is allocated to me . . ."

"I do know, Misty." Dishita spoke as if she was talking to a child. "But we already give you all we can. Please, try your best. Has Adam been to the station?"

There was a moment of silence, before Misty spoke again.

"No," she said in a small voice, as if failing to simultaneously monitor every particle of data in the Metascape Map was something to be ashamed of. *"I have no record of Adam Lang visiting that geo-temporal locale. But that's hardly my fault. How can you expect me to be useful when —"*

"Thank you, Misty," the professor interrupted, before turning to the others. "We've talked too much. We must act quickly to secure Sir Edmund. There will have been policemen in the station at the moment this picture was taken. If we're careful, we should be able to use them to get him safely away before Adam and whoever he's got helping him arrive."

"Let him come," Roman rumbled, his eyes blazing. "When Adam responds to this, we will be ready. We will crush him."

"If I really have to, I'd rather use the Inhibitor to block him . . ." the professor said.

"No!" Roman was shouting again. "That also blocks us."

"I won't see our founder used as bait, Commander," said the professor, jabbing the desk with his finger, "and I won't have another dreamwalker face Adam. They're kids, for pity's sake, not your private army. The hospital is full of broken minds as it is."

Everyone, including Roman, seemed surprised by the professor's outburst. The old man took a deep breath, adjusted his glasses, then spoke in more even tones.

"Dishita, what leverage do we have with Scotland Yard in December 1940?"

"From our research into the new sequence of events since Eddie's disappearance, we know that Eddie's mother had reported her son missing by the time this photo was taken, so we should be able to use that. If we can find a way to involve only the police who were already present at the railway station, we could arrange to have Eddie picked up without too much disturbance to the time line." Then she added, with a gleam in her eye, "Are you approving a violation of the Dreamwalker's Code, Professor? Officially?"

"What choice do I have? Yes — it's official. But I don't need to tell you to be careful, do I?"

"Then I'll need to dreamwalk immediately," said Dishita. "The preparations will take hours, and I couldn't sleep now anyway."

The professor nodded.

David wanted to speak, but he stopped when he saw Roman. The big man was gazing at some inward scene only he could see, and it was clear to everyone that he was more intent on the chance to attack Adam than on rescuing Eddie.

The professor sighed. "David found this picture," he said to Roman. "I think you should thank him. Admit it, there's more to David Utherwise than you thought."

Roman snapped out of his reverie and turned to David. His face began twitching as if he was chewing on something strange that wasn't meant to be eaten. He said nothing, but with a sudden movement he reached out and gave David a ferocious slap on the back.

"To work!" he boomed. "Misty, if you smell that dog Adam even near London, you let me know, okay?"

"Okay, Commander."

"When he shows up, we will crush him." Roman seemed bigger than ever as he left the room.

The professor stared after him with a look of anguish.

CHAPTER · 20
BE SEEN, BUT NOT NOTICED

David slept badly. The triumph he'd felt over discovering the photo of Eddie had soon given way to a dreadful worry that they wouldn't reach him in time.

Time.

It all came back to that in the end, and dreamwalking was giving David a new perspective on time that turned the common-sense world inside out. Everyone was worried about Eddie's future, about finding him and keeping him alive, but the bizarre truth of it was this: Right there and then, in the present, as David lay sweating on his bed, Edmund Utherwise *was already dead*.

And yet it was David who was the ghost!

When he eventually got up and dressed he couldn't face breakfast. He went straight to the Somnarium to see how preparations were going, but when he arrived he had the defi-nite impression he wasn't expected. Or needed, even. A young researcher with a harassed look took pity on him and showed him through to the Archive anyway.

The Archive of the Dreamwalker Project, a lofty rock chamber off the Map Room, was dominated by a Showing Glass almost as high as the window in the Lodge. Despite the room's name, the only papers David could see were the files and printouts around Professor Feldrake, as if the man somehow carried his own personal atmosphere of old-fashioned academic disorder wherever he went.

The professor was standing with a team of researchers to one side of the enormous screen, while two groups of three dreamwalkers stood directly in front of it. One group consisted of Petra, Dishita, and Théo, the other of people David hadn't met before. Before them, gigantic images passed across the surface of the Showing Glass: static photographs of trains, hurrying passengers, uniformed porters, and soldiers, all interspersed with short bursts of sound and film. The photo David had found briefly appeared, and David's eyes shot straight to the face of Eddie, looking lost in a crowd of evacuees. To the side there was a stream of smaller images showing 1940s clothing, cigarette cases, spectacles, and other personal items.

David walked slowly over to Petra as a photograph of an elaborate station clock towered in front of them, its hands moving by digital manipulation until they reached noon.

"What's all this for?" he whispered.

"To help us dream up our target date, time, and place," said Dishita, overhearing. "We need visual, geographic, and temporal references in order to dreamwalk accurately to a precise point in time and place. Some dreamwalks take weeks of careful preparation, but this one is actually quite straightforward. Paddington station is a well-documented building."

David knew the station quite well himself, but glancing up at the black-and-white photos of Paddington in the Age of Steam, he could tell he was going to see something extraordinary.

The briefing rounded off with a blizzard of technical details and schematic diagrams of the building that David struggled to follow. Then the researchers stood back and the professor raised his eyebrows at Dishita.

"We're ready," she said in a confident tone. "We'll get there."

A fair-haired boy who must have been the leader of the second team nodded agreement, but asked, "Is six of us enough, Professor? Shouldn't we send in a third team, just in case?"

"No, we need to keep this as low-key as possible. Dishita has been dreamwalking for hours already, laying the groundwork for the police pickup. All you need to do is watch over it and stop the Haunting from interfering. Beside, you won't be just six — David Utherwise is going with you."

The second team eyed him with curiosity and some suspicion.

"I don't want to be rude," said the fair-haired boy, "but might there not be, er . . . a training issue with David?"

One of his team snickered, and Dishita and Théo exchanged glances. David clenched his fists.

"He's key to this mission." Petra moved over to David's side. "More important than the rest of us put together."

"Well said." Professor Feldrake came and stood among them all. "Not only is he our only native Londoner, but his connection to Eddie more than makes up for his lack of experience. It would be foolish to keep him back."

"He is a liability," said a voice from the darkest corner of the room, and David turned to discover that Roman had been standing there the whole time. "And he'll be no use against Adam."

"I have made it very clear that no one will fight Adam," the professor said firmly. "These dreamwalkers are authorized to confront other members of the Haunting, but no one is to take on Adam himself. I would be grateful if you restricted yourself to security matters in the present, Commander, and left me to handle the past."

No one spoke in the Archive after that, but David saw Roman catch Dishita's eye before he left the room.

The two teams of dreamwalkers were led from the Archive to the Somnarium and got onto their beds in silence. It occurred to David that he should probably be nervous about going on his first live dreamwalker mission, but he was too preoccupied with a more fundamental worry. The lives of those he loved the most — their very existences — were on the line, and with this came the terrible dread that he himself might be utterly erased if something went wrong. He glanced over at Petra, and for a second he wondered if anyone would even remember him if he was snuffed out. To be so entirely destroyed that you were never even born was a fate worse than anything he could imagine. There was no question, he had to reach Eddie at any cost, forget rules and fancy briefings. If it came to it, he'd even fight Adam single-handedly. After all, what did he have to lose?

The professor gave them all a last word of encouragement. His anxious face was the last thing David saw before the nurse came over and placed the mask over his eyes.

She pressed the button.

David slept.

David was dreaming.

It took a moment to become fully aware, but the worry in the pit of his stomach forced his mind to focus. The chaotic jumble of the dream began to clear around the familiar figure of Petra. She was holding his hand, pulling him down a featureless hallway.

"You haven't been shown how to navigate yet," she said, "but it's not complicated. As with everything here, you just need to use the power of your mind. As long as you know where you want to be, you should be able to go there, but for now I'll help you. The others are waiting through here."

David allowed himself to be drawn through an open door. He found himself in a small room, entirely blank except for another door opposite him. It was closed.

"Welcome back to the dreamrealm," said Dishita. She motioned to David and Petra to stand with Théo. "The other team is already in place, so let's not waste any time. Misty?"

David was surprised to hear the computer's name here, but even more surprised by what happened next. A cascade of colored light poured down out of nowhere into one corner of the room and formed into a shape. Then the shape snapped into focus. It was a golden-haired girl in her midteens, dressed entirely in white, her hands behind her back and her head tilted to one side.

Her appearance was as enchanting as her voice and David was transfixed. It almost ached to look at her. Even as he stared, though, he felt that she was *too* beautiful somehow, too perfect to be real. But he couldn't help staring anyway. He heard a cough and tore his eyes off the lovely apparition for a moment to find that his mouth was hanging open. Petra and Dishita were glaring at him with eyes like daggers. Théo looked on, amused.

"*Yes, Dishita?*" said Misty, who then added with a wink, "*Hello again, David.*"

David started to mumble hello back but Dishita spoke over him.

"Misty, please confirm the weather and lighting conditions at Paddington station."

"*You are about to go out into a clear winter's day. The temperature at noon was 2.1 degrees Celsius. Sunlight will penetrate the building in some places, including platform one. You should be careful of that.*"

"We were all at the briefing." Petra put her hands on her hips. "We don't need you to tell us to be careful."

"*That's not fair, Petra. I'm only trying to help.*"

"The most helpful thing you can do is keep out of the way."

"*I think I should come with you on this mission. I can be very useful . . .*"

"No!" snapped Petra. "We'll call you if we need something."

"Thanks, Misty. You may go," said Dishita. Misty put her hands on her hips in an exact copy of Petra's pose and then melted out of sight. Dishita turned to Petra. "It doesn't help anyone if you treat her like that. You're teaching her all the wrong things, you know. When you're not just offending her, that is. She's our only link with the Map Room."

"Offending her? That faked-up Tinker Bell? She's just a dumb machine," said Petra. "The science guys would love to replace us all with dumb machines."

"Haven't you noticed how much like you she's getting?" said Dishita.

"That's not fair . . ." Petra started to say, but clamped her mouth shut. Dishita grinned.

"Now listen up. Our instructions aren't quite as simple as the professor made them sound in the Archive."

"What do you mean?" said Petra.

"Roman has the right to brief us as well." Dishita sounded defensive, as if she was preparing for an argument. "This is still a rescue mission, but the police will handle that once I've set things in motion. Our job is to make sure the Haunting doesn't interfere, but . . ."

". . . but Roman wants us to go after Adam," said Théo, nodding. "It is well. I am not afraid of him. We can hit hard too."

"Théo, no, don't talk like that!" said Petra. "Macho, like it's just a game. Adam's too strong. Remember Carlo? He wasn't afraid either."

"This isn't a discussion," said Dishita. "The professor's instructions are to help the police pick up Eddie, but Roman has given us separate orders. Théo and I will corner Adam. Petra, you'll back us up if . . . if needed."

"You're going to combine?" said Petra, and David caught a shy exchange of glances between Dishita and Théo.

"It's the only way to be sure," Dishita said. "It's not as dangerous as they say."

Petra shook her head and looked away.

"What about me?" David said.

Dishita gave him a cool look.

"Since you're here, you can help most by keeping your head down and your eyes open."

"I'm not just a piece of luggage. I want to do something."

"This dreamwalk is dangerous," said Dishita. "If it was up to me, you wouldn't be here at all. And don't question my authority, David; this is my team."

"The professor doesn't know about this, does he?" said David. "I thought we were just going to rescue Eddie. And what is combining, anyway?"

"You're a long way from needing to know about that," said Dishita. "And like I said, Roman has the right to brief us as well. We'll get Eddie, but it makes sense to strike at Adam while we can."

"Makes sense for *you*, you mean." Petra's hands were back on her hips. "Getting back at lover boy."

"Shut up, Petra!"

"No. You know I hate Adam as much as anyone, but he's too dangerous to fight. The professor's right: We should just rescue Eddie and let Adam sweat it out with his new haunter friends. He'll be nineteen soon; his dreamwalking days are ending. Don't make this personal."

"I said shut up!" Dishita snapped. "I'm not letting Adam get away again, and that's the end of it." She looked at Théo, who nodded back with a smile.

"Don't worry, we will get him," he said.

David said nothing, but he swore to himself that if there *was* going to be a fight with Adam, he wanted a part of it. The photo had been his discovery, and yet here he was being treated like a spare part, while everyone who was supposed to be saving

Eddie argued over how to do it. He looked at Petra but she was staring at the floor.

"It's time to go," said Dishita.

She gestured to the other door and it swung open, letting in the pale light of a long-ago winter. David stared through it, and then followed the others as, one by one, they stepped out into the year 1940.

CHAPTER · 21
UNINVITED GUESTS

The four dreamwalkers were standing in an empty compartment of a stationary train. It stank of stale cigarette smoke. Through the door of the compartment and the window beyond, David could see another train — chocolate brown with a coat of arms and a sooty cream roof. Outside the opposite window was the bustle and wartime hurry of platform one, Paddington station, on December 18, 1940.

The people were wearing mostly dark gray or dun-colored coats, muffled up against the cold, their breath mingling with steam. An elderly porter trudged past, pulling a trolley of leather cases, and two young soldiers clumped the other way, rifles and kit bags slung over their shoulders. Everyone wore a hat of some kind, and several of the women had fur coats. David stared at it all with a bewildering sense of both familiarity and wonder, as if he'd just walked out onto the set of a period drama and had forgotten how to get back.

The spell was broken by Dishita's voice. "You'll need to be disguised, David. You'll hardly blend in wearing that."

Looking at the others, David saw that he was now the only one not dressed to fit the time and place. Dishita had on a long coat and a green woolen hat and scarf, while Théo looked like an adult in his raincoat, hat, scarf, and leather gloves. Petra was wearing a dark gray fitted winter suit that seemed far too elegant for someone who wasn't supposed to be attracting any attention. She was even wearing lipstick, red like her beret. Somehow they all managed to make dressing in 1940s clothes look good. All three of them were looking at David expectantly.

David glanced down at the black dreamwalker suit he was wearing. "But how do I do it?"

"You're in charge of your dreaming mind now," said Dishita. "Decide how you want to be dressed and let your imagination do the rest. If you need inspiration, just look out of the window."

David concentrated and tried to visualize some of the horrible clothes he'd seen Eddie wearing. Nothing happened.

"Don't worry about it," said Petra. "Relax. You're trying too hard."

David thought again: creased trousers, cream shirt, V-neck pullover, and squeaky leather shoes — vintage Eddie style. Seconds passed but he remained exactly as before.

"I can't get rid of this stupid outfit."

"Remember, you are not wearing that outfit at all," Théo said. "Your mind has simply supplied it because that is what you were wearing when you went to sleep." But he was already watching the platform and clearly losing interest in David.

"Don't worry, I'll dream up something for you," said Petra, and suddenly David was dressed differently.

He caught a faint reflection of himself in the carriage window and felt even more like a film extra than before, in a blazer and stripy tie. For a moment it felt good to be dressed so smartly, but then he realized what he was wearing.

"A school uniform? Petra, thanks, but . . ."

"Ah, but I like you that way." Petra gave him her brightest smile. "A young English gentleman. Head boy at a posh boarding school, perhaps."

Théo smirked, and when David looked at Dishita there was no mistaking the doubt in her eyes.

"Never mind," she said. "I'm sure you'll get it in the end."

David wondered how long it had taken Adam to first master this trick of disguises. He felt foolish as he followed the three dreamwalkers into the corridor and out onto the cold, dingy platform.

The exotic mixture of smells struck David first. Coal smoke and bitter-tasting steam were by far the strongest, but cigarettes and oil were there too, as well as a leathery, varnishy tang. Thinking about old things and the past, he'd been expecting mustiness, but this world around him was as fresh and vital as the present. And of course, at that precise moment, for David and the other dreamwalkers 1940 *was* the present. He looked about in wonder until a loud metallic *whoosh* made him jump. A new cloud of vapor rolled out across the platform, the result of some steam-powered event beyond his understanding.

"Look at the time," said Dishita, pointing along the platform to where an ornate clock — the very one they'd seen back in the Archive — was visible above the vapor. "It's 11:35. David, are you listening? We need to split up and find Eddie as soon as possible, and Adam won't be far away when we do. The other team is already mingling with the crowds. Théo, you head to the main concourse — I've got to have a word with a policeman. Petra, find a good observation point over platform one. If we need to be in touch, call Misty, but only if you really need to."

"We won't," said Petra.

"Excuse me," said a voice, and they turned to find a girl with black pigtails looking up at David. She wore a blue school uniform with a golden dolphin on her blazer badge. Around her neck was a cardboard box, which David remembered from history lessons would contain a gas mask. "Please, do you know if this is the train for Bristol?"

"Er . . ." said David, who didn't have a clue. "Yeah, I think you're okay."

The girl looked at him with great curiosity.

"Ok-*ay*?" she said like she was trying out the word. "Are you an American?"

Dishita stepped forward quickly.

"I'm very sorry, but my Canadian friend here is mistaken. Please disregard everything he says. I'm afraid we really don't know where this train is going. Good-bye." And she dragged David away, leaving the girl staring after them.

"What are you doing?" Dishita whispered at the top of her voice. "What's the third law of the Dreamwalker's Code, David? What are the *first and second* laws, come to that? You might have sent that girl on the wrong train! We are guests in this time, remember? Uninvited guests. Haven't you got that yet? We mustn't do anything to disrupt the flow of history."

"Okay, okay, I'm sorry . . ."

"And stop saying *okay*. You should've been at the briefing earlier. No one uses that word in London in 1940. Petra, look after David. And keep his mouth shut. Right, let's go."

Dishita and Théo moved off along the platform until they were quickly lost in the crowds and steam. They seemed to fit right in as busy passengers. There was nothing ghostly about them that David could see, but close to the bulk of the train, platform one was a gloomy place, and winter clouds were blocking any sunlight that might enter through the high glass ceiling.

Petra led David along the platform and away from the massive, gasping locomotives at the end of the line. The platform was very crowded. As expected there were children there, being herded into groups, some in school uniform but many not. The only thing they all had in common, apart from the gas masks, were the cardboard labels they wore around their necks. David stared around, fascinated. But would Eddie really turn up among this lot? And why would Eddie be here, anyway?

Glancing nervously up at the ceiling, Petra continued to pull David until they came to a pillared opening to the street. Above the pillars, the Victorian clock showed the time to be 11:41. A pair of policemen with shiny buttons and tall helmets strolled beneath it. Petra scanned the faces of the people around them as she dragged David into the shadow of a massive stack of sandbags that partly blocked the entrance.

"So, what *is* the first rule of the Dreamwalker's Code, David?"

"Oh, don't you start. It's 'be seen, but not noticed.' I'm not stupid."

"I know you're not. But even in the shade a careful watcher might notice something unusual about you, like the fact that your breath isn't visible in the cold air like everyone else's. And there's more light coming through the roof than is good for us. You will have to learn these things on the job, David."

"So no walking through walls, then," David said. "I'd love to try it, though. What's the point of being a ghost if you can't do cool ghostly stuff? But I couldn't even change my clothes on my own. Perhaps I can't do these things at all."

"Nonsense!" said Petra. Then she gave him a crafty grin. "Come over here where we won't be seen."

She stepped into a narrow space behind the sandbags and David followed her. They were hidden from view, beside a patch of wall.

"Try it," she said, pointing at the bricks.

David reached out and touched the wall experimentally. He couldn't feel it exactly, but his hand seemed to be blocked by something solid all the same.

"The wall only stops you because your mind is reacting to it as if you were physically here. You need to tell your mind that this is a dreamwalk, David, that now you are only a ghost." And with that Petra stepped into the wall and vanished from view.

It was such a weird thing to see. David wondered if he'd ever get used to it. He reached out again and bumped his fingers against the solid barrier, but then blinked as he saw his fingertips slide a little way into the wall. He drew his hand back quickly. He'd have to take this one step at a time. He felt a presence at his shoulder and turned to see Petra behind him.

"Yuck! The men's lavatory," she said with her nose scrunched up. "But at least now we know Eddie isn't in there."

"It feels funny," whispered David.

"Yes, the first time. Your mind just needs convincing, that's all. But you're already making progress."

"How do you work that out?" said David. "I couldn't even dream up this costume. You had to do it for me."

"Yes," said Petra. "But I stopped helping you about three minutes ago. Now come, we mustn't waste any more time."

David looked down at himself. He was still wearing the school uniform Petra had chosen for him. Was he really dreaming it up on his own now? Despite this small triumph, he was still left with a strong need to prove himself, and he determined that if anyone was going to find Eddie today it would be him.

CHAPTER 22

THE PADDINGTON GHOST

Petra led David back onto the platform, and they hurried along it to the steps of a footbridge. From here they had a view down onto the trains, and the main part of the station beyond. Behind them was a huge arched window, but its panes were darkened by soot and crisscrosses of tape. David gazed ahead, recognizing the familiar vast space of Paddington station from his own time, but not the details of everyday life that it contained in 1940.

Petra raised her hand and pointed across the crowded platforms to where the green of Dishita's woolen hat could be seen slipping through the crowds toward the station clock.

The time was 11:49.

But where was Eddie?

"Shouldn't we get back down there?" David said.

Petra was about to answer when a voice cried, "Warning!" right beside David's head. He jumped with shock, turning to find Misty's golden eyes close to his. She was wrapped in a long dark coat, tightly buttoned up, and wore a hat that wouldn't have been out of place at a wedding, except that it was black. She might be in disguise, but she didn't seem able to hide her true dazzle.

"What are you doing here?" Petra's lip curled.

"We have detected Adam," said Misty. *"He has remained in this place long enough to be identified."*

She held out one slender arm. David followed her finger to a stationary train. Partly concealed in the dark open doorway of a carriage was the even darker silhouette of a man with a cane.

Adam.

"Someone's with him," David said, straining to see better. There was indeed a second figure skulking in the gloom.

"Misty, make yourself useful for once." Petra was straining too. "Who's that with Adam? Analyze."

"Charles Bartholomew Grinn," said Misty, looking down at the distant figures without the slightest hint of effort. *"Gangster, assassin, and manhunter. According to the Archive, he is responsible for seven murders, but is probably behind a further nine. He was born in 1895, will be arrested in January 1941, and will be hanged for murder three months after that."*

"Murder?" David cried. "Eddie's murder?"

"Calm down, David." Petra spoke without taking her eyes off the two figures. "Misty is just giving us the original history. This Grinn never killed Eddie, according to the records — none of us would be here now if he had. But Adam is trying to change all that. This is the man Adam has chosen to do his dirty work, and if he's due to be hanged soon anyway, Adam could promise him anything he likes. Misty, go and tell Dishita."

"Yes, Petra." Misty stepped away from them and melted from sight.

"Come on," David said. "We'd better get down there."

"No," said Petra. "We'll never get a better view than this. And look there . . . and there!"

David saw again the two policemen with their distinctive helmets taking up position close to the exit. Another strolled along the platform, his hands behind his back.

"Don't forget, Dishita's been busy," Petra said, "and Eddie's already been reported as a missing person. The moment we spot him, Dishita will point him out to the police. I doubt if someone like Grinn will try anything with the police here."

"But what if he does?"

Petra moved in close to David.

"Stop worrying, will you? We've done these things before, you know." She gave him a mischievous grin. "We're just here to keep watch, remember? We need to blend in. So let's pretend that we belong to this time and that you have just met me off a train. And let's pretend you missed me."

David didn't know if it was possible to blush on a dream-walk, but he felt himself redden.

"There you are," Petra giggled. "You'll be making your own clothes in no time. Now, you watch behind me, and I'll watch behind you. Eddie can't be far away now."

David stared down into the crowds over Petra's beret. Dishita was under the clock now, leaning against a pillar with a magazine in her hands, just a few paces from the two policemen. But why wasn't she doing anything? And where was Théo? Hesitant, David wrapped his spectral arms around Petra, thinking there were times when it was fun to be a ghost, and times when it wasn't. He forced himself to focus and stared down into the group of children below, scanning each face for signs of the boy who would one day be his grandfather.

The minute hand of the station clock crept toward midday.

A woman in a round hat came to join them on the walkway, her heels tapping as she climbed the stairs.

David glanced her way and saw that she had a steel camera around her neck. Was this the photographer who was about the take the very picture he'd found in Adam's room? David would have laughed if he hadn't looked down into the shadow of the carriage door and seen the dark figure of Adam raise his cane and point at the woman. The man called Grinn stepped forward.

"It's about to happen," David gasped, trying to step away, but Petra grabbed him.

"No, stay here! Keep watching the platform, there might be —"

"I can't just stand here . . ." David interrupted but stopped. Down in the shadows, Grinn had changed his stance. He was hunched forward in the carriage doorway, suddenly hard and intent, his face like that of a hungry wolf watching a lamb. His right arm was curled back. His coat was long and his hand mostly concealed, but even from a distance David caught the gleam of metal as something long and viciously pointed flicked forward.

A knife.

David followed the man's gaze, until his eyes stopped on the features he'd been so desperate to see. Eddie! His grandfather was there, down in the crowd, shoulders hunched and collar up. His hair was a mess, and there were signs of the fire all over him, but David would have recognized him anywhere. He could even see the rolled-up notebook in his hand. As Eddie walked slowly on, David saw the scene of the photo he'd found come together right in front of his eyes, about to be fixed permanently in the flash of the photographer's camera.

Grinn left the shadows, ducking between people.

David swore and pulled away from Petra, who cried "No!" after him.

He ignored her and ran to the stairs.

"David, come back!" Petra's whisper was almost a shout, but David was far from her now, leaping down the steps toward Eddie.

At ground level, he stopped and swore again. Suddenly the crowd was too thick, and Eddie wasn't visible. David pushed forward, dodging around people, frantic.

Where was Eddie?

Where was Grinn?

Then a group of children moved together. Beneath the vaulted glass roof a space cleared, and there, standing in dejection, was Eddie.

And ten paces behind him, his right arm pulled right back, was Grinn.

Time slowed as David saw his own destruction at the point of the knife in Grinn's hand, exactly as if the blade was about to be thrust into his own back. The faces of his father and sister danced before his eyes.

"Eddie! Eddie, look out!"

All around people turned to look.

Eddie's head snapped up and his eyes grew wide behind his sooty glasses.

"David?" The surprise in his voice echoed around the station.

David dashed forward, but he was so intent on reaching his grandfather that he didn't notice what was happening far above him. As predicted, the winter wind picked up and for a moment the clouds parted over London. The sun came out.

Someone screamed.

David spun around and saw several people looking at him, aghast. He held up his hands as if to ward them off. And then he saw it for himself. Winter sunlight was pouring down through the glass roof, and he was bathed in it. His hands, like the rest of him, were now transparent and suffused with a spectral blue glow.

"A ghost!" someone cried. A group of children began shrieking and flocked away from him, knocking into other passengers. Suddenly everyone seemed to be running or yelling, and David was left bewildered in an ever-widening circle of fear and confusion. He couldn't see Eddie anymore. He caught sight of Dishita's appalled face in the crowd and knew he had to get under cover quick. He turned. There was a sudden flash of light, and David saw the photographer on the walkway above, frantically fiddling with the enormous flash apparatus on her camera, clearly hoping for a second shot.

David ran. He darted out of the sunlight and glanced toward the carriage where Adam had been, but there was no one hiding there now. He looked back, hoping for a glimpse of Eddie, but his grandfather seemed to have melted into thin air. And there was no sign of the man called Grinn either, just dozens of wide eyes staring at him in fear. He swore even more emphatically, then pelted straight for the nearest dark corner, people yelling and falling away from him as he ran. He was so desperate that he forgot to slow down as he neared the station wall. He barged straight into it . . . and found himself on the other side!

It was a strange, indescribable sensation, but David had no time to congratulate himself for walking through walls. What a fool he'd been! He'd blundered right into the sunlight! And *then* he'd run straight through solid brick in front of crowds of witnesses. But even as he cursed himself, it did occur to him that at least he'd saved Eddie.

Or had he? Where was Eddie now? And the man with the knife? From the other side of the bricks, he could hear the commotion he'd caused, and a woman was still screaming. David swore again and again. He looked around at what appeared to be an engineer's workshop, wondering what on earth he should do now.

A sleek black cat crossed the floor, its dark eyes hard as they fixed onto David's.

Without warning, David felt an excruciating sensation in his left side, and he was flung across the room, pain pulsing through his whole being. The workshop and the machines in it grew faint, and he lost his bearings entirely. When he could finally focus again, he saw a girl about his own age standing by the wall where he'd come through himself. She had white-blonde hair, and David knew he'd seen her somewhere before. Her 1940s clothes melted away to reveal a strange, featureless suit, like those worn by the dreamwalkers, only silver-gray. The girl's hand was still raised exactly as if she had just struck him. Then he recognized her — it was the young nurse who'd tried to kidnap him from his school.

A haunter.

"Well, well," said the girl in precise English tones, "I didn't think I'd be seeing you again."

David struggled to stand, but his mind was drained and numb, his dreamself more like a puddle on the floor than a spectral body. The girl laughed. She rose into the air and arced across the workshop, her fingers extended like bright claws. She came to rest over him like a hawk on a mouse.

David tried to straighten up so he could look the girl in the eye, but the effort made the world grow faint again, and he slumped back down. He remembered the spear in the desert, and he knew that he'd just been hit by a mind pulse. He wondered if he was about to be knocked out of his dreamwalk as Dishita had been, and just how much it would hurt.

"You're supposed to be dead," said the haunter, "but this will do for now."

She drew her arm right back, her face terrible with concentration as she prepared to bring her spectral fist crashing down.

David flinched in terror. He was so weak from the first hit he knew that a second would be devastating. He thought of Carlo in his coma and Siri, who could no longer speak.

Then another arm flashed out from somewhere at the edge of his vision. The girl's raised hand was knocked to one side, her concentration broken. David turned groggily and saw Théo. The girl swung the fist of her other hand, but Théo dodged it and made an attack of his own, slamming both his hands into the haunter's side. The silver-suited girl shuddered as she was flung back, spinning out of control across the room. Her shriek was cut off as she vanished through the wall. Théo leaped across the workshop after her.

But he never got there. A shape sprang from the shadows of a hulking steam train like a pouncing cat and seized him in midair. Théo cried out, pinned half upside down in the center of the room by a tall, dark-haired figure in a silver suit.

It was Adam.

Théo tried to lash out, but Adam held him fast and high. Adam gave a fierce laugh as he forced his hands wide, twisting the struggling form of Théo in the air. Théo cried out again, this time in anguish. There was a sound like popping static as Théo's dreamself was ripped in two before David's eyes.

The beginnings of a scream echoed around the workshop as the remains of Théo's ghost disintegrated into nothing.

Silence fell over the room. Adam turned and looked at David.

"You?" he said. "They're so desperate they've even sent *you*?"

David struggled to his feet, his mind finally regaining a trickle of strength.

"You won't get him. Eddie, I mean. I stopped your man with the knife — Eddie got away."

David desperately wished he could have thought of something cleverer to say, but face-to-face with Adam he found it hard to speak at all. *Come on!* David yelled at himself. *This is the monster who wants to kill Eddie, to wipe out Dad and Philippa. Attack him!*

He took a hesitant step forward, forming his hands into spectral fists, but Adam was already striding toward him, his dreamself radiating mental power.

David raised his arms, trying to draw on pure hatred of Adam to supply the power his mind would need to fight. But it was no good. He was exhausted — the blonde girl had hit him too hard — and he slumped again.

"I don't care what you do to me," he managed, as Adam loomed over him. "Eddie's with the police. He's safe."

"You miserable little . . ." Adam began, his grin evaporating. "Yeah, I can see why you'd hope that. But thanks to your showstopping performance out there, precious little Eddie is gone again, so no, the police don't have him. But I have you. And you're the one who knows where he's hiding out. I'm going to enjoy making you tell me."

David staggered back, wondering whether he would still be able to pass through a wall in his weakened state. It was cruel, having to face his enemy without even the energy to defend himself, let alone anyone else. But Adam had destroyed Théo so easily that David knew there was only one thing left he could do. He turned and ran.

"Going somewhere, Davy boy?" cried Adam, leaping forward. He seized David and spun him back around. Instantly Adam's other hand fastened around his throat like a ring of ice. David gasped as he felt the ghostly fingers grip him and sensed his mind being quickly enveloped by the power of Adam's will. He tried to resist, but his world was already smothered by a crushing darkness, leaving nothing but the sound of Adam's voice.

"Tell me where he is!"

David managed just one word as his consciousness failed. "No . . ."

"Tell me!" Adam shouted. "Or I'll fill you with pain till you burst."

"David!" It was Petra's voice.

Adam looked to one side and something struck him. Then it was his turn to stagger back, releasing David as he did so. For a moment he looked pained and his dreamself grew faint, but with a dismaying lack of effort he snapped back to full, ferocious clarity. Petra was standing over David as Adam raised his arm to come back at her. But Petra wasn't the only newcomer.

"Enough," said Dishita as she stepped out of the shadows behind Adam. "It's over, Adam. The end of the line."

"The end of the *line?*" Adam laughed, nodding his head toward the railway station around them. "Was that some kind of joke, Dishita? Personally, I find the idea that two girls and a schoolboy can stop me much more amusing."

In reply, Dishita flew at him. Adam raised his arms and caught her hands, and the two of them spun crazily through the air, each wrestling to free a hand and hit the other. Petra looked down at David.

"I hope you weren't trying to impress me," she said, the hint of concern in her voice almost hidden by anger. "Because you didn't!"

David forced himself to look her in the eye.

"Where's Théo?" Petra said.

"Gone . . ."

"No!"

"I'm so sorry. But I couldn't just stand there . . ."

"What have you done?" Petra looked horrified. "Didn't you think Adam would have haunters with him? The station is probably crawling with them. Théo . . ."

David tried to speak, but stopped. Petra didn't appear ready to listen to him now anyway. She called Misty and shouted at her to bring the other team to help.

Adam and Dishita finally separated, each flinging the other away. They dropped back down to the ground at different ends of the workshop, both clearly drained by the effort.

"I doubt there's anyone there who could come, sweetheart," called Adam to Petra. Then, in front of them all, Adam's suit reappeared, as perfect and unruffled as if he'd just stepped out of a tailor's shop. He tugged the front brim of his hat low over his eyes and leaned nonchalantly on his gleaming black cane, the perfect picture of self-controlled malevolence.

"So you see, it's you who have reached the end of the line. My new colleagues have seen to that."

"How could you join *them*?" Petra spat back. "Murderers! How can you bear to work with them against your own friends?"

"You know the answer to that better than most, Petra," Adam said, "and since I know you won't be joining us . . ."

Before anyone could move, Adam flicked his cane forward and sent it flying straight at Petra. She cried out as she dropped back, the spectral cane zinging through the air above her. Dishita darted forward, but Adam was impossibly quick. David could only watch as he leaped high above Dishita then dropped down behind her. Before she could turn, a dreamwalker's door had appeared behind Adam. He knocked it open with his cane — miraculously back in his hand — and raised his hat.

"So long," he said, stepping through.

David acted instinctively. There was no way he could let Adam escape, not if Eddie really had disappeared again. This might be his only chance to save him. He flung himself at the door as it began to slam shut, and got one arm through. He pushed with all the force left in his battered mind.

Petra was with him in a moment.

"You can't hold it open that way."

"Can't let him go," gasped David. The door was pushing back harder and harder, crushing him as Adam willed it to close. Despite the pain, David could see what looked like water through the doorway — water and buildings, and was that a crane? And he could tell Adam was there somewhere, looking on with an amused smile.

Petra leaned into the door herself, but even together they couldn't do more than gain a little extra space.

"David, get out!" shouted Petra.

David pulled his arm back before it was too late.

The door slammed shut and vanished, leaving nothing but a faint tang of river air in the room.

CHAPTER · 23
GROUNDED

David sat in the Archive with an aching head and said nothing. The professor sat opposite him and the other dreamwalkers, while a motley assortment of technicians, assistants, and science types from the Map Room stood and looked on. But it was Roman who was asking all the questions.

Théo's chair was empty. Roman paced across the middle of the room with a look of fury as Dishita explained what had happened. When she came to the part where David broke cover and approached Eddie, causing a public sensation and ruining the rescue, the room became very quiet and Roman stopped right in front of David.

"If your own life wasn't so obviously at risk," said Roman eventually, "I would once again be asking myself just whose side you are on."

"Oh, come on, Commander," said the professor, speaking for the first time since the debriefing had begun. "David's hardly going to be helping Adam, is he? It was just a . . . a mistake."

"A mistake!" cried Roman. "Our founder is in danger — he needs help, not mistakes. He certainly deserves better than this." And he flung a newspaper down on the desk, right under David's nose.

The paper was yellow with age, sealed in plastic, and folded to page five. It was dated December 18, 1940. Under the title "The Paddington Ghost" was the photograph David had found in Adam's room. It showed the same view of the railway station, the trains, and the evacuees, but the detail was dramatically different. In the center of a scene of running figures and terrified faces, there was a vaguely human form, translucent, and with its arms raised. The quality of the photo was poor, but David didn't need to look too closely to recognize himself standing more or less in the place where Eddie had been in the original picture. Eddie himself was now nowhere to be seen. David glanced up and saw everyone in the room staring at him.

"You have turned a quiet historical moment into a freak show," said Roman in the tone of a judge about to pass a death sentence, "and wasted our best chance to catch Adam."

"We'll have to go back," called one of the technicians, and there was a rumble of agreement from around the room. "Try again."

The professor shook his head.

"That particular moment in time is too full of dreamwalkers already, ours and theirs. And with the panic and the crowds, we'd be going back into chaos. We might still be able to pick up Eddie's trail in the streets outside, but in the station that historical moment is far too unstable now."

"We could hardly have destabilized it more if we'd tried," said Roman. "It's high time we interviewed the boy again. I don't trust him."

"David is not working for the Haunting." Professor Feldrake's voice was raised now.

"No?" said Roman. "Maybe not. Maybe he really is just that stupid. But I knew we should never have assigned *her* to his case." And he pointed at Petra. She looked furious, but instead of reacting with a characteristic outburst she just sat there smoldering.

"That's an outrageous thing to say," cried the professor. "And grossly unfair. Petra is totally loyal."

For a moment Roman looked uncomfortable, as though he knew he'd said something he shouldn't have. Then he took refuge in an outburst of his own.

"Why must we work with kids?"

"We would hardly be working at all without them," countered Professor Feldrake.

The room fell silent again. The tension in the air said it all. David looked at Petra and wondered what Roman had meant when he'd pointed to her.

Jiro came into the room.

"We've finished the analysis," he said. "The events at Paddington station at midday on December eighteenth, 1940, have been substantially altered, though the short-term effects are negligible; it's just another ghost sighting, nothing to worry about. The photo was even branded a fake soon after it was published. We're still trying to assess the long-term impact. As for Edmund Utherwise, the other team tried to trail him, but he slipped away in the chaos."

There was a ripple of dismay around the Archive.

"Where's the other team now?" the professor asked.

"They were attacked, knocked out of their dreamwalk. Misty counted twelve haunters present at the end, not including Adam. They didn't stand a chance."

"And this man Charlie Grinn?" Roman asked. "Anything more on him? An address?"

Jiro shook his head. "We're searching the Archive, but there's not much. He could be anywhere."

"Adam knows how to contact him, though," Roman said. "And we have enough about Grinn to know he's just the man Adam needs. The worst of it is that Edmund Utherwise probably still isn't aware he's being hunted by a real flesh-and-blood killer."

"Why did you do it?" said Dishita, suddenly turning to David. She didn't seem angry, just completely astonished about what had happened. "Didn't you see the skylights? Théo was almost in position; we were seconds away from making a double strike. Adam was completely preoccupied, and the police almost had Eddie. I just don't get why you did it."

David was torn between rage and complete embarrassment at how badly things had gone. But he wasn't about to be made to look a fool.

"There was a man with a knife right behind him. The nearest police helmet was right across the station. I couldn't just . . ."

"Helmet?" Dishita looked incredulous. "There was a plainclothes policeman on either side of Eddie, David. What do you think I've been doing all night? I spent hours of delicate maneuvering to make sure there'd be real detectives there, only to have you prance about in front of them like something out of *A Christmas Carol!*"

Plainclothes? David was about to protest, but he shut his mouth. He simply hadn't thought of that. He put his head in his hands.

"It was his first proper dreamwalk," said Petra, trying to come to David's defense. "And I hear Théo will be okay. In time."

"But we don't have time!" Roman roared over her. "Théo is one of the strongest dreamwalkers we have left, and we need him *now*."

"That's out of the question," said the Dreamwalker Project's surgeon, a young woman seated beside the professor. "Théo has had a serious mental shock. He should make a full recovery eventually, but I won't be clearing him for dreamwalking for at least three months. And that's *at least*."

"And what about the three from the other team?" asked Roman, his eyes still on David.

The surgeon shook her head.

"It's too early to say, but again there's no way you can have them in the next few days. And you should count yourselves lucky I haven't signed Dishita off too."

Roman put his hands into his silver-black hair and rubbed his temples.

"Okay, let's start trying to clean this mess up," he said, turning away from David. "We always knew Adam would need help to eliminate Sir Edmund, and now at least we know who it is. We have to work on Grinn's location and then throw everything we have left at Adam when he next makes contact."

"But even the police at the time didn't know Grinn's address," said the professor. "Look at the file. He lived in an underworld, always in hiding. We can't waste time looking for him. The person we should be looking for is Eddie."

"Hunting for Eddie would be fine, Professor, if David here would tell us what he knows," snapped Roman. "But he won't."

"Not won't, *can't*." David took his head out of his hands. "Don't you think I'd have told you if I knew where Eddie was? It's just that . . ."

David found that everyone was looking at him again, and he stopped. What could he say? The professor put his hands together tightly, almost as if he were praying, and spoke.

"David, if there's anything you can remember, anything at all, now is the time to tell us. Even the smallest detail could help us find your grandfather."

David looked down again and shook his head. He'd have given anything then to help make up for the mess he'd just created, but he couldn't tell them what he didn't know. However, even as he thought this, he had once again that strange back-of-the-mind feeling that there *was* something he wasn't quite remembering.

Roman crossed the room and picked several important-looking files out of a messy pile beside the professor, like a man fishing coins out of a dustbin. The professor himself sat staring at the floor and said nothing.

"We have work to do," said Roman. Even David noticed that the authority in the room had shifted. Everyone was waiting for Roman to speak.

"I want two full research teams working on Grinn's location, and I want a report within the hour. Dishita says Adam escaped to a waterside location, and after the scare at the London docks earlier, we'll start there. All remaining dreamwalkers are on standby. I want to be ready for Adam Lang the moment we have something. Professor, you can finish up here."

He strode across the room, but paused at the door.

"Ah, and David Utherwise is suspended from the Dreamwalker Project. If he was ever *on* it, that is. He is confined to the Lodge until further notice. We will send someone to continue his interrogation."

Then he left, as did everyone but the professor and the remains of Dishita's team.

"That was very reckless, David," said the professor once the Archive had emptied. "How's the head, by the way?"

David had been suffering from a splitting headache since the attacks by the girl haunter and Adam, and he'd even been wheeled from the Somnarium on a gurney. However, within five minutes he was able to stand, and he'd insisted on being at the debriefing to face the music.

"It's fine, thanks," he lied. "Um . . . I'm really sorry, Professor."

"Well, it can't be helped now," said Professor Feldrake. "Roman hates having to work with you youngsters anyway. He resents you, I'm afraid. He has never got over losing his own abilities."

"Roman was a dreamwalker?"

"Oh, yes, one of the first generation. He worked directly with your grandfather and was quite a star. To lose all that and be forced to watch as others take your place, well, I can see why he's so unforgiving. Especially with Adam. But don't judge him too harshly, David. In the end, he wants exactly the same thing as the rest of us, even if I do think he's going about it the wrong way. The best thing you can do now is rack your brains."

"I do have the feeling there's something I'm not quite remembering."

"There you are, you see. Concentrate on that," said the professor, but his positive tone didn't sound quite genuine. "And I'm afraid you'll have plenty of time for thinking now. You won't be allowed back here in a hurry, or near the Somnarium."

"I thought *you* were in charge."

"Well, technically, yes, but things are getting serious, and Roman's been itching to replace me for years. He probably will too, at least while the emergency lasts. The truth is, my position has been shaky for some time, and the people who fund the Dreamwalker Project are terrified of what the Haunting might do with Adam on their side. I'm afraid I can't help you, David, not now."

"But I've got to find Eddie!"

"Leave that to us," said the professor, getting to his feet. "We'll do all we can to keep him safe, that I can promise you."

The professor ushered the dreamwalkers out of the Archive. Two security men who were waiting outside took up positions on each side of David and he was marched off with the others behind him. It was humiliating. As they crossed the Map Room and went up the stairs he felt everyone's eyes on him.

They were about to leave the gallery overlooking the Map Room when an alarm broke out. David turned and even the security guards seemed curious. Looking over at the great dazzling hologram in the center of the room he could see the ugly black mark he'd noticed earlier, creeping though the rainbow light like a spreading scar, and the whole sphere seemed to be trembling and fizzing louder than ever.

"Not again," groaned the professor, his knuckles going white as he gripped the railing.

"It's spreading?" said David.

"The time line is altering," said Dishita in a voice full of accusation. "Bit by bit. There are more changes now, more pressures on it than before. The longer Eddie's actions deviate from the past that founded all this, the deeper the rupture. If we can't patch things up soon, if Adam and Grinn find Eddie first, then the whole course of history will shift and force us into a new present. And if that happens there'll be no one left here to deal with it."

As they watched, the black scar branched, and a second jagged line began to deface the beautiful sphere.

The alarms were still blaring as David was led away.

CHAPTER · 24
LONDON, DECEMBER 18, 1940, 4:15 P.M.

Eddie tried to run again, but his chest ached so much he thought he'd faint. Surely he'd put enough distance between himself and the station by now?

He's still after you, said the voice of his doubt. *How did he know you'd be at the station? You've told him too much . . .*

Eddie didn't know what to think of that. How *had* David known where to find him? He coughed again and looked at the faces of the people in the street. They were watching him. Why were they looking at him like that?

Ahead was the entrance to a public park. Eddie slipped inside and hurried on until he saw a bench. He sat down and bunched his legs up under his chin. He pulled his hair a little. Soon his breathing became more measured and his mind clearer.

So, how had David known where he'd be?

Eddie flattened out his notebook, took a pencil from his pocket, and hunched down to write.

Dear Mother . . .

He paused, surprised. Where had that come from? He hadn't set out to write a letter. But perhaps that was the right thing to do. After all, his mother must be wondering where he'd got to. He chewed his pencil until he remembered what Kat had said about his mother being worried about him. Yes, perhaps he should have written before.

I am well. I will join you as soon as I can, but . . .

It was a brief letter, giving only the barest facts. The train Eddie had wanted to catch had been canceled, despite what it said on the timetable. A porter had told him it was being used to move evacuees instead, and said he'd have to wait a few days. Eddie had held the timetable up and pointed to where the times were clearly printed for anyone to see, but the porter had got angry with him then. It was shortly after that that David had appeared. But Eddie didn't want to mention this.

When the letter was finished, Eddie tore it out. Then he folded another page into a makeshift envelope with the help of his glue pot. He licked a stamp carefully — it tasted of the inside of his satchel — and pressed it firmly and squarely in place. Then he wrote his aunt's address.

The afternoon was already growing chilly by the time Eddie slipped out of the park. Would Kat be pleased to see him again? Surely she couldn't blame him for going back — he *had* tried to catch a train. And where else could he go now, anyway? But he'd have to keep quiet about one thing: There was no way he could tell Kat and her angry-eyed brother that David — the ghost who wanted him dead — was still after him.

The part of London where the theater stood was narrow and crowded, with a run-down air made shabbier still by fire and destruction. It wasn't like the leafy avenues and squares Eddie was used to seeing from his window, but then he remembered that the white walls and broad trees of his own street existed only in his memory now. It was a place he could never get back to, no matter how much he dreamed of it. He stared blankly at the heap of rubble and split planks of a bombed-out house and then hurried on, eager again for the warmth and company of the theater attic.

As he went, Eddie had the strangest feeling that he was being watched. He kept to the road when he could, despite the occasional motorcar, and tried to pick up his pace, one eye always open for a letterbox. It was just as he spotted that familiar Post Office red that someone grabbed his arm.

"Back again, are we?" said Tomkin, propelling Eddie in a new direction. "Changed your mind about that train, eh? Best not catch cold, though. Keep your collar up, there's a good man."

"Tomkin, what are you doing?"

"You haven't been quite on the level with us, have you, Eddie?"

"What do you mean?" It was all Eddie could do not to trip.

"Not here," Tomkin said, his voice low and hard now. They didn't stop until they were once again in the shadows beside the theater. Tomkin had obviously been busy, because instead of making for the rope, he turned to the side door. The planks were newly loosened, and he wrenched them back with a grunt.

"After you, squire."

Eddie ducked to enter, but Tomkin shoved him through, before grabbing his arm again and pushing him toward the stage. The dark was almost total there, except for a little brown light that filtered in through the boards above.

As they reached the ladder to the attic, Tomkin froze. A scraping sound came from the doorway behind them. Someone else was pulling back the planks.

Tomkin swore and shoved Eddie behind some scenery flats that leaned against the wall. In the silence that fell, they peered around at the wings as someone appeared there in a halo of yellow light.

But it was only Kat, carrying a candle.

"What's the matter with you?" Eddie shook Tomkin off. "You're acting strangely."

"Eddie!" Kat stopped short. "But . . . why are you still here?"

"*I'm* acting strange?" said Tomkin. "Blooming cheek! Anyway, how'd you expect me to act after discovering that someone's after us? Or rather, after you. Little Lord Creepy here has been telling us whoppers, Kat."

"Who's after me?" said Eddie, trying not to think of David. "My mother?"

"Er, no, Eddie, old son," said Tomkin. "I'm sure your ma doesn't know the dodgy geezer who was handing out these." And he shoved a crumpled piece of paper at Eddie's chest. Eddie held it up in the glow of Kat's candle. On the paper was a quick but accurately sketched portrait.

"That's you!" said Kat. "Eddie, what's going on?"

"We need to talk," said Tomkin. He grabbed Eddie by a fistful of collar and dragged him to the ladder to the attic.

When they reached the top, Kat put her candle to the fire she'd laid that morning. Eddie hung back, watching Tomkin warily, still clutching the sketch in one hand.

"Where did you get that picture, Tom?" Kat asked as the kindling began to crackle alight. The temperature in the attic was already close to freezing.

"From someone who's hardly going to be helping an anxious mum," Tomkin replied. "And it wasn't the coppers neither."

Eddie glanced at the sketch again. He'd need to stick it in his book, worry out the answers there. He looked at Kat and shrugged.

Tomkin shoved Eddie's shoulder.

"Oi, look at me, not me sister. This is my place you're in. Got that?"

Eddie nodded.

"Right." Tomkin stood over the fire. "Kat, I said yes to having Eddie here 'cause I thought he was just some nutty rich kid who might be good for a few suppers. But now it looks like there's more to our Eddie than even you realize. It was Rob Box gave me this paper."

Kat's eyes widened.

"That can't be right," she said. "Eddie, why would Box and his cronies be looking for you?"

"I don't know," said Eddie. "Maybe . . . maybe this is a drawing of someone else."

"Well, it certainly looks like you," said Kat, eyeing the sketch again.

Tomkin leaned in close.

"See that?" he said, pointing to a smudge on the drawing. "Smell it."

Eddie did as he was told and noticed the telltale alcoholic tang of a chemical copier.

"Yeah," said Tomkin. "So that means there could be hundreds of these drawings out there, and if the likes of Rob Box is handing 'em out, they're not going to the nice people your parents know. We're talking gangs here, crooks."

"You don't owe someone nasty any money, do you, Eddie?" Kat sat by the fire. "Heaven help you if you do, because we certainly can't."

Eddie didn't know what else he could say, so he pulled the notebook from his pocket, then fished around for a pencil.

"Jeez, give me a break!" Tomkin looked at Eddie in disgust, raising one fist. But after a moment he relaxed, shook his head, and plonked himself down beside the fire.

"All right, Eddie," he said. "Something doesn't add up here, but when I look at you I don't exactly see a crook, so maybe it *is* all a mistake or something. Let's sleep on it. But I warn you now, I don't like the way you look at my sister, and if I find you've been holding out on us, so help me, I'll brain yer. And *then* I'll hand you over to Rob Box."

Eddie sat down quickly and took his glasses off. He picked at the crack in the lens. He *was* holding out on them — he was keeping quiet about David.

"How much?" he said eventually.

"How much what?" said Tomkin, staring into the fire.

"Reward," said Eddie, holding the drawing up.

Tomkin looked at Eddie, the firelight dancing in his eyes.

"No flies on you, are there, Eddie? All right, if you must know, they were offering a hundred pounds."

Kat gasped.

"That's how much it's costing Kat and me to look after you, Mr. Edmund Butter-Wouldn't-Melt Utherwise. Just make sure you're worth it, all right? That sort of money buys a lot of comfort for the likes of us." And he put his arm around Kat, hugging her close.

Eddie put his glasses back on and briefly met Tomkin's gaze.

"Thank you," he said.

Tomkin waved his hand at him.

"Ah, forget it," he said. "They'd only beat us up and steal it back afterward," he added, clearly looking for a change of subject. "Anyway, there's something else I want to show you. I've been thinking about your ghost story, yeah, and — would you believe it? — there's only a ghost in the evening edition. Spooky, eh?"

Eddie took the crisp newspaper that Tomkin offered him. It was folded to page five. Under the title "The Paddington Ghost" was a picture. It showed platform one of the railway station, close to the clock and just where Eddie had been standing. Among the crowds he saw a ring of terrified faces turned toward something in the center of the shot: a vaguely human form with its arms raised. The quality of the photo was poor, but looking closely Eddie recognized the features.

"David," he said aloud, before he could stop himself.

Tomkin gawped at him.

"You have got to be kidding . . ."

"Let me see!" Kat snatched the paper. "Lord, it could be! But what was he doing there?" She looked at Eddie, her mouth open.

Eddie adjusted his glasses and fought back a cough. He risked a glance at Kat. She'd turned white.

"You were at Paddington today." She pointed at Eddie, then she jabbed at the ghost in the photo. "He was at the station because of you, wasn't he? But if he could find you there, then . . ." She turned to her brother.

"What! Come here, you mean?" It was Tomkin's turn to go pale. "Nah, give over! Don't wind me up, Kat, I'm not in the mood."

"I didn't know he'd be there . . ." Eddie began, but Tomkin snatched the paper back from his sister and shoved it under Eddie's nose.

"This," he said, "has been faked, so don't go getting all creepy on us again, or I'll sling you out right now."

"But, Tom . . ." Kat began. Her brother held up his hand.

"I mean it," he said, "Anyone can see it's been faked. I only showed it to you for a laugh. It's some kind of Christmas hoax — take our minds off the bombing or something, a government thing. Ghosts don't exist, plain and simple. If they did, the scientists would've got onto them by now, wouldn't they? There'd be proper stories about them in the paper, not fuzzy pictures like this."

Kat grabbed the paper again.

"You can't fake that!" she said impatiently. But then she added in a thoughtful tone, "Mind you, Eddie, look at him. I never saw your David ghost looking like this, all . . . glowing and see-through."

Eddie lifted his glasses onto his forehead and studied the picture closely. With his pencil, he began jotting quick notes down the side.

"Off he goes with his pencil again." Tomkin turned to his sister in exasperation. "The things you take under your wing, Kat. Aren't I enough for you?"

Kat smiled and kissed her brother on the cheek.

"Apart from the location . . ." Eddie circled part of what he'd written and crossed out the rest. ". . . I can only see one significant difference: sunlight. I only ever saw David at night. Here . . . you can see it is sunny. I remember it was sunny."

"What!" cried Tomkin, jumping to his feet. "You *remember*? You mean you were actually there when they took this? When were you going to tell us *that*?"

Eddie kept his head down, taking his writing off to one side and starting a new list. But he didn't get very far, because Tomkin seized the newspaper and flung it on the fire.

"I'll tell you this once, and I'll tell you this straight." Tomkin leaned in close to Eddie and jabbed his finger into him like a knife. "If you've done anything — *anything* — to bring danger to my sister . . ." Then he made a slow cutting motion across Eddie's neck, digging his nail in. "Understand? Now write that in your precious book and underline it."

Eddie swallowed.

Tomkin seized a scarf and woolly hat from the pile of salvaged clothes and stomped over to the ladder.

"I'm going out. Kat, tell your 'friend' he can stay tonight, but come the morning I want him gone. For good." Then he slid down the ladder and vanished from sight.

Eddie quickly rescued the paper from the fire. His hand was trembling.

"You should have told us, Eddie," Kat said.

Eddie started to write, but then he looked up.

"Your brother doesn't like me."

"He just doesn't like it that you're so mysterious, that's all," Kat said with a sigh. She picked up the kettle. "*He* wants to be the interesting one, out on the streets talking to all sorts, taking his chances. He wants you to be impressed that he knows people like Rob Box, but instead you always go one better with your ghosts and the like. Tom was always the jealous type."

"What does Tomkin do," Eddie said, "to know people like that?"

"I don't really know." Kat sounded troubled. "He won't tell me, but I think he's already mixed up in a gang himself. He spends less and less time selling papers, anyway."

"He's right," said Eddie, looking at the portrait of himself.

"What do you mean?"

"If someone *is* after me, I'm making things difficult for you by staying here."

"Eddie, look at me."

Eddie kept his head down.

"Eddie! Will you look me in the eye and promise me you never told David how to find this place?"

Eddie adjusted his glasses. It was nice to be able to give a clear and honest answer. He looked up.

"I never told him, Kat. I promise."

Kat clicked her tongue for a moment before speaking again.

"I'll talk to Tom. I think you should hide up here for a bit —

with those burns and that singed hair you'll stick out like a scarecrow, even around here. Maybe Tom will find out something, and I'll try to get in touch with your ma. But it'd be best not to show yourself for a while, all right? People don't hand out leaflets like that for nothing."

Eddie nodded. He carefully tore the photo of the ghost out of the newspaper and pasted it on a clean page of his notebook, positioning it squarely. He could tell Kat was still watching him, but he didn't know what to say to her, so he said nothing. Instead he looked at the image of David again, strangely lit and translucent, and wondered for the millionth time what it all meant.

CHAPTER 25

LONDON, DECEMBER 18, 1940, 11:52 P.M.

In Spurlington's Shipping Agency — at the late Mr. Spurlington's mahogany desk — an anxious Charlie Grinn sat absentmindedly spearing a singed notebook with his knife, while the whole building shook.

The telephone hadn't rung for nearly an hour. An air raid had been in progress for almost two.

"Bring me another," he yelled, pointing to the empty whiskey bottle that wobbled by the phone. Tater, who was standing behind the desk with a brow covered in cold sweat, sloped off into the gloom. The room was lit only by a small, sulfurous coal burner. In the corner a copying machine stood among split packets of paper. The smell of the spirits it used hung heavy in the dusty air. Outside, the distant wail of the sirens could barely be heard beyond the crash and rumble of the bombs.

Grinn wasn't happy. After the bizarre turn of events at Paddington — another ghost, for goodness' sake! — Adam had been furious. Grinn, though, had just been desperate to get as far away as possible from the sensation and the police who came with it, and was ready to give up the whole cursed affair as too risky. But Adam had other ideas. Grinn shuddered as he remembered the boy's reappearance in this very office that afternoon. He'd been terrifying and impossible to refuse. This whole business with Adam was becoming a nightmare, but by now there seemed to be only one way out for Charlie Grinn. Find this Eddie kid and stick a knife in him.

So far, the only clue was this half-burned notebook found in the ruins of Edmund Utherwise's house. At least, Adam claimed it was a clue. All Grinn could see in it were smudges and crossings-out, and what good was that meant to be? He jabbed his blade into it again.

Adam would return at midnight. And it had been clear from his tone that he expected to find the boy waiting for him, bound and gagged and ready to be killed. But even Grinn couldn't produce that kind of result, not in just a few hours. As it was, he was using all the contacts he had, calling in every favor, making the rashest of promises to some very dangerous people. Word had seeped throughout the underworld that Grinn was offering serious money to locate a lost boy, and every gang in London probably had someone out on the job, taking advantage of the raid and the empty streets. It was only a matter of time. But how much time?

"Tell me again what they said," Grinn snapped as Tater came back with the whiskey. "Could it be the boy we're after?"

"Can't say, guv," said the man as he poured his boss a glass. He splashed a little over the side as something exploded nearby. "It's just some kid they know. They say he's been lying to them. Thought you'd like to ask him yourself. They're sending their man straight over."

"Who is it?"

"Rob Box, guv."

"Box . . ." Grinn drained his glass and looked at the clock on the wall. ". . . is an insect. He really the best lead we have?"

Tater shrugged. He and the other minder were also looking at the clock, and the atmosphere in the room was growing tense.

Midnight struck.

"Well, Mr. Grinn," said an unmistakable voice. "Is it done? Is it seen to?"

Charlie Grinn remained composed. He'd already shown fear in front of his men because of Adam, and he had no intention of doing something so foolhardy again. He deliberately stayed in his chair, even as his minders fell back. Something moved in the shadows. Adam's face appeared first, pale and handsome, then the rest of him emerged from the gloom.

"Good evening, Mr. Adam," said Grinn. "Whiskey?"

"Don't waste my time, Grinn. What news?"

"We have everyone out now. All the most likely places — the docks, the Underground, the churchyards — are being searched, but there're more places than ever, what with the raids on, and . . ." Grinn stopped. He could feel the boy's gaze harden and take hold of his mind as it had done before.

". . . and we have a lead," he added quickly, gambling that the idiot Rob Box was really bringing something useful. "Someone's on his way here with a boy."

"Eddie?" Adam's face lit up and his eyes sparkled. "Is it him?"

"Well," said Grinn, "I think he's more in the nature of a witness, as you might say." And he was immensely relieved to hear a loud banging on the door, right on cue. Adam raised one eyebrow and stepped back into the shadows.

"Come in!" called Grinn.

The door was opened by one of the men he'd left outside. Grinn caught a glimpse of a motorcar's dimmed headlights before a hairy man dressed mostly in rags shoved his way through the doorway and began to struggle across the room. Locked in his arms, legs scrabbling for some foothold, was a boy in his early teens.

"Mr. Box," said Grinn. "And who's this?"

"Little runt's a biter," croaked Box. "Bleedin' toe-rag! He was seen wiv a kid like the one yer lookin' for, but lied about it. He knows somefink, so my guv'nor wants his 'undred up front." He released the boy and held out his hand.

"Thank you, Mr. Box," said Grinn, who knew that utmost politeness was wise when dealing with other gang leaders and their lackeys. "If this boy leads us to our target, I'll send the cash across in the morning. Your guv'nor knows the score."

Rob Box lowered his hand and glowered about the room. Grinn gave him a you-may-go-now look, and his men came and stood either side of their hairy visitor.

"First thing, mind!" shouted Rob Box, waggling his finger before he was led out.

When the door was closed, Tater came and stood over the boy crouching in the middle of the room. Still at his desk, Grinn switched on a flashlight and pointed it at their captive. It wasn't Edmund Utherwise, that was clear, but with Adam somewhere in the room, Grinn would have to be careful. He just hoped Box was right that this boy knew something.

"Name?"

"Never!" shouted the boy, standing up and tightening his fists.

Tater smacked him back down again.

"Tell us your name, and then tell us where to find Edmund Utherwise," Grinn said. "Help us and you can leave by the front door. Lie to us and you can swim home with a brick in your pocket."

"You don't scare me!" said the boy, standing up again. "Bleedin' pantomime, all this."

"Perhaps I don't scare you," said Grinn, "but my associate here just might."

The boy looked around in alarm, unsure which direction any new threat might come from.

"What is your name?" said a cold voice behind him.

The boy spun around and looked up into Adam's face as it materialized from the shadows. He shrank back almost as if Adam's gaze were driving him down forcefully. By the time he reached the floor his defiance had been replaced by pure dread.

"Name!"

"Tomkin" was the only word the boy could utter.

CHAPTER 26

DAVID REMEMBERS

David was sitting on the floor of his room, doodling dejectedly on an empty page of Eddie's old notebook and brooding on how everything had gone so wrong.

After he'd been escorted from the Map Room, the guards had delivered him and the other dreamwalkers to the Lodge. Dishita had marched directly to the Cave without a word, but David couldn't bring himself to go there. He could guess the kind of reception he'd get. Instead, he'd hesitated outside his room and had been grateful when Petra paused with him. It had seemed like a good moment to build up to some kind of apology. He'd been wrong about that too.

"I didn't ask to be part of this," he said to her. "Let's face it, I'm hopeless as a dreamwalker. Maybe Roman's right."

"Ah, stop feeling sorry for yourself." The lack of sympathy in Petra's voice should have warned him to shut up. "You survived, didn't you? Think of Théo. Your mind is stronger than you realize, David, it's the way you use it that lets you down. Go get some rest."

"It's just that, when you showed me David fighting Goliath, I thought . . ."

"What?" Petra's anger finally flared. "Are you trying to blame *me*? That David still had an army behind him, still put his trust in others. It's not my fault if you can only think about yourself."

"No, I didn't mean . . ." David began.

"Oh, just forget it." Petra had given him a look of disgust as she stormed off after Dishita.

And so David had not only messed up his chance to help find Eddie, he'd even managed to anger the only friend he had left. He scribbled furiously across the page. He was about to fling the book across the room when the buzzer rang. He got up and opened the door, hoping it wasn't Dishita — she'd no doubt go double ballistic if she caught him defacing one of Sir Edmund's precious notebooks on top of everything else. He was relieved as well as surprised to find Professor Feldrake standing there.

"I hope I'm not disturbing you," said the old man. "I just thought I should see how you were. You had quite a shock earlier."

"How do you think I am?" said David. "I'm not exactly a hero around here."

The professor gave a wry smile. He came in and sat down in the chair at David's desk.

"I also thought you should know that I have been formally suspended as director of the Dreamwalker Project. Don't blame yourself, though; it's been coming for a while now. There are more than a few people who think an old duffer like me isn't up to the job. They say I only got it because I was a long-standing colleague of Sir Edmund's."

"You worked with Eddie?"

"Oh, yes, almost from the start. He hired me as a historian to help with the very first research missions into the past. But that was years ago. I'm just an old dinosaur myself now, I suppose. It's good to see you writing in his book, by the way."

"You put it in my room, didn't you?"

Professor Feldrake grinned.

"I'm sorry, Professor," said David.

"Oh, don't be. You're his grandson, and a blank page is meant to be written on . . ."

"No, I mean I'm sorry you've been suspended. It's so unfair."

"Oh, don't worry about that. I still have faith in this place, even with Roman in the driving seat. And so should you, David."

There was an awkward pause.

"What will happen now?" David asked.

"Well, Roman has reduced the research team looking for Eddie. He says that without help from you it will be impossible to find him anytime soon, so the new focus is firmly on locating Adam and eliminating him. The Map Room sounds more like a military command post right now. Too much fighting talk for an old academic like me."

"But Adam's too strong. I saw what he did to Théo. He nearly did it to me. We've lost too many dreamwalkers fighting Adam already."

"*We?*" said Professor Feldrake. "Are you finally accepting your true part in all this?"

"There was a man behind Eddie with a knife!" David struggled to control his temper. "I'm sorry about what happened, but I thought he was going to die. My part in all this is to save my family. It's not my fault if no one told me there would be plainclothes policemen there. Trust has to go both ways, doesn't it?

Maybe if people didn't keep things from me, I would have done things differently."

"That's a fair point," said the professor. "A very fair point indeed. You remind me of someone I used to know."

"Right," David said, not very interested in this. "Just as long as it's someone worth being compared to."

The professor gave David an unexpectedly bright smile, then removed his glasses. As he cleaned them on his tie, he spoke again.

"You know, this place was never supposed to be like this. The Dreamwalker Project didn't even have a security advisor in the beginning. We were just a bunch of starry-eyed scientists and wonder kids, opening the lid on history for the first time. And your grandfather was the greatest dreamer of us all. Unsleep House was just the château back then, no need to dig down into the mountain or put soldiers at the gate. But the Haunting have changed all that; they've made us paranoid. No one has stars in their eyes now. I just wish you could have seen what we were, David, and not what we've become."

"Misty told me you don't even know who's behind it," said David. "The Haunting, I mean. But how can you not know? Surely you at least know the name of the person Adam's working for now."

"The King of the Haunting," the professor said, almost to himself.

"What?"

"Oh, it's nothing. Just a rumor. There is a word — a name perhaps — that's come up time and again over the years, but, well, one word isn't going to get us far, is it?"

"His name is King?" David said. "Or do you mean . . . ?"

"That he *is* a king?" the professor chuckled. "Or perhaps that's just what he calls himself. Or perhaps it's a code word, or . . ." The professor replaced his spectacles. "Don't waste your time thinking about it, David. As I said, it's just a rumor."

David stared at the old man, and wondered if the professor knew more about this mysterious king than he was letting on.

"So, what happens next? Does Roman really think we can stop Adam with force?"

"Roman hates Adam more than you can know," said the professor. "And maybe he's got it right. We no longer outnumber the Haunting, but some sort of final showdown between us is at least logical. And we still have some pretty talented dreamwalkers on our side. Dishita in particular wants revenge for Carlo and the others. And Petra will no doubt surprise us as usual."

"Petra?" said David, trying not to sound too interested in one dreamwalker over the others.

"Oh, yes. There's more to her than meets the eye. She's fluent in five languages, you know. Or is it six? In any event, she's very capable."

"But what good are languages against Adam?" cried David, losing control of his voice.

"I know, I know," said the professor quietly. "But it's out of my hands now. The people who fund the Project are desperate for an end to the crisis, and they're backing Roman all the way. As far as they're concerned we have an all-out psychic war on our hands, and Petra is just one of the troops."

David tried to imagine Petra facing Adam in a mind fight. The thought made him feel sick. It wasn't just the dreamwalkers

Adam had recently beaten; in the years when he'd worked for the Project he'd defeated dozens of haunters too. Petra would lose that fight, and David couldn't shake off a vision of her in a coma, growing old and mindless on life support. And would Dishita really do any better?

"But if we did find Eddie," David said, "we could still get him to safety, couldn't we? I mean, well out of London and away from Adam? We could still solve all this without anyone getting hurt?"

"Well, yes, we could move him to some secret spot Adam would never guess. We've helped people stay alive before. Why?" The professor looked suddenly hopeful. "Have you remembered something?"

"I don't know." David drummed his fingers on the wall. "Like I said, I just have the feeling I've seen or heard something that could help. I might remember it . . ."

The professor gave a weak smile.

"That's the way. Keep thinking positively. You never know what might turn up. I have to go, but I promise I'll let you know if anything happens. I'm sure you'll have a part to play in all this before the end."

The professor stood to leave, but when he reached the door, he turned with a strange, almost crafty look.

"Oh, and don't let being under house arrest bother you, David. Since when did a locked door stop a ghost?"

The professor stepped out, but paused in the doorway. He waited for a moment, as if weighing something in his mind, then spoke again.

"After all, whatever you dream you can do, Davy, you can do."

The door slid shut. David stared at it in astonishment. The professor's words sounded exactly like something his father used to say. What *was* the connection between his dad and this place? He rushed to the door and opened it, but the professor had already left the corridor. David ran to the main door from the Dreamwalkers' Lodge, but his way was barred by two security guards. The professor had gone.

David returned to his room and crashed on the bed. His mind, overloaded, wandered crazily over the events of the last two days. Could he, even now, remember something useful?

He picked up the old notebook again.

"Eddie, where would someone like you hide?"

David thought of his lost friend and tried to visualize him as his own grandfather. It wasn't easy. After all, David had only ever seen him as a boy. The one picture the professor had shown him of Eddie as an old man was all he had to go on.

David sat up. Something was nagging at his mind again. He went to the Showing Glass and switched it on. It took him just a few moments to find that very same picture, attached with many others to Sir Edmund's official file. He increased its size so that it filled the whole glass wall.

Sir Edmund Utherwise, distinguished scientist and founder of the Dreamwalker Project, looked back at him, surrounded by shelves, leather spines, and framed photographs. David wondered where the picture had been taken. The base was so modern that this paneled study couldn't possibly be part of it. Even Professor Feldrake's office, with all its clutter and books, was obviously built recently. He looked again at the room behind the old man. Books. Photographs . . .

David went very still.

He reached out and zoomed the image down to one particular black-and-white photo. It showed a small group of people standing on the steps of a large town house. In the center was a man in a Second World War officer's uniform. Beside him were a woman and a boy. It was Eddie, looking just as David remembered him, except perhaps slightly less sad. So this man must be Eddie's father, going off to war, and the woman Eddie's mother. There were five other people around them, some of them at least looked as if they must have been servants.

And one of these was a girl.

David zoomed in closer. She had a strong, defiant gaze that didn't quite fit the housemaid's pinafore she was wearing. When he tried enlarging her image even more, the picture became too much of a blur, but he was left with the strong feeling that he'd seen this girl somewhere before. Who was she?

And finally it came to him.

He knew then that at all costs he had to get a closer look at this photograph.

CHAPTER 27

THE CHÂTEAU

David stood in the hall and buzzed Petra's door, bracing himself for the worst. After a moment it slid open.

"Hi," he said. "Um . . . can we talk?"

Petra let him in without saying a word. David wasn't sure how best to handle this frosty reception, so he just came straight out with it.

"Petra, where was Eddie's study? I mean, Sir Edmund Utherwise's study? You know, the one in the photo the professor showed me when I first got here. Was it in Unsleep House somewhere?"

"Yes," said Petra. "His study is on the top floor of the château. Sir Edmund hated it down here. He called it 'the mole hill' and refused to be moved. Why?"

"*Is?* You mean it's still there?"

"Yes. They just locked it up when he died. The science guys want to keep it exactly as it was. A sort of museum for them, I guess. What is this, David?"

"Listen, I need to get into the château. I want to look in the study. How can I do that?"

"You can't," said Petra. "You're under house arrest, remember? You can't even leave the Lodge without an escort."

"But what if I weren't under arrest?" said David. "How do you normally get to it from here?"

"There's a tunnel from the upper level of the base that leads into the cellar of the château," Petra said. "But you would never get there. The upper level is heavily guarded these days."

"Isn't there some other way? There must be a fire escape or . . . or whatever. It's very important. I think I've found something."

"Oh?" said Petra, her face stonier than David had ever seen it. "Like what?"

"Look, Petra, I'm sorry about what happened at the station, about making a fool of myself, about . . . everything. I just want a chance to put things right. Help me get into the château and I'll show you."

Petra stared at him for a long time before she spoke.

"They assigned me to protect you, David. That's all I've ever done. If I'm going to help you now, I need to know that you will trust me from now on, without hesitation. So will you?"

"I will," David replied. "I couldn't wish for a better body-guard than you, Petra. And I really am sorry."

Petra thought about this for a moment. Then she gave David a brilliant smile.

"Good," she said. "Because I already have a plan."

"I hope you don't mind other people's underwear." Petra grinned.

David tried to keep calm as she wrapped a sheet tightly around him. He couldn't take his eyes off the laundry chute hatch in the corner of her room. What kind of plan was this?

"Are you sure this is the only way?"

"Yes, stop fidgeting." Petra seemed to be enjoying herself. "There's always a pile of dirty clothes at the bottom. Well, almost always. You'll be fine."

When Petra had finished he had to hop to reach the hatch.

"This is ridiculous," he protested, trying to hide his alarm. His arms were bound tightly at his sides, and he suddenly realized he was going to have to go headfirst.

"You want to get out of the Lodge, don't you?" said Petra, not quite suppressing a laugh. "I'll meet you in the laundry room in five minutes."

"But is it steep?" David peered into the dark of the hatch as Petra held it open. He was going to fit, but with only a finger's width to spare. The chute sloped away at an alarming pitch.

"I thought you said you were going to trust me." Petra pointed into the chute.

David shut his mouth and put his head into the hatchway. He pushed farther and farther into the square metal hole, then yelped as two hands closed around his ankles and heaved. Petra's laugh was cut off as his body filled the chute, and he was falling. He found himself hurtling down into the dark in what had to be a near-vertical drop.

In seconds he was out and facedown in a heap of dirty clothes. In the pitch black, David rolled frantically to free himself, but when he finally got the sheet off he banged his head on a low metal ceiling and fell back into the dirty linen, stunned.

It seemed to take Petra much longer than five minutes to get there, and when a doorway finally opened and that familiar tangle-haired silhouette appeared, David could tell she was still laughing.

"Come on out now," she said. "You have passed the test."

"Test? What test?" David asked as he crawled out of the laundry cupboard.

"You really do trust me. That was mad, what you just did," said Petra. "But let's not wait around here. Come."

He followed her out of the laundry room, too glad to see her smiling again to be angry at being played with. And she had got him out of the Lodge. They moved swiftly down a corridor and then climbed two flights of stairs to the level where the canteen was. Petra ran here, silent in her boots, and David did the same. He followed her into a recess. She opened a service door at the back and they ducked through into a deep cupboard.

Petra walked straight to the back of it, pushing past mops, buckets, and brooms. In the gloom, David heard a metal panel being popped free, and weak light broke through from beyond. Behind the cupboard was a narrow rock passage that seemed prehistoric after the clean, modern surroundings of the rest of the base.

"What is this?" asked David.

"When they extended Unsleep House, they just went straight down into the mountain beneath," said Petra. "There was a vast cavern there already, and even now there are still some unused natural passages like this one. It joins with the main tunnel entrance to the château's cellar."

"Is this how you get into the château normally?" said David, surprised. The only light came from a few flickering neon strips hanging from bundled cables that ran along the ceiling, and there were places where water dripped through.

"No," said Petra, stepping into the passage. "I don't know what this passage is, or why it is lit — it seems to have been forgotten. But this is the way I sometimes come when I want to go out."

"Out?" said David as he followed her. They made their way along the tunnel in single file, Petra leading the way.

"Sometimes I need to be on my own," said Petra. "Or at least not down in the base. Like your grandfather, I don't like being cooped up underground all the time. The château is more like a real home."

"But don't you ever go home?" said David. "To your parents? Théo said that not all dreamwalkers live here. What about Christmas, holidays?"

Petra slowed down and then stopped walking. She stood with her back to him. David waited, wondering what he'd said. Eventually she turned.

"This is my home," she said in a small voice. "David, I am going to tell you something, something that you will hear sooner or later. I want you to hear it from me, okay?"

"Okay."

"When I first dreamwalked, I was only nine years old. I had no idea what was happening, of course; I thought it was just a wonderful dream. But I soon found out the truth."

"Someone from Unsleep House came and picked you up?" said David. "They 'activated' you?"

Petra shook her head.

"They spotted me on the Map, but they didn't reach me in time. Others were watching too."

David said nothing. The air around him seemed suddenly chilly.

"The Haunting got to me first." Petra looked at the ground. "They raided my home. I was taken."

"Taken?" said David. "What about . . . ?"

"My family? The Haunting only take what they want, David, and they only want dreamwalkers. They can't afford to leave witnesses."

David didn't know what to say.

"I was held for over a year," Petra continued, forcing the emotion out of her voice. "They made me dreamwalk. They forced me to terrify people, to be a ghost. They told me my family would be hurt if I didn't. So I became one of them."

"You . . . *you* were a haunter?"

"Yes." Petra's face had disappeared behind a curtain of curls. "They told me it was my destiny, that this was what dreamwalking was really all about — being a ghost, haunting the past in order to change it. They promised me riches and power, and if I questioned them, they threatened to hurt those I love. They made me into a monster."

"The statue! In the museum!" David said, suddenly remembering the terrifying image of the Gorgon with the snake hair and piercing eyes. "That really was you, wasn't it?"

"That was the form they needed from me. I didn't have any choice."

"But you were rescued . . ."

"I escaped!" snapped Petra, her hair flying back so that her eyes flashed in the gloom. "I am the only one who has ever escaped from the Haunting. I drifted for a while, but then Unsleep House took me in. That's how I found out that my family had been murdered. I did all those terrible things to protect them, but they were already gone."

David stared. He felt numb inside.

"The King of the Haunting," he said eventually, without really intending to say it aloud.

"Where did you hear that?"

"The professor said something about the Haunting being led by a king," David said. "Did you . . . did you ever . . . ?"

"Meet him?" Petra's eyes flashed again. "No, David. If only I had!" Then she spoke more coolly. "When I got here, I did all I could to destroy the Haunting; I told the professor everything I knew. But it wasn't enough. *King* is just a word, after all, and no one knows what it means. So the Haunting are still free to keep doing what they do. They still take dreamwalkers as slaves. They still murder those who get in their way."

"Petra, I'm so sorry," said David in a whisper, "about your family."

Petra looked at him with moist eyes.

"It is not for you to be sorry. You didn't know," she said.

"But I do know what it's like to lose someone close," said David.

"Your father. Yes." Petra stepped closer then and took David's hand.

"We're dreamwalkers," she said, looking up into his face. "Life is different for us, as you've seen, but death is too. When we lose someone it's not the same as it is for other people. When someone dies they come to the end of their time, but that time — the time when they lived — is still out there somewhere. It still *happened*. And we are the lucky ones who can slip back and visit that time again and see those we have lost. It's a wonderful thing we can do, David. The Haunting is wrong. *This* is the greatest gift of the dreamwalker."

David blinked at her. He really hadn't thought of it like that.

"So you do this?" he said eventually. "You visit your family as a dreamwalker?"

Petra smiled again, but her face was still sad.

"Once," she said. "I did it once. But it was too hard. I wanted them to see me, but that would have been so wrong. How would they have reacted? How could I have explained? No. Instead I just stood there in a shadow and watched and . . ."

It looked to David as if she was about to cry, and he was amazed she hadn't yet. He put his arms around her, unsure if this was really the right thing to do, or if he was allowed. Petra accepted his touch for a moment, but then gently pushed him away.

"It's okay," she said. "I'm okay."

They looked at each other for a moment.

"I don't need to see my family again," she said, "not like that. But knowing that I *could* visit them, that they are still out there somewhere, happy and unaware in their own time, that's a great comfort. You might find it a comfort also."

David put his hands in his pockets and looked at the floor. Part of his mind was dealing with the unexpected thought that he could see his father again, in a sense. But another part of it was thinking of Petra and how close she was standing. Then she spoke again and broke the strange moment.

"You will find that some on the Dreamwalker Project still don't trust me. You heard what Roman said in the Archive — once a haunter, always a monster, that's what they think. I just wanted you to know the truth from me before you hear any stories, that's all. Now let's go find your grandfather's study. Come." She turned on her heel and set off down the corridor again.

CHAPTER · 28
SECRETS AND BETRAYAL

David and Petra arrived at the end of the dripping stone passage.

"Ah, here is the way in."

They stopped beside a small metal door that looked as though it was rarely used. There was a vertical bar up one side with a padlock through it. Petra gave David a crafty look, then kicked the bottom of the bar with her foot. The padlock dropped off, and David saw that it had been broken at some point in the past.

"Did you do that?" he asked.

"I don't like locks," said Petra. "Unless I've locked them myself. Come."

The door led into a larger passage, still cut roughly from the rock, but in better condition. The light was more stable here. Soon David noticed that the ceiling had become vaulted and was made of white stone, greenish-gray with age and damp, and hung with cobwebs. They had reached the cellar. It was pitch-black from there on and David cursed himself for not thinking to bring a flashlight.

"This way," said Petra, walking out into the shadows. She moved her arm, and a shaft of light sprung from a flashlight in her hand.

The cellar was enormous, with arched side bays full of boxes and crates, and high, cobwebbed racks, the odd wine bottle still resting there. Petra clearly knew where to go, and soon they were walking up stone steps, picking their way carefully in the little patch of light pointed at the girl's feet. At the top was a large wooden door. Petra turned the handle and pushed it open.

"Wait a moment," said David. "Aren't there security cameras or anything?"

Petra shrugged. "I have never seen such a thing here."

They stepped through the door and walked out from under an enormous carved staircase that dominated a paneled hallway. In front of them was a broad, glass-paned double front door, and on each side of the hall there were further doorways. Through one of these, David caught a brief glimpse of furniture draped in dust-sheets, stacked files, and an overhead projector, and he remembered that the Project had actually used this building until quite recently. Now, though, it felt abandoned.

Petra handed him the flashlight.

"The study is on the top floor," she said. "This was your idea. You lead the way."

They began to climb.

When they reached the first floor, David glanced uneasily down the long corridors. The ground floor had appeared well kept, but up here the building seemed in poor condition. The shards of light that entered between the wooden slats left crooked bars of shadow on the wall. David felt cold as they continued up the stairs, the wooden steps creaking beneath their feet.

On the next floor the shutters were also closed, and the flashlight illuminated great looping cobwebs and lost its brightness in the dust. Petra, who had kept behind David as they climbed, suddenly walked straight to a window in the middle of the landing. She climbed up onto the wide sill and undid the catch.

"What are you doing?" whispered David.

"I want to see the view," said Petra, not whispering at all.

She gave the tall shutters a determined shove. They fell wide open, and David welcomed the freshness of the cool mountain air after the air-conditioned base. Beyond was a far-reaching view along a valley, ringed with the snow-capped peaks of the Alps. The late afternoon sun spilled on to the landing, and Petra stood in its light, breathing deeply. David saw that there were some things on the windowsill — magazines and books, a cushion, and an empty teacup.

"I haven't been here for a while," said Petra, jumping back down. "But now you know all my secrets. The study is along there on the left."

Leaving the window open, they continued down the corridor until they arrived at a closed door. It was locked.

"I don't suppose you know where the key is," said David, without much hope.

"Why bother with a key?" Petra said. "I didn't have a key when I first came to the château. And you're stronger than I am."

"Break in, you mean?" David was surprised. "But what about alarms? And won't Misty notice? I thought she was everywhere in Unsleep House."

"Only in the new bits. There's no Misty up here."

David looked at Petra and remembered that he still had a lot to prove to her. He turned back toward the door. It was old, and the wood was dry. He could feel Petra watching him, but even if she hadn't been, there was too much at stake to let a few boards of decaying oak stop him now. He stepped back and hurled himself at the door.

He'd expected to be flung back with a bruised shoulder, but instead the brittle wood just split right down the middle, disintegrating into splinters and dust. He shone the flashlight inside.

Everything in the room was covered in white sheets, but there was one large rectangular object in the middle of the room that was obviously a desk, and several others that could have been armchairs. The bookcases were also covered.

David smiled. He was standing in his grandfather's own room, and really standing there, not dreamwalking. This was the strongest physical connection he'd yet had with the boy from his dream, though it was also the closest he could ever get to him in the present. Sir Edmund Utherwise had lived out his natural span — dreamwalking was now their only means of contact. David found himself fingering the notebook still in his pocket.

"Are we looking for something specific?" said Petra, breaking his thoughts.

David walked over to the nearest bookcase, pulled the dustsheet down, and swung the flashlight across the shelves. Books, nothing more. He walked to the next case and did the same.

This time his flashlight revealed the wall of photographs he'd seen behind Sir Edmund in the photo. He quickly scanned the frames until he found the one he was looking for. It was exactly where it should have been. He took it down and shone the flashlight at it.

"Here, look," he said. "You see this group of people? I think that must be Eddie and his mother saying good-bye to his father. It dates from around the time I first started visiting him. The end of 1939, I think, when the war started. Anyway, you see that girl there? I've seen her before. She was a maid or something at Eddie's house."

"You come from a rich family," said Petra.

"Me? No! Well, in Eddie's time maybe — *I* don't live like this. But listen, this girl's name was Kitty or Kat or something. I saw her come to Eddie's door a few times. He never let her in when I was there, but I think she saw me at least once. The thing is, they didn't behave like she was just his servant. It was more like they were friends."

"I see," said Petra, taking the photo. "I do remember her from my time watching you and Eddie, but she was just listed in the Archive as a resident in the building and was not part of my briefing. I was only there to watch you, David, and I was very careful. Eddie already had one ghost; he didn't need another. You think she might be a clue to finding Eddie?"

"Well, yeah. Everyone assumes that because Eddie was such a loner, I must be his best friend or something, but why shouldn't he have had someone else? I mean, how much does anyone here really know about Eddie when he was my age? And if *you* kept seeing a ghost, wouldn't you want to tell someone? Ever since the professor first told me Eddie had gone missing, I've been trying to remember something Eddie said when I last saw him. It came back to me when I saw this picture. Eddie said he shouldn't have trusted me and that someone named Kat had told him so."

"Meaning this girl?" said Petra.

"I think so. The point is, *I* don't know where Eddie's run off to, but maybe she does. I want to go back in time and talk to her."

"The professor needs to know about this," said Petra. "We should get back."

David followed her to the door, shining the flashlight once more around room as he went. He stopped.

"Wait."

He walked back to the wall of photos and picked up another. It showed a man and a boy shaking hands in the Map Room of Unsleep House, and behind them, looking on and smiling, was the elderly Sir Edmund Utherwise. The boy was Adam Lang, and the person he was shaking hands with was someone David knew instantly. It was his own father.

He held the picture up to Petra.

"If Misty isn't here, perhaps you can give me a straight answer now," he said, unable to keep the anger from his voice. "What has my dad got to do with this place?"

Petra came back over. She looked awkward and embarrassed.

"I never wanted to lie to you. They told me that you shouldn't know, not until the crisis with Adam was over."

"Know what?"

Petra bit her lip.

"Tell me!"

"David, you grew up thinking that your father was a soldier, but that is not true. He was part of the Dreamwalker Project."

David said nothing. He'd kind of worked that out for himself. But seeing his dad with Adam was horrible.

"He was a trainer," Petra continued. "He taught us dream-walking technique. He was a dreamwalker himself as a boy, and like many he stayed on to work here as an adult. They had to think of something to tell your family, so the soldier thing became his cover story. Sometimes the only way to keep a secret is to tell a lie."

"But why keep it from me now?" David said. "He was my dad. Why shouldn't I know?"

"Richard Utherwise, your father, was Adam's mentor. He was personally responsible for training and guiding the Project's best dreamwalker, and he spent a lot of time working closely with Adam. Security thought this would upset you and cloud your judgment. The professor agreed. I'm sorry."

David looked at the photo again and felt sick.

"If my father wasn't a soldier," he said after a long silence, "how did he die?"

Petra stared at her feet.

"An accident. He fell down some stairs in the base. Just a stupid accident."

David looked at the picture again, then threw it across the room. It shattered against the wall.

"I want to get out of here."

Petra said nothing as she took the flashlight and led the way back down the corridor. David followed her in silence. All he could think of was the fact that his father had spent far more time with Adam than he had with his own son. And no hero ever dies just falling down the stairs.

No hero at all.

They reached the top of the steps but David was too lost in his own thoughts to notice what was happening. Then, as he took the first step, he saw that Petra had gone, and the flashlight beam was nowhere to be seen. He froze.

"Petra?"

Nothing.

He looked back down the corridor to where they had been. It was dark, easily dark enough to hide someone. And David thought he could see a shape in the gloom, but there was no way it could be Petra. A sudden wave of panic chased away the misery over his father's betrayal, and he ran down the stairs to the hall.

"Petra! Where are you?"

Without the flashlight, the dark closed around him. Desperate to get out, he made straight for the front door where the last of the evening light was still coming through the glass. He grabbed the door handle.

Something dark and man-shaped stepped across the outside of the door. David staggered back and turned.

A head suddenly appeared in a blaze of light right in front of him. David let out a whimper.

"Boo," said the unsmiling, flashlight-shadowed face of Roman.

Lights came on and David saw that he was surrounded by armed security men.

He was actually relieved.

CHAPTER 29

PETRA'S FAREWELL

The walk back to Unsleep House was humiliating. David's hands were handcuffed behind him, a gesture of utter pointlessness that David found hard to take seriously. Then he was marched through the cellar of the château and paraded around the base like a prize. As he passed, people stopped and stared, but no one challenged Roman, and David was taken down to the security wing and straight to a cell. There his handcuffs were removed, and he was shoved inside. Roman stepped in behind him.

David had remained silent up till then but he turned on the commander the moment they were alone.

"This is so stupid!" he shouted. "You'll regret this when you hear what I've just found. And I have rights — you can't just keep me here!"

"Keep you here?" said Roman, his anger making his accent much stronger than normal. "I have no intention of keeping you here. We have kept you long enough."

David wasn't expecting this.

"What's that supposed to mean?" he said, still shouting.

"We are sending you back to London. There is a plane leaving in the morning. You are going to be set free."

"Set free!" David said. "I'm not an animal." But then he remembered that his life was supposed to be in danger in London. "Wait, does the professor know about this? I thought someone was trying to kill me!"

"Don't worry," said Roman with a sneer. "Your precious self will be looked after. Personally I think your usefulness has been exaggerated all along, but we will hold you in our London sub-branch for a few days, just until the security risk can be assessed. Then you are on your own."

David found his anger subsiding, but this new development confused him. After all, he was being given what he'd wanted so badly just a short time before: the chance to go home. But at the same time he was too involved with the events at Unsleep House to want to leave now.

"You've always had it in for me," he said to Roman. "What's your problem anyway?"

"My problem?" Roman came and stood right over David. "My 'problem' is with little kids who don't understand, who don't care. Kids like you, shouting about rights and laughing at the rules. You don't understand dreamwalking, you don't . . . *deserve* it." He took a deep breath. "It is a miracle, boy. And no miracle should be left in the hands of children."

"Yes, you were a dreamwalker too." David rolled his eyes. "I do know."

"You know nothing!" Roman grabbed David. "Nothing!" He twisted him roughly, pointing to the logo on David's back: the image of the sleeping face with a third eye open in the fore-head. "Now you have the gift, boy. *Now!* But one day you will know how it feels when this third eye closes. Then maybe we will speak again."

And with that he dropped David and strode out of the room.

"Wait!" David called. "I found something. I think I might know how to find Eddie."

Roman waved this away with one enormous hand and swung the door shut. Electronics whirred as the heavy bolts slid home.

David kicked the door in fury, raging at how powerless he was, and at how easily he had been caught up in these dangerous events only to be just as easily flung out of them. What would happen to Eddie now? And where was Petra? Perhaps they would listen to her. Perhaps a dreamwalker could still talk to the girl named Kat and find Eddie. It might still be okay. But David was desperate to be part of it. He sat down on the fold-out bed and felt frustrated, miserable, and alone.

He was left with his thoughts for a long time before he finally fell into a fitful sleep. It was only his second night in the base, but he'd been through so much during this short time at Unsleep House that his body was exhausted. He eventually awoke to the sound of the bolts flipping back and the door reopening. He stood up, half hoping that the professor had come to get him out, but it was two security men. One of them handed David a small suitcase.

"Your things," the man said. "You can get changed on the plane. It's time to go."

David picked up the bag and tested its weight. It contained everything he'd had on him when he was first brought here, including his clothes. He really was being thrown out, then. And for doing what? Breaking the door of his own grandfather's study?

"I need to see Professor Feldrake," he said.

One of the men shook his head. The two guards led David out of the cell and through the security wing to a broad spiral staircase he hadn't seen before. From far above came a loud, cavernous sound, and a cool breeze descended. David was taken up the stairs and out into a vast space. The size of it was hard to fathom in the gloom, but at one end daylight poured through a huge triangular opening. From here a long, narrow strip of artificially flat rock spread out and along the top of a ridge. It was a runway. At the top of a mountain! Despite the circumstances, David was amazed.

Standing in the center of the cavern was a small passenger jet. It was the kind of plane he'd never dreamed he'd ever travel in, the kind only used by rich businessmen or government agencies. It stood, looking sleek and powerful, while several engineers checked it over and its engines whined in readiness.

Waiting by the plane was a small knot of men and women clutching computer bags and briefcases. One woman held an armful of antique scrolls, wrapped in plastic. The people peered at David with curiosity but said nothing as he was led to join them. They must be his fellow passengers, sent to London on Project business that he would never know about. He stood with them, the security men on either side of him, and wondered if he should still try to tell someone about Kat.

As he waited, his hands in his pockets and the bag on the floor between his legs, he heard the sound of feet running on the metal floor. He looked up.

It was Petra.

She was alone, and though the two security men looked at her suspiciously, no one stopped her. David walked to meet her, and also to put some space between them and the guards.

"I wanted to see you," said Petra, glaring back at the guards. "I was worried they might have hurt you."

"No," said David, "but they're kicking me out. What have they done to you? Are you okay?"

"Ah, they shouted at me for a while, nothing new. I heard you were leaving. They don't trust you. They don't trust me either, but they need me. They need every dreamwalker they have left."

"And I don't count, I know," David said. "Did you tell them about Kat?"

"I tried, but like I said, they don't trust me," Petra said, keeping her voice lower than the engine whine. "Roman has ordered us to give up on trying to find Eddie completely. Now we are being sent in groups of three to hunt Adam down. Roman's orders are to combine the moment we see him."

"What *is* that? Combining?"

"A double mind pulse. When two dreamwalkers merge together."

"But Adam broke Théo like he was snapping a twig," said David. "Will even that be enough?"

Petra gave David a resigned look.

"We'll soon find out. And he can't get us all. Some of us might survive long enough to hit him hard."

"What does the professor say?"

"He's disgusted. He hates all this mind pulse stuff anyway. But they won't listen to him anymore."

"Petra, what about the photo, what about Kat? Surely there's still a chance to find Eddie and avoid all this."

Petra glanced again at the guards and shrugged.

"I'm dreamwalking again soon with Dishita. With Théo out of action we are just going as a backup team of two. They'll probably make us babysit Misty, but there will be two other groups in place for when she detects Adam. *If* she does. They are the ones who will do most of the fighting."

"This is crazy!" said David. "Now we know about Kat, I've got to get back there. Maybe I can dreamwalk tonight from wherever they're sending me."

"Maybe," said Petra, "but you're going to be held prisoner until this is over."

"I'm not going to sit in some prison cell and wait to be wiped off the face of history!" cried David. "I should be here, with you."

"Yes," Petra hissed under her breath. "Yes, you should be here." But, glancing over at the guards, she said aloud, "It's over, David — I'm sorry. Good-bye."

David looked at her in surprise, but was even more astonished when she rushed forward, threw her arms around his neck, and kissed him on the cheek.

"We'll wait for you, David," she said in his ear, and before he could reply he felt her fingers push something up into his collar. Then she stepped away and ran off across the vast cavern without once looking back. The guards quickly lost interest in her.

David returned to stand by the other passengers and resisted the temptation to reach for his collar. He was very aware of the place where Petra had kissed him and felt fuzzy and strange. As he waited, the preflight checks were completed and the passengers were finally allowed to climb up the fold-down steps. Inside the plane he was taken to a seat near the back. Both security men were clearly going to take the flight with him.

"What do you think I'm going to do?" David snapped at them. "Jump out with a parachute?"

He sat down by a window and turned his back on the guards. Soon afterward the order came from the pilot to fasten their belts. David did as he was told and felt himself pressed back into the seat as the plane accelerated and rushed out of the dark into the golden light of morning.

In no time at all they were airborne, and he found himself looking down over the Alps, watching the rising sun brush the snow on the peaks. But his mind was buzzing with thoughts of Petra and the small object she had hidden in his collar. What could it be? Ten minutes later, when he had sunk down low in his seat and made sure that no one was watching, he reached behind his neck and drew out a thick square of tightly folded paper.

Glancing at the guards one more time, he turned back toward to the window and carefully opened it. It was the photograph from the study, folded so that Kat's face wasn't creased. And rolling around inside were three small yellow tablets.

David spread the photo facedown and flat. Across the back was a drawing: a snaking double line with wavy marks drawn inside. As a Londoner, David recognized it immediately as the River Thames. And there at the center was a detailed little sketch of Tower Bridge. Beside was written an exact date and time: 5 P.M. on the 19th of December, 1940.

A rendezvous? Was Petra telling him where and when to meet her?

He looked at the pills. They had DREAMWALKER PROJECT stamped in tiny letters around the rims. A small voice in the back of his mind whispered *poison*, but he could never believe that of Petra, not now. So there was only one thing they could be: sleeping pills. Of some special kind, adapted for dreamwalkers?

He took one more look at the map, memorizing the date and time written in Petra's spiky handwriting, then he swallowed the pills.

He thought again about his friend Eddie, all alone and in danger in a bombed-out city. He thought of his father and his sister and of how their lives were indistinguishably bound up with Eddie's and his own. He thought of Adam with his black hat and cane, prowling through the ruins of London with murderer Charlie Grinn at his side. He thought of Petra and the others, preparing to fight for their lives.

His thoughts began to merge and break down. His last clear image was of Eddie, scrambling away across the burning rooftop a moment after they'd last spoken.

"Hold on, Eddie," David murmured. "I'm coming."

The only answer was the vibration of the plane.

Then David slept.

CHAPTER 30

LONDON, DECEMBER 19, 1940, 4:27 P.M.

In the theater attic, Eddie was laying a fire on the thunder sheet. He had drawn a neat diagram of it in the open notebook beside him. Concentrating on the need to combine heat, fuel, and oxygen in a structured way was helping him forget that a few days ago an uncontrolled fire had almost roasted him alive.

Tomkin hadn't come back the night before, and Eddie could tell Kat was worried. But all he felt was that it was better having Kat to himself. And she would want to be warm when she got back. He picked up two sticks and considered the most efficient place to set them. It was as he was doing this that he suddenly realized he wasn't alone.

Eddie froze, still holding the sticks. He squeezed his eyes tightly shut.

"Who is it?"

No one answered. The silence was absolute, and yet Eddie knew he wasn't mistaken. He forced himself to raise his head and slowly open one eye.

Someone was watching him from the shadows of the attic.

Someone who had appeared in absolute silence, without climbing the ladder or entering through the hole in the roof.

Eddie felt a chill grip his spine.

"Who's there?"

Both of Eddie's eyes were open now — he couldn't have turned away even if he'd wanted to. He tried desperately to make the dark shape he could see into some innocent object. The theater attic was full of moldering stage props after all. Could it be a mannequin? A puppet? A costume he hadn't noticed before?

But it was no use. He knew there really was someone there, and he'd only ever known one other person who could appear in silence like that.

"David?" Eddie swallowed. "Is that you?"

The figure stirred and stepped forward, becoming more visible against the dark. What had seemed to be nothing more than a shadow now revealed itself to be a boy — somewhat older than Eddie — in an extremely sharp suit, with a hat and a cane.

"I didn't mean to startle you," said the boy.

"The ladder made no noise," said Eddie, picking up his notebook and rolling it tightly. "When you came up it. It always makes a noise."

The visitor shrugged.

"As I said, I didn't mean to startle you. I was merely passing. I have to go now. But have no fear, Eddie. Please forget you ever saw me."

And he moved toward the trap door.

"You know my name?" said Eddie. "How do you know my name?"

The boy stopped and turned, bringing an intense gaze onto

Eddie. Eddie looked down, gripping the notebook so tightly in his hand that he almost crushed it.

"You are Edmund Utherwise, aren't you?" said the boy. "Well, good evening, Eddie. I was told you'd be here, that's all. By a boy called Tomkin."

"Tomkin," Eddie said in an almost-whisper, "didn't come home last night."

"It's fine, Eddie. Tomkin's just . . . staying with some friends of mine. There's nothing for you to worry about. And now I really must go."

The boy walked again toward the hatchway.

"Just one more thing. These friends of mine, they'll visit this place shortly. To pick up some things for Tomkin. But you won't let them worry you, will you, Eddie? Just stay here nice and safe, and you'll be fine. Agreed?"

Eddie nodded his head, but inside it the voice of his doubt buzzed like a swarm of bees. He wished Kat were there to talk to this strange boy.

"Good," said the visitor. "And now I really do have to be moving on." He began to lower himself down the ladder.

"Wait!" Eddie called, more to hear the reassuring sound of his own voice than anything else. Then a question burst out of him, almost of its own accord.

"What's your name? If you know mine, you should tell me yours. It's polite."

The strange boy was almost gone; his head and shoulders alone remained above the floor. He paused and turned his ferocious, dark gaze on Eddie the way a cat would look at a mouse.

"Adam. My name is Adam. And now — finally — good-bye, Edmund Utherwise."

When Eddie looked again he was gone, without a single creak or groan from the rickety ladder. Eddie was alone again.

With a shaking hand he lit the fire.

CHAPTER · 31
THE FREED MIND

David was dreaming.

Unsettling images turned in his mind — an empty château, dusty photographs, yellow pills — making little sense.

But wasn't there something he had to remember about dreams? Wasn't there someone he was supposed to meet?

He made his mind focus and saw the image of a girl. He remembered her name was Petra. Then he remembered the map she'd drawn, and Tower Bridge, and the wartime world of the boy who would one day be his grandfather . . .

Eddie!

The chaos of the dream fell away, and David saw that he was there, standing on the bridge, looking up at the twin Gothic towers as the last rays of a winter sun painted them a weak yellow. He was dressed once again in the school uniform and felt the chill air of a long-past December seep into him. A motorcar rumbled past, all black wheel arches and round lamps. There were barrage balloons tethered above the city, soldiers in the streets and sandbag stacks on either shore of the Thames. A small plane thrummed low across the sky. It was a Spitfire.

For a moment David spun slowly on the spot, taking in the scene. He'd done it! He'd left his body back in the present, asleep in a jet plane somewhere over Europe, irrelevant. It was his mind that mattered now. And his mind was precisely where it needed to be.

"I'm here!" he cried out loud, shaking his fists at the sky and laughing. Pedestrians on the bridge tried to ignore him, but from behind there came an accented voice.

"Do you always keep a girl waiting?"

David turned to see Petra, dressed exactly as she'd been at Paddington station.

"You're late," she said, showing him a 1940s wristwatch whose hands showed it to be five past five. "But maybe I'll forgive you."

David was so pleased with himself that he jumped at Petra and gave her a hug. He'd forgotten he wasn't yet used to the dreamwalking state, and in his excitement his dreamself began to blend into Petra's, so their ghosts overlapped in parts. It felt very intimate and dizzying.

"Calm down, will you!" said Petra, pushing him away. "Combining like that can be dangerous. Let's save it for Adam — if we meet him."

"I'm sorry!" said David. "I'm just happy to have got here, and happy to, er . . . see you."

"Oh?" said Petra, flicking the hair from her eyes.

"Well . . . I mean . . ."

"Let's not waste time." Petra grabbed David's hand and pulled him along. "Come. We must join the others."

David allowed himself to be led along the darkening bridge. The streetlamps that would normally have lit this scene in his own time, and which would certainly have been in use in the

1940s, weren't switched on, and it was only spotting the sand-bags again that reminded him why.

Petra came to a halt at the base of the nearest tower and pointed at the stone wall. A door was suddenly there, a dream-walker's door.

"But I've only just got here," said David. "Where are we going now?"

"Things have changed since we last spoke," said Petra.

"But . . . but that was only a little while ago. Just before I boarded the plane. Can things change that fast?"

"You forget that you are now in the business of time-travel," Petra replied. "For me it's several hours since you left Unsleep House. Misty has detected Adam's presence in London several times, though each time he moved before she could pinpoint him. It's clear he's been busy. But then, so have I. David, I think I have found Kat."

"Really?" he said. "You've spoken to her?"

"No, I thought you should be there when I did that. Come, Dishita is close by. But get ready to talk fast — she won't be happy to see you, I think."

Petra opened the door and stepped through. David followed her.

On the other side, he found himself in a very dark place, but the jagged silhouettes around him were clearly ruined build-ings, black against the deep twilight of the sky. And the atmosphere was horrible. The air was filled with the acrid tang of recent fires and the destruction of things that aren't supposed to burn.

"Where's this?"

"I'm not surprised you don't recognize it," said Petra. "This is Eddie's street. His house used to stand just over there."

David peered through the gloom at the twisted shapes and rubble heaps. It was unrecognizable. Then he saw something move at street level — two figures emerging from the dark.

"Someone's coming," he hissed.

"Relax," said Petra. "It's just the others."

"Petra!" came the stern voice of Dishita, in full I'm-in-charge mode. "Where have you been? I told you to stay close. And who's that . . . ?"

Dishita became clearer as she approached, her eyes catching light from somewhere as they grew wide. It was obvious that Petra had told her absolutely nothing about what had happened on the runway.

"David? But . . . how can you be here? They sent you home . . . Petra! What have you done?"

"David deserves to be here for the end of this." Petra put her hands on her hips, ready for the argument. "I just made sure he would be, that's all."

"And what does that mean, 'made sure'?" demanded Dishita. "David, explain yourself."

David told Dishita about the note Petra had given him, and the yellow pills.

"Somnium pills!" Dishita gasped, turning to Petra. "You gave him somnium pills? More than one?"

"It was the only way. It's nothing — he can take it."

"But it's years since we used those. They're not safe. And if David took two, then . . ."

"He took three, actually," said Petra.

"*Three!*"

"Er . . . Should I be worried about this?" said David.

"No, no," Petra waved his concern away. "Dishita is being unimaginative, that's all. Before the sleep machines were invented, the science guys came up with pills to do the same job. You'll be fine, David, just asleep for a very long time. And we'll need that time if you are going to help us find Eddie."

"I have to report this to the Map Room," Dishita said, shaking her head. "Misty, you'd better tell Roman that David's here."

The other figure in the dark stepped up alongside Dishita and pulled back the hood of a black evening cloak. Streams of golden-white hair fell down to her shoulders, and a complexion free of any blemish shone out. Even the faintest scrap of light was reflected back from the perfect face of Misty.

"*I already have. David, your presence is not part of the mission plan. Roman is very angry. He wants you to end your dreamwalk immediately. Is there anything you'd like to say to him?*"

David shrugged. "I suppose they'll wake me up now. So all this was for nothing."

Petra gave a gleeful laugh. "David, they can't wake you up, not with those pills. You're in a sort of mini-coma. There's nothing Roman can do about it."

"A coma!" David stared at her.

"Hey, don't forget you promised to trust me," Petra replied. "This is what you wanted, isn't it?"

David couldn't argue with that. He ought to be grateful to her, especially if Roman couldn't touch him. And surely his body was still okay, or his mind wouldn't feel so clear. He turned back to Misty, enjoying the feeling that Roman was powerless.

"Tell Roman that I'm going to do what he should be doing. I'm going to find Eddie and make him safe. Tell him he doesn't need to worry about any more mistakes — I've learned a lot, the hard way. And tell him to lighten up — he's had his dream-walking time, now I'm going to have mine. Oh, and tell him I want an apology when I succeed."

"Roman didn't like that," said Misty. *"Here's his reply."* And she put on a perfect imitation of Roman's voice. "You have a big mouth, boy. But I'm not going to punish you. I don't need to. Because if you mess up again and ruin this mission, if you let Adam reach Sir Edmund first, by God, you will have done the job for me. You will have written yourself out of history. The rest of us will be left leading very different lives but you, boy, you will be nothing. No, *less than* nothing. Even your father will never have been born. Would you like to take a moment to reflect on that?"

David felt his confidence drain away. He said nothing.

"Silence?" went on the voice of Roman. "Yes. Silence suits you better. Now keep your head down and do exactly what Dishita tells you! Dishita, stick to the mission brief, but do not let David Utherwise out of your sight."

Misty paused for a moment and then continued in her own enchanting voice. *"David, the professor told me to tell you he's monitoring this from his office. Would you like to speak to him?"*

David shook his head. He suddenly didn't want to hear anything more from Unsleep House. After what Roman had said, he was just desperate to find Eddie.

"Thank you, Misty," said Dishita. "Okay, David, you heard Roman, no more games now. This is my team, and thanks to you I don't have Théo. You'll just have to stand in for him the best you can, but remember that the professor is not running this anymore: Roman is. We can't waste time looking for Eddie; it's hopeless. Our target is Adam. Now —"

"David knows how to find Eddie," Petra interrupted. "Roman wouldn't listen, but Dishita, *you* must. This is your command. David, tell her."

David quickly explained about the photo and his memory of Kat's name being spoken by Eddie at their last meeting. Dishita listened in silence.

"And Petra said something about finding Kat," David finished.

"I think I know where she is, yes," said Petra. "As a servant, Kat lived in the same house as Eddie, so obviously she was also made homeless by the fire. But she must have had somewhere else to go. I spent the last hours before this dreamwalk trying to trace Kat in the Archive, because if David's right, then Eddie could well be staying with her."

"*Could well* be?" said Dishita, clearly unconvinced. "And even so, we still don't know where that is."

"True," said Petra, "but I have managed to track down Kat's aunt."

"Go on," said Dishita, her voice betraying a first hint of interest.

"Kat's aunt is a cook in a house just two streets away from here. Kat can't stay there, I've checked, but her aunt has managed to get her some temporary work in the house. There's not much in the Archive, but at this time of day I think Kat should still be there. Dishita, we must forget about Roman and his crazy orders and go and see Kat. And we don't need Misty anymore — with David, our team is complete."

"Are you sure, Petra? You know I like to be helpful."

"You will make every man who sees you stare right at us," said Petra. "And every woman too. Those science guys are really dumb. They know nothing about dreamwalking."

"Misty, have you relayed any of this about Kat to the Map Room?" Dishita asked.

"Not yet. Would you like me to do it now?"

"No," said Dishita. "No, tell them nothing. Not until we're sure."

"I will have to tell them if they ask."

"Then give them no reason to. If they want to know what we're doing, tell them we are in position near Eddie's house."

"I really don't think I can lie, Dishita."

"It's not a lie; we're only going a few streets away. Now cover yourself up. Okay, I'm going to give this lead one chance. Petra, show us the way. But David?"

"Yes."

"I'm going to leave the job of talking to Kat to you."

CHAPTER · 32
MISTY'S MOMENT

David crouched in darkness beneath the front steps of a grand town house and squinted through the little basement window. The glass was misted by condensation, but as it formed drips and ran, he could glimpse what was going on inside through the clear channels left behind. The kitchen beyond was bathed in warm light from lamps and a roaring stove. The heat of the room radiated through the glass, and above, gravy-rich steam rolled out through a ventilator and into the cold night.

"What can you see?" Dishita's voice was so low it was barely audible.

"A woman, the cook I suppose she'd be, and another woman. But I can't see Kat."

"Let me look," said Petra, and she pressed herself forward to the window, her head right beside David's.

"Yes, that is Kat's aunt. The other woman I don't know, maybe . . ." She stopped talking as a third figure entered the kitchen, carrying a basket of laundry.

"It's her!" said David. "Kat!" But he must have spoken too loudly because the two women looked over at the window.

"Bloody kids at the bins again," said the cook. "Chuck a bottle at 'em, Alice."

The woman called Alice stalked to the window. She rubbed the condensation away in one brutal swipe of her hand and pressed her nose up to the glass. David sensed sudden movement behind him. He glanced back and saw that the other dreamwalkers had gone, making themselves disappear into the brickwork. He hadn't been fast enough. The woman at the window was looking straight at him, though in the gloom it wasn't clear how much she could really see.

"Clear off out of it!" she shouted.

David kept very still, but he knew this wouldn't be enough. He couldn't risk another blunder, not now, so when the idea came into his head to frighten the woman with his ghostliness, he knew it was a temptation he had to resist. He remembered the first rule of dreamwalking; he'd been seen, so now he had to make sure he wasn't noticed.

"All right," he said loudly. "I'm off." And he scampered up the steps. He waited in the street above, crouching to keep out of sight and feeling foolish. After a moment the mean, pinched face vanished from the window, and David crept back down.

"Quick thinking, David," breathed Dishita, reemerging. "If only you moved as fast."

"I'm doing my best," David whispered back. "But the girl we saw before — with the basket — she's definitely the one I've seen at Eddie's house. That was Kat."

"She's gone again," said Petra, peering into the kitchen once more. "Let's all go in and find her."

Dishita waved her finger to silently indicate *no*. Petra's eyes flashed defiance back at her, and she was about to speak, but Dishita spoke first.

"David must do this alone. It's going to be a shock for Kat to see a stranger in the house, but at least David's a Londoner. Even so, he's going to have to work hard to persuade her, so everything must be as normal as possible. I don't know how many Indians are in London in 1940, Petra, but there certainly aren't many Germans."

"It's okay, I can do it," David whispered, "but I would like someone with me, just in case. Can I take Misty?"

Petra's reaction was so loud that David expected the angry face to return to the window.

"David, no! She's just a useless machine!"

"Are you sure?" Even Dishita, who was the only dreamwalker David had seen treat the computer with any respect, seemed surprised. "Misty's useful at times, but she was never designed for an active mission role. I don't see how she can help you."

"All the same, I think she'll be useful now," said David. "Misty, will you come with me, please? But keep yourself covered up and out of sight unless I call you, okay?"

"Okay, David," said Misty from inside her hood, and there seemed to be another quality to her voice now: a hint of satisfaction. A light flashed briefly from inside the hood as if from a too-perfect smile. *"I have always said I like to help."*

David could tell that Petra was beside herself with silent rage. He just hoped he'd made the right decision. He walked to the wide door under the steps — a tradesman's entrance, presumably — and pressed himself hard against it. He knew the others were watching, and he thought back to the moment in Paddington station when Petra had shown him how to walk through walls, and how he'd later done it himself accidentally.

He felt his dreamself bump against the solid barrier of physical matter. It resisted him. But then he focused his mind on the one, wondrous fact at the heart of dreamwalking: He wasn't physically present at all.

In a single fluid motion, he slipped through the wall.

He found himself in a dark corridor on the inside of the house. In a moment Misty was standing there too, waiting for his lead, her hood still down. David guessed that with such a companion he would have to take all the initiative himself. He held up his hand for her to wait.

To the right was a half-opened door with the kitchen on the other side. Peeking through the gap at the hinges, David could see the cook and the woman called Alice, still talking about thieving tramps at the bins.

There was no sign of Kat anywhere, and David prayed she hadn't gone upstairs. He really didn't want to have to search the entire house for her. There were two more doors farther down the corridor, so he decided to check these first. He slipped past the kitchen and hurried along.

The first door was closed. David glanced nervously back to the kitchen before forcing his spectral head right through the wooden barrier, ignoring the unpleasant sensation this produced. The room was dark and appeared empty, but he heard a faint *thump* from beyond the wall to his left. Someone was in the next room. He jerked his head back into the corridor and slipped farther along. When he came to the next door, he held up his hand for Misty to stop, then peered inside.

The room was clearly a laundry. There were baskets of linen standing about and sheets drying on lines that crisscrossed between the walls. The atmosphere was thick, with a strong smell of rough soap. There were wide ventilators in the upper walls, though little fresh air seemed to pass through them. One small, fizzing lightbulb was all that lit the room. In the center of the far wall, her back to the door and her arms in hot soapy water up to the elbows, stood a girl, rubbing hard at something in a sink.

It was Kat.

Leaving Misty in the corridor, David stepped into the doorway but hung back a little so that the sheets and the shadows would obscure his features. There was nothing for it — he'd just have to speak.

"Please don't be frightened. I'm a friend."

Kat spun around with a splash of bubbles and water. She stared at David in shock, frantically pushing her hair back from her eyes with her dry upper arms.

"Who are you?" Kat seemed torn between fear and uncertainty, and David remembered that she was new to this house. She must be half expecting surprise encounters all the time. But he wondered whether it was wise to tell her his name too soon.

"I'm a good friend of Eddie's. I'm very worried about him. I think he's in trouble, and I want to help."

Kat's expression hardened — fear was overcoming the uncertainty in her eyes. She turned to face David directly, one hand searching for a long-handled something that he could see sticking out of the sink behind her. He had to act fast to keep control of the situation.

"It's Kat, isn't it? Can I call you Kat? Eddie told me about you. Is Kat short for something? Katherine?"

"Katrina." This was said with a gulp and a slight tremor. *"Who are you?"*

"Before I tell you my name, let me tell you two things first. It's important. You seemed scared of me, Kat, but I want you to understand that you don't need to be. Okay . . . I mean, all right?"

She gave a jerky little nod.

"The first thing is that someone impersonated me in order to hurt Eddie. Someone incredibly dangerous," David said. *"I* didn't do anything to harm him. And second . . ."

This is it, he thought.

". . . second . . . everything you think you know about ghosts might not be true."

"David!" Kat's mouth was almost too dry to speak. "Oh, my God."

"Kat, please, don't be scared." David stepped in front of the hanging sheets, doing everything he could to radiate goodwill. "Yes, I am David. But more than that, I really am Eddie's friend."

"Get away from me!" Kat cried, and she flung the long-handled object. Before David could move he sensed it pass right through him and clatter against the wall in the corridor outside. It was clear that Kat would have screamed if fear hadn't constricted her throat. David had to act fast — he was losing her.

"Kat, please, look at me. We're about the same age, I think, like Eddie. He's your friend too, isn't he? I'm not what you think I am. I'm not a real phantom, I'm just a boy who needs your help. Please don't be scared of me."

Kat had gone very still, though the moment of abject terror seemed to be passing. But now David had a cold, hard stare of intense mistrust to deal with.

"Ghost! Monster!" Kat cried suddenly. "You are a devil. Eddie told me about you — you wanted to kill him, to make him a spirit like you. I'll never tell you where he is, even if you bring all the demons of hell. Now get away from me!"

She was shouting loudly, and it would only be a matter of time before someone heard and came to check on her. And then what would David do?

"Kat, I swear to you that I'm not a devil or a monster. I'm not even a dead person from hell, if that's what you mean. But there *is* a monster out there, someone who wants Eddie dead. He's the devil, not me. I'm on the side of the angels, I promise. Look, Eddie has some very special friends." And he beckoned out into the corridor.

Misty stepped into the room and lifted back the hood of her cloak, letting her lustrous hair spill out once more. Her face caught the mean little light from the electric bulb and threw it back around the room like the gleam of firelight on gold. The grubby walls and linen baskets seemed to shrink back in shadow as she gave Kat the full benefit of a bewitching smile.

Kat had clearly forgotten to breathe. When she could finally speak, nothing coherent came out, but David was just pleased that the hostility had gone from her face.

"Kat, will you help us to help Eddie?" He spoke cautiously, hoping to avoid breaking the spell he'd guessed Misty would cast over someone like Kat. "He's in terrible danger. Maybe you are too. But you and Eddie have friends now, powerful friends."

Kat couldn't turn her eyes from Misty. David tried to imagine the effect the hologram was having. For Kat, with her scrubbing brush and washboard life, beauty and glamour were a distant, probably unobtainable dream. Misty must seem to her like a vision from another world, a world of miracles. As, in a sense, she was.

"Are . . . are you an angel?" Kat asked Misty, her hands clasped together.

"Er, sort of," said David hurriedly, before Misty could answer. He didn't want the moment ruined by the computer's difficulty with little white lies. "Kat, we don't have much time. Please, take us to Eddie. We need to get him away from London as soon as possible, away from danger."

Kat stepped forward, her eyes still drinking in the beauty of the apparition before her. Then, finally, she looked at David again.

"Someone *is* after Eddie. But how do I know I can really trust you?"

"Kat," said David, indicating Misty, "my beautiful friend here always tells the truth. Ask her why we are here. She's incapable of lying."

The girl looked at David, and then back at Misty, her face a mix of emotions.

"Eddie's a good person." Kat spoke calmly now, but there were tears in her eyes. "I haven't met many of those in my life. But now my brother's disappeared, and I don't know . . . I . . . all I want is to do the right thing. Angel, have you come to help us?"

There was a pause, and David prayed that Misty wasn't

being taken too near an untruth. Would the computer even realize that Kat was addressing her?

"*Yes,*" said Misty at last. "*I like to be helpful.*"

At the sound of Misty's pearl-drop voice, the last shades of mistrust left Kat's face.

"All right," she said. "I'll take you to Eddie."

CHAPTER 33

London, December 19, 1940, 5:53 P.M.

Eddie sat alone in the attic after the strange boy named Adam had left, trying to decide what to do.

You mustn't go out, said the voice of his doubt, and this is what Kat had said too. *Stay here. Hide. You mustn't go out . . .*

But Eddie wasn't so sure. He looked again at the page in his notebook where he'd scribbled his way through the options. There was now only one thing left that was legible:

Silence. Only David can appear in utter silence.

The conclusion was obvious, even if he'd been deliberately avoiding it: The boy called Adam was a ghost like David. If *ghost* was the right word.

You promised Kat that David wouldn't find you here! The words rang in his head. *If David and Adam are the same, then a ghost has found you here. You have broken your promise . . .*

Eddie shut his book. That was right, wasn't it? So there was only one thing he could do now. He stood up and grabbed his satchel, putting his few possessions inside. He'd go back to Paddington, study the timetable again. He'd get to his aunt's house, even if he had to sleep in the waiting room until a train became available. But as he was putting his satchel over his shoulder, he heard a sound far below.

The stage creaked loudly.

People had entered the theater, as Adam had said they would, people much bigger than either Kat or Tomkin.

Eddie quickly dragged a stool to the spot under the hole in the roof. His injured ankle and weak lungs meant he hadn't used this way out since the night he arrived, but there was no time now to worry about aches and pains. He grabbed the edge of a freezing, rotten beam, heaved himself up, and looked out across the roof.

With the last dregs of light in the sky, Eddie saw the silhouettes of two men in overcoats on the roof of the building next door. One of them had his arm raised, the unmistakable shape of a revolver in his hand.

Eddie dropped back into the attic and looked around wildly. The only other way out was to go down, but already he could hear someone climbing up to the trapdoor. The top of the ladder was bouncing against the edge of it with the weight of an adult. Eddie ran to the hatch and looked down.

In the beam of a flashlight shining up from the stage far below, a face peered back at him — a face with a thin mustache.

"You aren't friends of Tomkin's." Eddie felt foolish saying this, but he needed to hear his own voice.

"No," said the man. "No. But I do have business here, that much is true."

"Business?" Eddie backed away. He was breathing so fast that his damaged lungs burned. "Who are you?"

The man reached the top of the ladder and looked over at him.

"My name is Grinn — Charlie Grinn — and I'm nobody's friend. Someone wants you rubbed out, Eddie, and I'm the man who'll get it done."

Grinn climbed out of the trapdoor and reached into his pocket. He pulled out a bone handle and released the knife's blade with a wicked *snick*. He stepped toward Eddie.

"But why?" Eddie's voice went high with fear.

Grinn shrugged.

"Does it really matter?" he said. "No funny business, now. How much this hurts is up to you."

Eddie backed farther into the theater attic and grabbed the nearest object, a papier-mâché Roman helmet. He flung it at Grinn, but the gangster simply swept it aside. Eddie reached again, but there was nothing there of any use, nothing at all — even the stage swords were just painted balsa wood. Grinn was only a few paces from him by now, already pulling back his arm.

Then he was obscured from view.

Something — no, some*one* — was suddenly standing between them, facing the gangster.

Grinn's jaw dropped with astonishment. An apparition had just risen up through the solid wooden floor! He stepped back in shock, tripped over the thunder-sheet hearth, and let go of the knife.

"Run, Eddie — *run!*" shouted a voice Eddie knew.

"David?"

Grinn started to get up again, but fell back at the mind-numbing sight of more figures rising into the attic through the floor, and another one floating down through the beams of the roof. And then Kat was there too, climbing off the top of the ladder. Grinn seized his knife and scrabbled back across the floor, staring in fear and confusion at the group of people suddenly there.

"David!" Eddie said again, rubbing frantically at his spectacles. "Is that really you?"

"It is, it is," said David. "At last, I've found you."

"That man wants to kill me. But . . ." Eddie took a step back again. ". . . isn't that what *you* want?"

"No! Eddie, it would take too long to explain now, but we've been looking for you ever since the fire at your house. Someone does want you dead, Eddie, someone extremely dangerous, and he must know where you are or his knifeman wouldn't have come. We have to get you away."

"There are men on the roof with a gun, and more downstairs . . ." Eddie began, but David shook his head.

"The ones downstairs have run off, scared out of their wits, and we've dealt with those on the roof too. Being ghostly can be quite useful sometimes."

"But, David, *what are you?* Are you really a ghost?" Eddie felt his mind racing, and on an impulse he swept his hand at David. It passed right through him as if he weren't there at all.

"Later, Eddie." David was grinning. "We've come a long way to help you, but time is against us."

"It's true," cried Kat, coming over to Eddie. "At least, I

think it's true. David and his friends are here to help you, Eddie, and they even have an angel!"

Eddie looked back over at Grinn, who was crouching in the corner of the attic like a frightened animal, staring up in terror at the three figures who stood over him.

"An angel?" he said. "So that would explain . . ." And he pulled his notebook from his satchel and started flicking through the scribbled pages. Yes, that would fill in a lot of blanks. "David, *are* you an angel?"

"Don't answer that!" said a voice, and Eddie saw one of the three figures hurry over. She was a tall, dark girl in her mid to late teens, with a foreign accent. "You mustn't tell him anything, David. The second rule, remember?"

"But, Dishita . . ." David began.

"No names!" snapped the girl. "Eddie, I'm sorry to present you with all these mysteries, but you will need to work all this out on your own. You must leave the city immediately. We have cleared your way out of the building, but you are in terrible danger if you stay here. Come with us now, and we'll guide you. Can you drive?"

"Drive?" Eddie was surprised. "I've never tried, but I understand the principles." He pushed his glasses firmly up his nose. "The internal combustion engine . . ."

"Warning!" called out a clear voice, and everyone turned to look at the figure in the long cloak who was still standing over Grinn. She had raised her hood.

"That's the angel," whispered Kat to Eddie, whose eyes were boggling.

"What is it, Misty?" asked David. "What's happening?"

"Adam. I have detected Adam. He is coming. We . . ."

Misty stopped speaking, her face frozen in midspeech. Her final syllable rang out in one continuous, squealing vowel sound. A long black stick was protruding from her chest. Before anyone could act, Misty dissolved, falling to pieces in countless tiny points of light that skittered across the floor and flickered away to nothing. She was gone, and standing in her place, his cane still raised, stood Eddie's mysterious visitor.

Adam.

For the first time, David found himself in the same room as both his grandfather and the boy who wanted him dead. He stepped protectively in front of Eddie, who was clinging on to Kat, but he also wondered what Adam would do, what he *could* do. After all, no dreamwalker, no matter how strong, could actually touch Eddie.

"Adam," Dishita said, "you've failed. We're taking Eddie now, and your only ally in this time is over there, cowering on the floor. It's finished."

Adam snarled. Then he turned to Grinn. "Get up, you idiot!"

The gangster stood slowly, with his knife held out in front of him.

"Mr. Adam," said Grinn in a hoarse voice, "for God's sake, what is all this?"

"Ghosts, Grinn, nothing more. No one here can harm you; they can't even touch you. But you, Grinn, are no ghost. *You* can still kill the boy. Now stop gibbering and grab him! Finish the job!"

Grinn took a small step forward.

"Stay where you are!" called Petra in a voice that was terribly altered. She rose off the ground, her hair rippling out from her head like a Gorgon's snakes. She gave Grinn a pitiless look that should indeed be petrifying. Sure enough, the gangster stepped back again, white as a sheet.

"Ignore her!" shouted Adam. "Close your eyes if you have to. She can't touch you. No one here can. *Kill the boy!*"

Some kind of realization seemed to come over Grinn. A dreamwalker was a terrifying thing if you didn't know any better. But the moment you understood they were actually powerless over the physical world, everything changed. And unfortunately, it looked as if Adam's words were finally getting through to Charlie Grinn. Adam had to be silenced.

It was clear that Dishita thought the same thing.

"Now!" she shouted at Petra, and Petra swooped back toward her. The two girls stepped into each other and began to combine, their separate dreamselves rapidly blending as they brought their forces together. Alarm passed across Adam's face.

"No you don't!" he cried, and he leaped forward, raising his cane to try and hit them first.

For the briefest moment David had a clear image of the two dreamwalkers merged into one. The combined figure they made was primarily that of Dishita, yet Petra was there too, and their double-dreamself crackled with mental energy, filling the attic with a high-power sound. And when the figure moved to counter Adam as he smashed his cane down, it was as if four arms lashed out, not two.

There came an ear-ringing *smack* and *crack* as the dream-walkers clashed. David saw Adam flung back, his face a blank of pain, his whole dreamself faint and rippling. He was turned head over heels in the air by the doubled force of Dishita-Petra and sent spinning straight through the wall at the end of the attic with a cry of dismay.

Dishita-Petra stood in triumph in the center of the room, facing the wall in readiness, her multiple arms raised.

Nothing came back through. Adam was gone.

But David had seen exactly what happened, and he knew that Adam had managed to strike too. As he watched, the principal half of the double-dreamself began to fade, and two of the arms fell. The part that was Dishita toppled forward, separating out from Petra, who seemed to be trying to hold her up. But still Dishita continued to fade as she fell through Petra's arms to the floor. Petra knelt beside her.

"Dishita? Can you go on? Can you hear me? Dishita?"

Dishita stared up at nothing.

"It hurts . . . I can't . . . I . . ."

Then she faded away to nothing.

"No, no!" Petra was distraught. She turned to David. "Dishita was in front. She took the full force of it. It was bad, David, very bad — Adam really meant it."

"And Adam?" David asked. "Did you hit him hard enough?"

"I . . . I don't know. We didn't have time to combine properly. I just don't know."

David looked back to where Dishita had just been. She was gone, her dreamwalk brought to a sudden and brutal end. What would be happening back at Unsleep House? Hundreds of miles and nearly eighty years away, was Dishita's mindless body being wheeled out of the Somnarium?

"Misty!" David called. *"Misty!"* But Petra was shaking her head.

"Misty's gone too. And without her, even the Metascape Map is useless," she whispered, glancing across to where Kat and Eddie were huddled beneath the hole in the roof, one looking fearful and confused, the other taking every detail into his quick mind. "We're on our own."

"Then we have to get Eddie out of here."

"David." Something in Petra's voice made him turn.

Charlie Grinn was firmly on his feet now, looking at them with new resolve. He tossed his knife in the air and grabbed it back. Then he walked toward Eddie.

"Eddie, Kat — get out!" David said. Petra rose off the floor and swooped down at Grinn, her hair wild once more. But this time the gangster stood his ground. He lashed out, and his knife went straight through her.

"No one was ever hurt by a ghost," Grinn declared, half hysterically. He advanced again toward Eddie.

"Bleedin' spooks! I'm sick of it! Mr. Adam was bad enough, but you lot . . . walking through walls, staring, floating . . . tricks! Just a bunch of smoke and nothing, that's all. But I'll get the boy, and when Mr. Adam comes back, I'll be rich, and then I'll retire to some place where there's no war, no coppers, and no BLEEDIN' *GHOSTS!*"

Petra flew back to David. There was nothing they could do to stop Grinn. By now Eddie had pushed Kat up onto the roof and was dragging himself after her. Grinn lunged forward, and David felt sick with powerlessness as the gangster grabbed Eddie's ankle, sending the stool flying. Suddenly being a dream-walker was the worst thing in the world.

"Eddie, kick him!"

David didn't need to say this; Eddie was lashing out with all his strength, and Grinn was forced to let go. David saw Petra slip up through the beams of the roof and he followed her, rising out into the night. Kat was there, pulling Eddie up onto the roof tiles. Down below he could hear Grinn snatch the stool back up and bang it down on the floor beneath the hole.

"Where's the angel?" Kat cried to him. "I thought you said you were powerful. Help us!"

David didn't know what to say.

"We can help by showing you the safest way," Petra told them. "Keep calm and move carefully."

Grinn's head appeared through the hole as Kat and Eddie stumbled away from it.

"Get back here, you little bleeder!"

"This way!" David called, and without thinking he took to the air, heading for the roof of the building next door.

It was exhilarating! Even in all the stress, he was thrilled. Looking back, he saw Kat pulling Eddie along, and saw that Eddie was dragging one ankle. David flew on, right out into the space between the buildings. He had a moment of vertigo at the sight of the deep shadows in the side passage five floors below before he dropped down onto the neighboring roof. *I can fly*, he thought.

Then he remembered that Eddie and Kat couldn't.

The gap between the buildings was well over five feet, maybe nearer ten. Eddie and Kat stumbled to a stop at the edge. Behind them, the silhouette of Charlie Grinn heaved itself onto the roof and stood up straight. He took his knife from his clenched teeth and walked slowly in their direction.

"Go on, kid!" he shouted. "Jump! Make my job easier."

CHAPTER · 31
GRINN GETS IT DONE

Kat jumped first. As she stepped back and then ran at the gap, David was impressed by her courage. She leaped at the very last moment, her skirts raised and her trailing foot pushing down hard against the edge of the guttering. She hit the other roof with a crash, one leg hanging over into the void. David crouched beside her, powerless to do anything but encourage her to her feet. She'd hurt herself, but she didn't complain, she just looked back and called to Eddie.

"Come on, it's not far. Eddie, jump!"

Eddie stepped back. He adjusted his glasses and glanced at the top of the broken iron ladder he'd climbed when he first came to the theater. It was clear he'd rather not jump at all, but go down that way. David followed his gaze downward, and was dismayed to see that someone was actually coming up the ladder from the street. Could it be one of Grinn's men? They'd scared off a few, but how many more would the gang boss have brought with him? Grinn himself was getting closer, but Eddie was still just standing there.

"Eddie!" Kat and David were both shouting now.

Eddie threw a last wistful look at the ladder and then took off his glasses. He stuffed them in his inside pocket, along with his rolled-up notebook. Grinn was just a few paces away when he began his run up.

Eddie jumped.

He hit the edge of the neighboring roof with a hard clatter, the edges of the tiles digging into his stomach. His lungs emptied themselves in a single *ouf* of escaping air, and he clutched at the tiles in desperation. One of them came away, and Eddie fell back. Kat grabbed his coat and heaved. Somewhere far below the tile hit the ground and shattered.

Grinn reached the edge of the roof, panting furiously and just a couple of feet away from where Eddie was struggling. He looked at the knife in his hand, clearly considering whether or not to throw it. David couldn't imagine what crazy calculations must have been going on in the man's head by then, but there was nothing he could do but watch in horror as Grinn came to a decision, raised the knife past the right side of his head, and flung it straight at Eddie.

The knife struck Eddie, and he cried out. Kat heaved one last time and dragged him onto the roof, with the knife still sticking out near his collar.

"Kat, take it out!" David shouted. "Oh, God, take it out!"

Kat grabbed the handle and pulled the blade clear, her eyes wide at the sight of it in her hand and of Eddie's blood running onto her fingers.

"It's done!" cried Grinn, dancing up and down on the very edge of the roof. "Ha ha — done! Mr. Adam, it's been seen to."

"Adam is gone for good," Petra said. She was standing behind Grinn. The gangster turned around.

"Go on, girlie, push me off," he sneered. "That's what you'd like, isn't it? But you can't. It's like you're not even here. Bleedin' spooks! Go on, clear off, and don't forget the Utherwise boy's ghost on your way. Ha ha!"

"Not dead yet," said Eddie, sitting up and wincing back at Grinn. "Thick coat."

David could have cheered. Eddie had obviously been hurt, but not as badly as Grinn had thought. The gangster yelled in rage and got ready to jump across.

"Stop!" Petra called out, swooping around in front of him. "You'll never make it. You are risking your life for nothing. Adam is finished. You can let the boy go, Charlie Grinn. Whatever Adam promised you has disappeared with him. It's over."

Petra's voice was hard and she was staring into Grinn's eyes with great intensity, bringing all the power of her will to bear. Grinn even hesitated, but not for long.

"Mr. Adam's vanished before," he said, "but he always comes back. And I'll have something for him when he does, even if I have to strangle the life out of that scrawny weasel with my bare hands."

He moved back to take a run at the gap. But before he started, a voice called up from the iron ladder.

"Wait, boss, I'll get 'im."

"Who's that?" Grinn said. "Tater? Is that you?"

Grinn swept right through Petra and strode back to the edge to look down into the gloom, eager to see one of his men.

"Got a shooter?"

"Yeah, I'll get 'im," called the voice. "Give me a hand up, boss!"

The shape of an arm appeared at the top of the ladder. Grinn reached down, his teeth gleaming in the dark. David's heart sank. On the roof, with Eddie injured, there was nowhere to hide from a man with a gun.

Then Grinn gave a shout.

David saw the gangster struggle in the dark. Then he staggered, toppled over the edge and vanished from view. For a second there was a cry, before the night was filled with a dull bone-breaking *thud* from the cobbles of the side street below.

"Ha!" said a voice, and a boy climbed to the top of the ladder. "He had that coming and no mistake."

CHAPTER · 35
GOOD-BYES

"Tom!" Kat cried with relief.

As the three non-dreamwalkers slumped onto the tiles and struggled to get their breath back, David and Petra crouched beside them. Even in the dark it was clear to David that all three had been hurt, and Eddie was bleeding steadily despite Kat's attempts to staunch the wound. She was working at his shoulder with the hem of her dress, but kept glancing at her brother with something like awe.

"You killed him," she kept saying. "Dead! You pulled him off the roof!"

"Friend of yours, was he?" said Tomkin in a thick voice, making him sound like he'd taken a recent beating. "What do you care? Chucking knives at you, wasn't he? A nasty one, that Grinn was, and I know more about it than you, believe me. A lot more. Charlie Grinn never let anyone go."

"I don't think I could have done it." Kat was still shaking her head, despite the sense in her brother's word. "You killed him, Tom. Dead!"

"You're all I've got left, ain't you?" said Tomkin, stroking his sister's head with a burst of furious affection. "I'll kill anyone who tries to hurt you."

"Tomkin, where did you come from?" Eddie winced as he spoke — Kat was pressing his shoulder very hard.

Tomkin turned a cold stare onto Eddie.

"We was fine till you showed up. Then suddenly we've got the likes of Grinn in the attic, and worse still. You and me're gonna have a long talk about ghosts, Eddie Utherwise. Right before you clear off for good, that is. No hard feelings, you understand, I just want you out of mine and Kat's lives before you bring any more trouble our way. Got it?"

"Don't be a numbskull, Tom," Kat said. "Just tell us where you've been?"

"They nabbed me, didn't they?" said Tomkin. "Long story — tell you later. Anyhow, I was in a motor outside the theater. That Grinn made 'em bring me in case I was lying."

"Lying?" Kat stared at her brother. "No, Tom, you didn't . . . you told them where to find Eddie?"

Tomkin hung his head for a moment.

"Yeah, all right, I did. But I had someone's boot on me face at the time, didn't I? Like I said, you don't know what that Grinn was like. I'm sorry I squealed, but I had to say something so I could get back to you."

Kat reached out and gripped her brother's knee.

"How did you get out of the car?" Eddie asked, apparently not noticing Tomkin's hostility toward him.

"It was that one," said Tomkin after a moment, pointing to Petra. "She dropped down through the blinkin' roof! Scared the living daylights out of the two heavies guarding me. Me too, if I'm honest. Some sort of trick, I suppose," he added, calling over to Petra, "though how it's done I've no idea."

"No trick," said Eddie, glancing at the two dreamwalkers. "Not in the way you mean, Tomkin. This is David, the ghost I told you about, and his friend."

"It's best if you don't know my name," said Petra. "I don't want to be mysterious, but there are things you mustn't know about us."

"But we owe him something," David protested. "Eddie, I mean. We can't just vanish and leave him without an explanation."

"No!" Eddie cried, only partly out of pain. "You can't! David, tell me what you are. What you are really?"

"Yeah, I'd quite like the answer to that too," said Tomkin.

"I'm sorry," said Petra, "but that's precisely what we can't tell you."

However, when she saw the miserable look on Eddie's face, she continued. "Listen, Eddie, you are being hunted by someone who wants you dead — that should be clear to you now. Why this is and exactly what David and I are, you will have to figure out on your own, but I promise that you will understand one day. You could say it's your destiny to understand."

"Where're you from?" said Tomkin, eyeing Petra with suspicion. "You sound German to me."

As if to illustrate Tomkin's worst thoughts, air-raid sirens started sounding all around the city. They echoed through the streets, mingling with the clamor of people hurrying for the shelters. Searchlights had already begun raking their beams across the sky, as night and another wave of warplanes closed on London.

"All I can tell you," said Petra eventually, "is that I have nothing to do with the people who are about to bomb this city."

There was an awkward silence, and David could see that Petra would have loved to say more.

"I dunno," said Tomkin eventually. Already they could hear the far-off stop-start drone of aircraft and the *thump* of a distant anti-aircraft gun. "British, German . . . I'm still trying to get my head around the fact that I'm talking to a ghost! I must be losing my mind."

"It is against the rules to tell you more," said Petra. "Just don't give up hope for the future, Tomkin, that's all."

"I will discover your secret one day," said Eddie, and with such vehemence that everyone looked at him in surprise. "Perhaps you have already said too much. There's only one way you could sound so optimistic about the future. Am I right?"

Petra glanced at David, then replied, "How is your shoulder? Can you move?"

"Nothing in my past explains why someone would want to kill me," said Eddie, ignoring the question and pulling his notebook from his pocket, "so maybe the reason lies in my future. Such things are said to be impossible, but then ghosts are meant to be impossible too."

"I think the shock's gone to your head, mate," said Tomkin, tapping his forehead. "The sooner you get back to Castle Creepy or wherever you've come from, the better, I'd say."

"Yes," said David. "Eddie, we have to get you away from here. There might still be some of Grinn's men around."

"Where's the angel?" said Kat. "I felt safer when she was here."

"Angel!" Tomkin tried to laugh, but it sounded hollow. "Whatever happened to common sense? Anyway, yeah, Grinn's got half the gangs of London looking for you, Eddie, so Mr.

and Mrs. Ghost here are right that you'd better move on. Been nice knowin' you."

"Eddie, when we asked earlier if you could drive," David said, "it sounded like you were saying yes. Is that right?"

Eddie glared at him but said nothing.

"Tomkin, do you think the keys will still be in the car you came in?" said Petra. "Eddie needs to get out of the city, and fast."

"There's ways to start a car without keys," said Tomkin, tapping his nose. "And if it means getting rid of Eddie all the faster, then I'll even drive the car myself."

A roar of sound washed over the little group on the rooftop as a firebomb erupted. It was south toward the river but the closest explosion yet, and it lit the sky with a spike of yellow light. The noise of the sirens was mixed now with the jangle of fire engines.

"Eddie, you have to move," Petra said. "Can you stand?"

Eddie struggled to his feet, but toppled back down, landing heavily on his knees.

"He's still bleeding." Kat sounded worried. "I don't see how he can jump back to the theater, let alone climb down to the street, and we can't carry him. Tom, we'll have to fetch help. The firemen could bring him down."

"What?" Tomkin look incredulous. "Don't you think firemen have enough to do without mollycoddling the likes of him? Look, I'm sick of all this. All I care about is getting you to a shelter, Kat. I'm done with Lord Creepy."

"We can't leave him," Kat said, as a shriek in the air ended with another explosion, this time just a few streets away. "We'll get help for Eddie, and then we'll go to the shelter, all right? I promise."

Tomkin swore. Then he turned to Eddie.

"You got your claws into my sister, right enough. But this is the last thing we'll do for you." And he grabbed his sister's hand. Together they ran to the edge of the roof. Without hesitation they jumped back across to the theater, their silhouettes briefly highlighted by yet another explosion.

David grinned as he watched them go. He made a mental note to look Kat and Tomkin up in the Archive when he got back to Unsleep House. Perhaps they were even still alive in his own time, old and wrinkly somewhere. He could drop by and chat about all this over tea and crumpets.

Then he remembered this was something he'd never be able to do with Eddie.

He looked back at the boy who would become his grandfather. Eddie had managed to get to his feet and was hobbling away from them, toward the edge of the roof. Beyond him the skyline to the south was ablaze, but Eddie hardly seemed concerned.

Petra came to stand beside David.

"I got Misty to check on the way here," she said. "This building was never hit during the war. Eddie is as safe here on the roof as he will be anywhere, at least from the bombing. But we should stay with him until Kat and Tomkin bring help. And you should say good-bye now, David. There might not be time later."

David said nothing. He'd guessed that some sort of final farewell was approaching, that this might be the last time he and his grandfather were together. He walked over to join him at the edge. For a moment they both watched the devastation that was being wrought on London. Even though David knew that for him this destruction was historic — a past event in the city he lived in — he found it hard not to think of the people who lived here now. How must it feel to belong to this time, to face terror raining from the sky every night without the comfort of future knowledge a time-traveler has? He couldn't even begin to imagine. He turned to Eddie.

"How's your shoulder?"

"Ache in my scapula, right side," Eddie said, "and a hole in my coat. That man Grinn should have jumped. This knife is not designed for throwing."

David looked down at Eddie's hands and saw in the gloom that he was holding Grinn's switchblade, apparently unconcerned at the sight of his own blood. David shook his head. The boy who would one day be his grandfather could be really strange at times.

"David, you have to tell me." Eddie turned to him. "What kind of ghost are you? You talk of rules. That suggests organization. Do you work for some kind of agency?"

David had to laugh. "Eddie, you don't need me to tell you anything. You'll have worked it all out by breakfast."

"I'll keep asking you," Eddie said, not laughing back. "Whenever we meet. I'll get to the truth somehow."

"After this I don't think I'll be allowed to visit you again. I think you've seen all the ghosts you're supposed to."

The fearful sounds of the air raid grew around them. A black cat crept along the guttering.

"I'm sorry I doubted you," Eddie said.

"None of that matters now," said David. "This is good-bye." He looked back to make sure that Petra wasn't in earshot, then leaned in close. "But promise me one thing, will you? If you ever have a son, tell him to spend a bit more time with his own children."

Eddie's eyebrows jumped above his spectacles, and David could almost hear the smooth machinery of his mind whirring as it seized hold of this new piece of information. David knew he'd just said too much, that he had probably just broken a rule of dreamwalking or something, but he didn't care anymore.

"David —" Eddie began, but his words were cut off.

Something dark reared up into the space between them. Eddie stumbled back in surprise. A shape like a man was suddenly blocking David's view and towering over Eddie. Eddie let out a cry and missed his footing. The shape moved and David could see Eddie again, his arms reaching out for balance as his left foot slipped off the guttering.

Five stories up, Eddie Utherwise fell backward off the roof.

CHAPTER · 36
DREAMWALKER NUMBER ONE

Eddie vanished from view, and David heard a dull impact below. Then something struck David and he was thrown back across the roof, exploding with pain.

"At last!" cried Adam, standing on the edge of the building and raising his fists in triumph. "At last!"

"Adam?" David picked himself up and stared, frantic. "*Eddie!*"

Adam turned. He snarled when he saw David.

"But if *you're* still here . . ." he began, then he shot over the edge of the building where Eddie had fallen. David flew out after him.

Eddie was sprawled on a narrow ledge, just one floor down from the roof, visible only because of the reflected glow of nearby firelight. The slightest movement could send him toppling the rest of the way to the ground, but Eddie wasn't moving at all. David swooped down beside him, searching desperately for signs of life.

Adam was already there, raging over Eddie's body.

"Why won't you just die?" he cried. "Curse you, Utherwise! Curse you!" He scrabbled at Eddie's neck, his spectral fingers clawing at the boy but having no effect whatsoever.

David took his chance and lashed out at him with every shred of mental energy he had. It was his first mind pulse, and he thrilled at the sense of power it gave him and at the sight of Adam being flung back from Eddie's body.

"Get away from him!" David shouted. "Why can't you just leave me and my family alone?"

Adam turned in the air and braced his dreamself, shrugging off the effect of David's attack. He produced his cane out of thin air and rushed at David with a wild shout. But before he could reach his target, Petra caught Adam in midair, locking her arms around him and carrying him off at a crazy angle. Together they spun down into the shadows of the passage. David was about to go down after them when he heard Petra cry out. She came flying back, faint and out of control. Adam rushed up after her, his cane raised. By the time David reached the roof, Adam was already standing there, and Petra was lying at his feet.

"So close." Adam was hardly coherent with fury and frustration. "It shouldn't be this difficult! But once I've crushed you two, I'll finish him. I'll find one of Grinn's men . . . I'll finish the Utherwise family for good."

Petra slipped back out of Adam's reach and shot around behind him, forcing Adam to turn his back on David. David didn't need to be told this was a deliberate move. He rushed at Adam, leaving the tiles and crossing the space between them like a rocket. Adam turned back only just in time, and stepped to one side. David swore as he flew straight past him and came to land about twenty paces from Petra.

"Eddie's hurt."

"I know," Petra called back. "But we can't help him now. Kat and Tomkin are his best hope. Our job is to destroy Adam; nothing else matters."

"But the professor said . . ."

"Forget what the professor said," said Petra. "We have no choice. And you know what we have to do, don't you?"

Adam was between them again, his eyes swinging from one to the other, radiating hateful intent.

"I know what you're thinking," he said. "And you know I can't let you combine. But if you don't, you also know you cannot defeat me. And so . . ."

In midspeech, Adam flung himself at Petra with astonishing speed. Petra shot up from the roof, her dreamself blurring with effort, only just avoiding Adam's grasp. She arced across the space between herself and David and reached out for him as she did so. David jumped toward her, eager to bring together their mental power. He felt her dreamself touch his own and blend into him. He had a sudden overwhelming sense of her fiery, untrammeled mind and all it was capable of, and an intoxicating mix of rebellion, determination, and sadness. It was the very essence of Petra. David felt the power of his own mind grow with the strength of it.

"Gotcha!" cried the voice of Adam, and David felt Petra's presence leave him just as suddenly as it had arrived.

"No!" David jumped after Petra, but Adam lashed out at him with his cane, sending him flying back. In his other hand he held Petra fast, though she struggled so much he could hardly keep upright. But Petra's dreamself was already beginning to fade as Adam crushed her mind with his.

"I'm stronger than any of you," he purred to himself, before shouting, "any of you!"

David shrugged off the effects of the hit and launched himself at Adam with what strength he could find. But Adam was ready for him. He threw his cane at David, and although it was a weak, distracted mind pulse, it was still enough to send David staggering back. David tried yet again to recover, desperate to reach Petra. Adam had her in both hands now and was raising her above his head.

"David, run!" Petra shouted.

Adam brought her crashing down over his knee. She cried out and was gone, her dreamself broken in two and cast aside in a cloud of spectral scraps. Before David could do anything, Adam was standing alone, facing him, his cane back in his hand.

CHAPTER 37

THE DREAM OF ADAM LANG

David felt a weakness like he'd never known before, a numbing fatigue of the mind. He'd been hit several times, and he wondered how much of his ability to withstand Adam was down to the pills Petra had given him.

Petra.

At the thought of her and what he'd just seen happen, despair almost overcame him. He was alone now, in 1940, facing Adam with no help and with his own grandfather unconscious on a ledge, inches from falling to his death. He forced himself to ignore his feelings for Petra and concentrate. Could any help come now? Surely Jiro had seen where they'd all been on the Map before Misty went down. Why wasn't help coming? When Adam spoke, it was as if he could read David's mind.

"There's no one left, Davy boy. I've seen to that. Unsleep House wanted a showdown, and by God, the Haunting's given them one. I doubt there's anyone left capable of dreamwalking right now. And by the time they recover and get Misty going again . . ." Adam began to advance on David. "Well, they won't get her going again. Edmund Utherwise will be dead before then, and those half-wits and do-gooders you work with will have been wiped from the face of history."

"I'll stop you!" David shouted back. "I'm still here! Tell that to the King of the Haunting!"

Adam looked amazed for a moment and faltered.

"My, my, someone's been doing their homework. So you've heard of the king, then?"

His tone was mocking, but there was something in his face and voice that he hadn't been quick enough to hide. And suddenly David saw what it was.

"You don't know who it is, do you?" he cried. "You're working for him — doing all this — but he hasn't shown his face. Even *he* doesn't trust you . . ."

"Shut up!" Adam roared. "It doesn't matter, anyway. The Haunting have been useful to me, sure, but I'm playing for bigger stakes than even they can dream of."

"I'll kill you for what you did to Petra." David's voice was diamond hard, but as he tried to summon the strength he'd need, he knew that his mind wasn't. Adam merely laughed.

"You sad little boy. You Utherwises are so pathetic." Adam came closer, pointing his cane. "Your grandfather, so proud of himself and his work — well, look at him now. You — untrained, unwanted, and stuck here all alone. Even your father was an easy kill in the end. What a family!"

David had been poised to throw himself at Adam, but at those words he stopped.

"What did you say?" he demanded. "My father . . . a *what?*"

Adam looked surprised again, but then gave a sudden, mad laugh.

"I see I'm not the only one who isn't trusted. They didn't even tell you the truth about that? Oh, priceless! I thought it was revenge keeping you here, but no, that idiot Feldrake didn't even bother to tell you how your own father died."

"You . . . *you* killed him?"

"Of course I did. You don't think a man like that would just fall down a flight of stairs without being pushed, do you?"

David wanted to shout something back, but his mind was frozen with horror at what he was hearing.

"Of course, Feldrake didn't actually know himself until I left the Project, and then only when I admitted it. Bunch of losers! I actually feel quite sick when I think of all the years I wasted on them, all that tiptoeing through history and 'leave no stone turned' crap. To think I didn't discover my full potential until it was almost too late."

"But why?" David found his voice again. "My dad . . . why?"

"Your old man may have been great in some ways, Davy boy, but he was as unimaginative as the rest of them. Always the first to call on your precious Dreamwalker's Code. 'Don't tell anything, don't scare anyone, blah, blah.' Pathetic! But he was smart enough to see I wasn't satisfied. He wrote a report on me, recommending I be retired early, saying I'd become unstable. Me? Retire *early*? When I was only following his advice? 'Anything you dream you can do, you can do,' he said. Well, is it my fault if my dreams were greater than anyone else's? Is it? I made sure that report never reached Feldrake, and I'm afraid Daddy had to go." Adam grinned and began to advance again. "But don't worry, Davy boy. Once I've found one of Grinn's men and put a bullet in little Eddie's head, all this pain of yours will just wash away. It's almost an act of kindness."

"But Dad was right about you!" David yelled, grief and fury

raging in him. "Listen to yourself — you *are* insane! Who are you to decide who gets to live or die? You're barely older than I am! You're just a . . . a kid, not a . . ." But David couldn't bring himself to say it.

"Not a what?" Adam's eyes glittered like black fire. "Were you about to say *god*?"

Adam began to grow.

David stepped back in astonishment as his enemy swelled and stretched, his dreamself rising and extending impossibly, expanding until it towered above the rooftops, blotting out the air-raid sky. Within moments Adam was astride the city, a colossus, bending back toward the earth through banks of cloud and smoke. His face filled David's field of vision, and his laughter ruled the sky. David almost fell to his knees.

Then, in a moment, the terrible vision passed. Adam was once again on the roof, the size of a mortal man. But the impact of what David had just been shown was undeniable. He knew that it had been nothing more than a dreamwalker's trick, an illusion spun out of the power to control one's own dream, but the sight had been truly terrifying.

Adam advanced on him again, his voice rich with manic delight.

"Even now you don't get it!"

David began to retreat.

"The power to save those who died before their time? The power to kill those who should have lived? Can't you see? If I can choose who lives and dies, if I can reshape history, then I *am* a god. And when your family is obliterated and I have my time over again, that is how the world will know me. With all of history at my feet, I'll find believers enough. The Romans perhaps, or the ancient Chinese, or . . ." Adam stopped. He raised one long pale finger to point into the clouds above, to where the deep stop-start drone of the bombers shook the heavens.

"Yes! The people who sent those planes know how to worship. Just think what I could tell *them!*"

David was so bewildered and wretched he didn't notice that he'd retreated off the edge of the roof and drifted out into space. He looked down at Eddie lying still on the ledge and tried to think clearly. Adam seemed unstoppable, but surely even now there was something he could do. If he could just find another dreamwalker to combine with, he'd wipe the smug grin off Adam's face, then smash him again and again, once for each of David's family and friends that Adam had hurt in his selfish quest for power. But there was no other dreamwalker there. His only option appeared to be a desperate solo attack followed by inevitable oblivion. At least then the nightmare would end.

"Little Davy, all alone," said Adam in a mocking voice as he rose up off the roof and raised his cane. "It's time to say good night." And he swept down.

David darted to one side, only just avoiding the zinging cane that sliced through the night air. He was desperate to escape, but his mind was also alive with a sudden idea. Adam's words had reminded him that he wasn't alone, not entirely. There was still someone here who could help him, someone who was already unconscious.

Eddie.

And according to Dishita, Eddie had had the dreamwalker's gift too.

David's mind raced. He'd never actually called up a dream-walker's door before, but he had got back to this time on his own, and Petra and the others had always said it was easy. He just needed to know where to go to, that's all. And there was only one place he could imagine Eddie's unconscious, dreaming mind would be right now. After all, where else would a hurt and frightened boy want to be?

David's door, when it appeared, was set in the wall of the building right beside Eddie's stricken body. David threw himself toward it as Adam turned and came for him again. Willing himself across the space as fast as he could, David kicked open the door and shot through, twisting around to slam it shut. There was a moment of intense pressure pushing against him, but he felt the door close firmly. It dissolved to nothing.

David slumped down, but he couldn't rest yet. He forced his head up and checked that he was where he'd planned to be. He was crouching in a room with patterned brown wallpaper. There was a brass bedstead and a desk beneath a window. On the desk were pens, a lamp, and a pile of crisp new notebooks. It was Eddie's bedroom, just as it used to be before the fire. In front of the desk was a chair, and sitting on the chair was Eddie, his head in his hands. Beside him stood a woman. She was stroking his hair.

"Eddie!" David cried. "Eddie, I need you."

Eddie glanced up and gave his friend a confused look.

"Who is this, Mother?"

The woman gave Eddie a gentle smile but said nothing. She ignored David completely.

"Eddie, you're dreaming," David said. "None of this is real. It's just a dream."

"A dream?" Eddie looked uncertain. "You're . . . you're David, aren't you?"

"Yes! But don't you remember? This place was destroyed; your house got burned down."

"I . . . don't want to think about that." Eddie shook his head and his mother made a there-there sound.

"Wait." He looked up again. "David, wasn't I talking to you just a moment ago?"

"Yes, but then you fell off the roof. Oh, come on, Eddie, you must remember! You were knocked unconscious. Now you're dreaming, stuck inside your own head. Don't you see?"

"I suppose I must be," said Eddie, not sounding very interested. "Dreaming about you. It's just a dream."

David stared at his friend and wondered how long it would be before Adam worked out where he'd gone. He'd been collected from his own dream by Petra on several occasions, but each time he'd been prepared for what was about to happen. Eddie, however, knew nothing about dreamwalking or Unsleep House or anything, and David couldn't tell him what he needed to know without breaking the Dreamwalker's Code. He could have cried out in frustration.

Instead, he came to a decision.

He picked up a pen and a notebook from the desk.

"There's no such thing as 'just a dream' for people like me and you, Eddie," he said, and he could see that he finally had Eddie's full attention. "You want to know what I am? You want answers, to know what's been happening to you? Well, you of all people deserve the truth." And as Eddie sat and stared, David opened the notebook and in a few quick lines he wrote out the secret of dreamwalking.

David opened a second door close to where he'd made the first one at almost exactly the same moment he left. He stepped out into the night air just in time to see Adam throw himself against the first door. David pulled Eddie's dreamself out after him.

Eddie gasped, staring across the space above the back street.

"This is your secret?" Eddie was blinking furiously. "Projected consciousness . . . through dreams?"

Then he caught sight of his own body sprawled on the cold stone, blood pooling beside it from the knife wound.

"Oh. I don't look very well over there, do I?"

"It's not your body you have to worry about right now, Eddie," said David. "It's your mind we need if we're going to finish this for good. Look!"

But David needn't have pointed. The dark form of Adam's dreamself was sharp and sinister in the gloom as he turned to face them. The look on his face was all bewilderment and fury.

"No!" Adam snarled. "No, no, no!" And he flew at them, his cane raised.

David grabbed Eddie and pulled him straight into the air, ignoring his startled protests. There was no way to make this easier, no time to introduce him gently to the miracle of dream-walking as David had been. Adam missed but turned in a second and rocketed after them. David pulled Eddie's dreamself higher and higher into the sky. The ledge fell back below, but Eddie's crumpled body could still be made out, lying there like a broken doll.

"Eddie, we are ghosts now, you and me, right?" David gasped as he strained upward, racing ahead of Adam.

"Right, right," Eddie managed.

"Though we aren't dead. But if we want to keep it that way, you will have to trust me, okay?"

Eddie seemed to nod, but it was hard to tell in the dark, with an icy wind roaring and the wail and crash of an air raid all around. Far below the dark city turned, the light from fires the only clear points of reference beyond the amber-lit dome of Saint Paul's Cathedral. And still David strained higher and higher. But Adam was closing fast. He reached out with one pale, grasping hand to snatch David back down.

It was time.

David hauled Eddie up and allowed their two dreamselves to combine.

The first thing David felt was Eddie's continued astonishment. But close behind this was the intense sensation of joining his own mind with something extraordinary. He'd always known Eddie was smart. He'd been told again and again at Unsleep House that his grandfather was some sort of genius. But nothing could have prepared him for the strength and clarity of Eddie's pure mental form. His own mind was exhausted and battered, but as it began to combine with Eddie's he felt a wave of untapped power flooding into his own dreamself, giving him all the force of his grandfather's brilliance and potential.

But then Adam seized him.

David acted quickly, twisting in the air and lashing out at Adam. His twofold mind pulse caught the eighteen-year-old square in the chest.

There was a ringing sound and Adam was flung back. He somersaulted far from them in an uncontrolled spin, vanishing into the night with a trailing cry. But within moments he was back, bursting out of a growing cloud bank like a furious crow and hurtling toward them.

David, doubled with Eddie, braced himself for the attack. Time seemed to slow as their combining became complete. David knew that he was in control, that Eddie was too confused to make decisions, and he drew forward all the mental energy he could from two minds working as one. But even as he did so he felt something else, as if there was a third mind there with them, someone who was intimately linked to both David and Eddie, a bridge between the two. For a moment David sensed the vivid and unmistakable presence of Eddie's unborn son — his own lost father.

Adam crashed into David, but David was immovable now and simply grasped Adam in a grip of iron. All the energy of Adam's attack was thrown back at him, and his dreamself almost exploded with the strain of it. He cried out in agony, but David didn't let go. Adam tried to fight back, to force David's grip to break, but his dreamself was growing ragged and losing its features. The suit and cane had gone, to be replaced by a rippling black abstraction of a body.

Then, with a supreme effort, Adam got one arm free and smashed his spectral fist into David's face. David hardly felt a thing. Instead, he merely hit back, and as he struck he could feel Adam's mind start to crumble.

"Curse you, curse you . . ." Adam's thoughts would have been clear to David even without the words. He grabbed Adam with both hands and began to pull. He twisted him as he'd seen Adam himself do to Petra and Théo. Adam cried out and began heaving, desperate to get away. But he couldn't. He could do nothing but yell helplessly as David twisted and pulled him to breaking point and . . . *CRACK!*

There was a sudden release of mental power, an explosion of dark light as Adam's dreaming mind finally snapped. David was caught off guard and felt Eddie's mind wrenched away from his own. David's solitary dreamself was carried away by the shock wave, and he lost all sense of place and time. His last thoughts were of the certainty of Adam's destruction, but also of the loss of Eddie.

Then his mind shut down, and everything went black.

CHAPTER · 38
PHILIPPA'S GIFT

When David opened his eyes the light was too bright. He had to keep them half closed for a long time until they'd adjusted. Then he tried again.

The room he was in was white and clean. Above him were several box-shaped objects with wires and cables beneath them. There was something else there too, strange yet familiar. David looked for a long time before he recognized it. It was a teddy bear.

I've seen that before, he thought to himself, *but not for a very long time.*

He lay there staring at the teddy before he finally realized that he didn't know where he was. He tried to sit up. His body didn't respond. Not even his fingers. He wondered if he should be worried about this, but somehow he knew there was nothing seriously wrong. He was very tired, that was all. Very tired and as stiff as a plank. He heard a faint, papery sound, and with an effort he managed to tilt his head slowly and look. Someone was sitting there, her nose in the pages of a tattered old book.

"Hi," said David, and he was surprised at how weak his voice was.

The person looked up. It was his mum. She met his eyes for a moment and then cried out.

"David!"

She jumped up and pressed a button that hung on a cable beside the bed. Her book fell to the ground, its dust wrapper slipping off as it went. This reminded David of something, but he couldn't quite remember what. Within seconds there were other people in the room, white coats and clean smells and intent gazes. His mum was speaking quickly, and someone pulled the blinds down, easing the pressure on David's eyes. Someone else was holding his arm. Was that an injection? Was someone crying?

"Where . . . ?" David croaked, but he couldn't manage any more.

"It's okay, David." His mother was trying to sound calm and steady. "You're in the hospital, but everything is going to be fine. You had an accident at school. They brought you here in an ambulance."

The next time David was able to think clearly, he was propped up in a half-sitting position. He looked around the room. He was obviously still in the hospital, so it was a surprise to see so much stuff that he recognized as his own. Beside the bed was a pile of books and magazines, all of which he'd read before, as well as his games and music player. There were posters on the wall that he'd last seen tacked up in his bedroom, a stack of DVDs on the floor, and a portable CD player that he hadn't used for years and had covered in stickers. It'd seemed like a good idea at the time, but now it looked a bit lame.

"How are you feeling?"

His mum was sitting in the chair again, watching him with a half smile.

"Fi —" David started to say and had to swallow and try again. "Fine, thanks."

"I brought some of your things."

"How . . . how long have I been here?"

His mum pursed her lips and said nothing. David knew then that he'd been lying in this bed for a long time.

"Why did you bring that?" He pointed feebly at the teddy bear.

"I didn't, it was Philippa," his mum replied with an awkward smile. "I said you wouldn't want it, but you know what she's like. I was just grabbing a few things, and she suddenly appeared with that, insisting you'd want it. You've probably forgotten all about it but, well . . . I brought it anyway."

She shrugged, looking even more uncomfortable.

"They told me to bring things you would recognize. I'll take it back home if you like. I suppose it's a bit embarrassing for a teenager."

"You think?" David laughed. Then he looked serious. "When can I go home?"

"Not straightaway, so the doctors say. They need to keep an eye on you for a bit. Is there anything I can get you?"

"Mum, what happened to me? I can't remember anything clearly."

"An accident at school. It was quite serious. They explained it to me, but . . . it's funny, I can't quite remember exactly what it was now. Isn't that silly? I'll ask them to explain it to you later."

"How long have I been here?"

"Almost two weeks," said his mother, looking him straight in the eye. "Listen," she added, clearly wanting to move on to something positive. "There are some people here to see you. From your school. Goodness knows how, but they've found out that you're awake again. They must have spies here or something."

David's memory stirred again.

"Spies?"

"Well, not like James Bond, but you know what I mean. Anyway, they're waiting outside now. I told them it'd be better if they came back another day, but the doctors think it will do you good to see as many familiar faces as possible. Just tell me when you're ready, and I'll go and fetch them."

David groaned. He really didn't want to see any of his school friends. And as for the teachers . . .

"I don't really fancy seeing Mrs. Fernley right now."

"Oh, it's not her. They're from your new school."

"*New* school?"

"Yes. I tell you what," she said, getting up, "I'll go and get them now. They've already been waiting over an hour."

After she'd gone, David lay still and silent, trying to identify something elusive that was teasing his memory.

There came a knock at the door, and an old man walked in. "Hello there!"

His eyebrows were leaping like a pair of crazy caterpillars. He had a box of chocolates under one arm and a roll of printout paper sticking out of his pocket. One of his pens was leaking blue ink onto his jacket.

David stared at him for a moment.

Then he remembered everything.

CHAPTER · 39
THE KING OF THE HAUNTING

David and the professor sat in silence. Having made his entrance, Professor Feldrake appeared to have difficulty knowing what to say. He opened the box of chocolates and put it on the bed. Then he helped himself to one.

"Coffee cream. My favorite! I can't manage the toffees anymore, not with these old teeth. Would you like one, David?"

David waved the chocolates away. "Professor, what happened exactly?"

"Ah. I was hoping you wouldn't ask me that, because we're not one hundred percent sure. There are a lot of questions we're hoping you can help us answer."

"But we did win, didn't we? We stopped Adam?"

"Yes, David, we did. *You* did!"

"And what about Adam?"

"Not a sign. Not for two weeks now. In fact, the Haunting has been keeping its head down. Without them hounding us we've been completely free to work in peace: deep historical research missions, archaeological intervention . . . bliss! But as for Adam, well, he hasn't been detected since they picked him up fighting with you. Given his age and the extraordinary power of your attack, even if he does recover it'll be far too late for him to bother us again."

"Professor, what happened to Eddie? He was injured, badly I think, on a ledge."

"Relax, David," said the professor. "Don't forget, though it may feel like you were just there, we're talking about events that actually took place many, many years ago. Your grandfather survived — after all, you'd hardly be here now if he hadn't, would you? We can fill you in on the details when you're better."

"But I need to know now!" David sat up straight. The professor tried to push him back.

"All right, all right," said the old man. "It was Kat and . . ."

"Tomkin!" said David. "Kat and Tomkin were Eddie's friends. Funny name, Tomkin."

"Some sort of nickname, I expect." The professor looked distracted for a moment. Then he continued. "Anyway, yes — Kat and Tomkin contacted the police, and Eddie was taken to hospital. On the police files it says he was injured during an air raid. When he was discharged, he went out to live with his mother at his aunt's house, and the rest, as they say, is history. It's remarkable how resilient the time line can be."

"Kat and Tomkin!" David smiled. "They seemed really interesting, but we hardly got to speak. I wonder what became of them."

The professor put the chocolate box down.

"I'm afraid they were . . . unlucky."

"What does that mean?"

"Just after they brought help to Eddie, they were caught in an explosion. On their way to an air-raid shelter, I understand. I'm sorry to say Kat was killed instantly, and her brother . . . well, the Archive tells us precious little about either of them."

David's smile died. He felt numb. He'd always known that thousands had lost their lives in the London Blitz, but it felt altogether different now that he'd met some of them.

"It's part of history, David," said the professor. "Try not to get too involved. It's not for us to question what's already happened, remember? I know it sounds hard, but Kat wasn't destined to survive the Second World War, that's all. A great many weren't."

David shook his head.

"And someone else died," he said. "I saw it. A man called Grinn."

The professor shrugged.

"Again, he only had a few months left to live anyway. As I said, the time line is a tough old thing. Even the great Adam Lang couldn't do more than dent it in the end. Thanks to you."

"So Eddie's okay?" said David after a moment. "*Was* okay, I mean. I can't wait to see him again, but I suppose I'll have to find some other time and place —"

"David." The professor's voice had a hint of warning in it. "You shouldn't think about dreamwalking yet, your mind is still very weak. But more than that, I'm afraid there's no question of visiting Eddie again."

"But —"

"No." Professor Feldrake held up his hand. "According to the time line we've fought so hard to preserve, Eddie's ghostly visits stopped after his house was destroyed in the fire, and that's how it's going to stay."

David looked away. In his mind he'd already decided to go and visit Eddie again on the quiet, but when he looked back at the professor it was clear the old man knew exactly what was going on in his head.

"Forget it, David. After this scare we decided to use the Inhibitor on Eddie. You remember the Inhibitor, don't you? It blocks all dreamwalking around a given time and place? Well, we've applied it to every single point in Eddie's life, including the theater attic, now that we know about it. There'll be no more ghosts for Eddie. His life is locked into its own time, and no one from his future can ever go back and interfere with him again."

"I wasn't interfering." David frowned. "We really were friends, you know."

"I know, David, I know." The professor's voice lost the hard edge it had acquired. "But history comes first. And even the greatest friendship has to come to an end sooner or later."

David was silent. He was angry to be blocked like this, but he also remembered what Petra had told him in the tunnel to the château, and somehow the simple thought that Eddie was still out there somewhere was a comfort — on a different part of the time line from David, yes, but not so very far away when you thought about it.

"Anyway," said the professor, rummaging in his pocket, "after your arrest, Sir Edmund's study was thoroughly searched, and this was discovered. I'm positive it wasn't there before, so it's very real and concrete proof that some changes to history did occur. It's addressed to you." And the professor handed a sealed paper packet to David. "Naturally, no one has opened it."

The small packet was surprisingly heavy. As David tore it open, something slid out and landed on the bed. It was a bone handle with cruel steel ends. David felt a sensation of horror as he recognized it: the knife that Charlie Grinn had flung into Eddie's back. Holding it carefully, he pressed the small steel switch, and the blade flicked out.

The professor jumped.

"This blade," said David, turning the metal in the cold hospital light and enjoying the professor's discomfort, "nearly destroyed us all."

"Good heavens," said Professor Feldrake, as pale as a ghost.

David put the knife down and reached into the packet. Inside was a letter, in the steeply sloping handwriting of an energetic but elderly man. It was written on a page torn from a notebook and dated to just a few years ago.

Dear David,

Please accept this grisly keepsake. It is a reminder that our existences are fragile, a fact that has certainly helped concentrate my mind over the years. Now, as my time is coming to a close, I would like you to have it, to remember me by throughout your own life. And may it be a long and happy life too.

We didn't say a proper good-bye. Of course, I realize now that we could never have met again, but at least this simple piece of paper can do what science and dreamwalking no longer can — finish my apology to you and allow me to express my thanks for saving my life, and for something else too. But first, the apologies.

David, though I have long since dedicated my entire life's work to you, I'm both ashamed and sorry that I couldn't have done more after you were born. Given that your early dreamwalking experiences and my own disturbed childhood were so intimately tied up with the foundation of the Dreamwalker Project, the risks to the time line were deemed too great for me to make contact in the present, and I bowed to this ruling like a weak old fool. I am a lousy grandfather, as well as a doubting friend, and I apologize.

With even greater bitterness, I must also apologize for my failure to prevent the death of your father, my son. Naturally I would have done anything to save him, regardless of the consequences, but I simply couldn't remember or didn't understand enough from that terrifying night on the rooftop to prevent Adam's admission into the Project, nor the sorry string of events that led to our terrible mutual loss.

Because of these failings, I hardly deserve the enormous gift you gave to me when we last met. David, thank you a thousand times over for that first taste of dreamwalking. The *recollection itself was almost obliterated from my mind by the stresses of the moment, and I have struggled to recover the precious memories of those events ever since. But that brief point in time, high above the city with our united minds unconstrained by the confines of physical law, was the defining moment of my life and the foundation of everything I have done since.*

David, thank you.

Edmund Utherwise

David lowered the page and stared at the knife, not knowing what to say. The professor was clearly itching to see what was in the letter but was too polite to ask. Instead he helped himself to another chocolate.

When David looked back at the letter, something bobbed into his mind — a jumble of recent memories, fragments of fact, and unanswered questions that were finally resurfacing in the troubled sea of his memory. Only now he could see the connection between them, and it was a connection that made his eyes go wide. He lowered the letter and stared at the professor.

"David, what's wrong?"

"I think I know who it is!" he blurted out. "The person behind all this. The King of the Haunting! Professor, it's —"

"No! Don't say it!"

David's eyes went wider still.

"You know, don't you? You knew all along! But why . . . ?"

"I suspected, David, that's all. But if we're right, then there's nothing we can do, is there? That person's history is too closely entwined with Eddie's now for anything to be done about it, not without enormous risk to ourselves."

"But, Professor —"

"No. We have no choice but to keep our defenses up and wait for time to rid us of that particular threat. Until then, I urge you to keep any suspicions you may have to yourself. Tell no one, David, is that clear? Don't even tell the other dreamwalkers."

David stared at the professor. Could he really just say nothing? But then, it all seemed so incredible that maybe he'd got it wrong. On the other hand, if he was right, and if the professor really was too scared to do anything about it, then there was one thing he could do himself, wasn't there? At least being stuck in a hospital bed gave him time for a little private dreamwalking. It was certainly something to think about.

"How are the others? Dishita, Théo?"

"Oh, they're mostly fine," said the professor, clearly pleased that the conversation had moved on. "There were some casualties, as you'd expect, but we're lucky not to have lost more. Misty is back up and running too. Théo says hello, by the way. Says he's looking forward to working with you again. And Dishita is singing your praises to anyone who wants to hear. She has asked to debrief you personally. I think she's desperate to hear more about your battle with Adam. We all are."

"And Petra?"

The professor frowned.

"Poor girl." He sighed. "It's a terrible shame. Such a loss to the Project."

David felt his spine go cold. The professor was helping himself to another chocolate when David lost his cool completely.

"What do you mean, 'loss to the Project'?" he shouted. "She's a person, not one of your machines! If she's dead, or —"

"Dead!" said the professor in surprise. "She's not dead! Good heavens, no. It's just that . . . well . . ." But the old historian seemed to have run out of words.

"Look," he said eventually, "there's someone else here who can explain it better than I can."

He got to his feet and put his head out of the door. After a moment he stepped back. A girl wearing a long winter coat and sunglasses walked in.

It was Petra.

"Hello, David," she said, with a smile almost like her old one. "I'm glad you're awake."

"Hi" was all David could manage.

The professor rocked back and forward on his heels and looked awkward again.

"When I said 'loss to the Project,' I was referring to Petra's injury. PPD, you see — Psychic Projection Disorder."

"You science guys," said Petra. "Just call it what it is: burnout. What the professor is trying to say is that I can't dreamwalk anymore. Adam did too much damage. I'm no longer a dreamwalker."

David was shocked. He tried to think of something to say, but when he began to speak, Petra stopped him.

"Don't. In some ways it's quite liberating actually. I'm free."

The professor looked at them both.

"I'll give you two a moment," he said, stepping toward the door again.

"Wait," said David. "You haven't told me how Roman is doing."

The professor seemed bewildered. Then he saw the look on David's face.

"Don't be too hard on Roman," he said. "You didn't see him at his best, and the pressures on him were very great. In the aftermath of the Adam Lang emergency he has even been awarded a medal, and I'm pleased to say he mentioned you in his acceptance speech. I realize you might find that a joke, but Roman cares for Unsleep House very deeply, and he's a better judge of people and events than you might think."

"Better than my dad?" asked David, fixing the professor with a steady gaze. The professor sighed.

"All right," he said, "all right. I apologize for not telling you about that."

"But he was murdered! And I had to hear it from Adam, of all people — his killer."

"Oh, I was worried that might have happened." The professor was clearly distressed. "David, I'm really very sorry. We just didn't know how you'd react if you found out during the emergency. Your father was a key member of the Project, and we also felt his loss very bitterly. We couldn't imagine that he'd been murdered or that one of the dreamwalkers was capable of doing such a thing. I suppose everyone was so dazzled by Adam they never stopped to question the effect his work was having on him. Everyone except your father, that is. Oh, dear. I promise that when you have recovered, I'll tell you all I can about your father."

David lay in his bed and said nothing. Petra gave the professor a disapproving look. The old man seemed desperate to get out of the room. He stood and picked up the box of chocolates.

"I'll just go and see if your mother would like one," he said and darted out of the door.

Petra had taken off her sunglasses and David could see signs of strain in her eyes.

"I still need these," she said, waving the glasses. "But I'm much better, really. Don't look so worried. I like your teddy bear, by the way."

David went red with embarrassment and threw the old toy at his mother's bag, which was still by her chair.

"My mum brought way too much stuff."

"Well, she has been coming here every day," said Petra.

"Every day?"

"You look surprised, but I don't see why. You are lucky, David Utherwise," Petra said, and perhaps because these words were more revealing than she'd intended, she gave him a brief flash of her mischievous smile. David smiled back, but he couldn't quite meet her eyes.

"Petra, I don't know what to say."

"Then say nothing."

"But I could have stopped him, I could have hit Adam harder, got him away from you."

"You did all you could. Even now you don't give yourself enough credit for what you have done. You won, David: You defeated your Goliath. I believed in you all along, and I was right to, wasn't I?"

"But you've lost . . . so much," said David, wishing he could think of something better to say.

Petra gave him a stern look.

"Not as much as Carlo or Siri or some of the others."

"What will you do now?" David asked eventually. "Leave Unsleep House?"

"I've been thinking about it. I have some money, and the Project look after their ex-dreamwalkers very well. I might travel. I mean really travel — taking my body with me this time. Perhaps I will even try sunbathing. I'm not sure what I have to stay for, and I don't miss dreamwalking as much as I thought I would."

"But you do miss it."

Petra looked at him.

"I have been offered a job. On the linguistics team at Unsleep House. They always need language teachers. So, I have the chance to stay, and maybe I will. At least for a while. But I'm still deciding . . ." Petra let the sentence trail off. "They'll ask you, you know. You are still dreamwalker number five until you tell them otherwise. You are going to have some decisions to make soon."

"I can really say no?"

"Yes, you can," she said, watching him closely. "You have a home to go to, remember? If it helps, I hear they're planning to make some changes after what has happened, to go back a bit to how things were in your grandfather's time."

"A few more windows would be nice," said David, "and I think Roman needs to go on a long, relaxing holiday. Perhaps he could go with you."

Petra made a face but laughed.

The door opened, and the professor put his head around.

"Sorry, Petra, but we ought to go. The helicopter's ready. Good-bye, David — get well. We'll speak again very soon."

Petra nodded and made to follow the professor out. At the door she turned back to David and gave a small wave.

David felt the urgent need to say something to her, but he just couldn't think what. His ears were hot. He blurted something out.

"I'd like to see you again soon."

"Ha!" said Petra, looking down her nose. "In your dreams!"

David was crushed and embarrassed, but then he saw the mischievous look again.

"I meant that," she said with a smile. Then she put her glasses back on and stepped through the door.

LONDON, THE
PRESENT DAY

David stood in the shadows, silent as death. His dreamself was so far back in a corner it was partway into the wall, but his head was still in the room. He could see what was happening. He could hear what was being said.

The King of the Haunting looked even older than he had expected, his body frail and ruined. Only his bald head and right arm moved as he manipulated a joystick on the armrest of his gleaming electric wheelchair. With a *whirr*, he rolled across the tiled floor toward a nervous young man with a goatee who sat at a bank of portable computer equipment in the center of the vast space. Far above, the roof was glass and steel, letting in the last of a winter sun. But the structure of the building was much older than the modern fixtures it now contained. This was a twenty-first-century office in the shell of a Victorian theater.

On a gurney in the center of the room lay the body of an eighteen-year-old boy. There were electrodes attached to his temples. David couldn't stop staring at him. He had short black hair and a handsome profile, but he was still — stiller even than David.

Adam Lang.

Beside him wheezed the artificial lung of a life-support machine.

The old man stopped his chair.

"Any improvement?"

Goatee Man tugged at his beard as he shook his head.

"Nope, nothing but flat lines on the EEG — no higher brain function at all. It could be years before he recovers. If ever."

"He'll be no good to me by then," said the old man, looking at a watch on his good arm. "Just like he's no good to me now."

"Sir . . ." Goatee Man fidgeted in his seat. ". . . I still don't get it. Why have we brought him here? It's not safe for you. And here, of all places!"

"I told you, I have an appointment. Any moment now, if I'm not mistaken. Until then, we wait."

"It's just that . . . sir, I'm picking something up."

"So? That's what you're paid to do."

"Yes, but it's centering on this very spot, getting clearer by the second." Goatee Man's eyes were darting over the screens in front of him. "A knot in the Psychic Field. Sir, I think there could be someone dreamwalking in the area."

"Oh, there's someone dreamwalking in the area all right," said the old man. "There has been for about three minutes. I'm just waiting for him to stop messing about and show himself, that's all."

Then, before David could react, he whirred his chair around.

"Isn't that right, David Utherwise?"

David waited for a long time while the old man's eyes played over him in the gloom. He wasn't sure why he'd come, or exactly what he'd wanted to say — he probably shouldn't have come at all — but now that he'd been seen, it would be cowardly to just turn and flee. He stepped out of the dark.

Goatee Man jumped when he saw him, his hand darting to a telephone handset, but the old man stopped him.

"Relax. He's not here . . . officially. Are you, David?"

David said nothing.

"Well now, how are you feeling?" The old man's face broke into a leering smile that was probably supposed to be friendly. "You're certainly in better shape than poor Adam here. Hospital food not too bad, I hope? I'm sure they'll let you go soon."

"I know who you are." David tried to keep his voice steady and strong.

"'Course you do. You wouldn't be here otherwise, would you . . . *Otherwise?*" And the old man chuckled at his own joke, croaking like a kettle full of frogs.

"I came here . . ." David said, ". . . I came here to tell you to keep away from us, from my family —"

"Nah, you didn't," the old man interrupted. "You came here because you couldn't keep away from me, because you're curious. Like all my best boys and girls. And that's why I waited so patiently to see you."

"You knew I'd come?"

"'Course! Smart kid like you. Take after your grandpa, don't yer?"

"Leave Eddie alone! I came here to tell you to keep away from my family. They call you the King of the Haunting, but I know who you really are. I worked it out."

"Yeah, you said. But let's skip to the end, eh? You're here 'cause you got questions. So ask away."

David moved from one foot to another, keeping his dream-self in clear view but out of the light. It was already a habit.

"Why?" he said eventually. He couldn't believe he was getting into a conversation, but the old man was quite right — he did have questions. "Why go for Eddie at all? What did he do to make you hate him so much?"

"Philippa," replied the old man immediately. He stared at David with a look of cold, lizardlike intensity before continuing. "Your little sis. Oh, yeah, I know all about Philippa. And your mum, and even your school friends, such as they are. But it's little Philippa I want you to think about now. Got a clear image of 'Phizzy' in your mind? Good. Now imagine me strangling the life out of her!"

The old man raised his livid right hand and made a crushing motion in the air. David's fists bunched instinctively, and he stepped forward, but the old man's ugly croak stopped him.

"There! Answered your own question, din't yer. You'd kill me if I hurt your sister, wouldn't you? Or you'd try. Well, your Eddie as good as killed mine. It's as simple as that."

"He didn't! It wasn't his fault! She wasn't going to survive the war anyway — the professor said so. You can't blame Eddie, Tomkin."

"Don't call me that!" the old man spat back. "Little Tom! I haven't been Tomkin for years. It's Thomas King now, as it always was. Kat's the only one who can use my nickname. Only she can't, can she? My little Katkin! She died fetching help for your precious Eddie. And so precious Eddie has to pay."

"It was an accident! Just let it go. Eddie's dead now anyway. Leave his life in peace."

Thomas King rolled toward David, stopping just a few paces away. He looked David square in the eye.

"Yeah. Yeah, he is dead, isn't he? But you're still here."

"What do you mean?"

"When that bomb landed, it did more than take away my sister and my legs, it nearly took my mind as well. After, I could still remember Kat, but it took me years to get the details back. I couldn't even remember having lived in this theater till Adam found Eddie in it. All I could recall was one thing: the bespectacled face of your granddad leering at my Kat. Disgusting!"

"He liked her, that's all. And maybe Kat liked him back. Did you ever think of that?"

"Shut up! She didn't like him, she just felt sorry for the little runt. She was so kind . . ." King's voice caught in his throat. ". . . *too* kind. And look where it left her! See what kindness does? I hate your Eddie more than you could ever understand. He might as well have killed me along with Kat!"

King's clawlike hand was raised again, twisted into a fist. Then it dropped.

"But I'm tired, David. So tired of it all."

In the old man's face David could see the proof of this clearly enough. Years of anger, bitterness, and the restless thirst for revenge had left Thomas King with the pinched face of a gargoyle. And a heart of stone to match.

"And you're right." King narrowed his eyes with a crafty grin. "I *am* still here, aren't I? While Eddie's all dead and rotted to worm food, I outlived him. Stole his discoveries and survived him. So maybe, I'm saying to myself, maybe this last failure is what you might call a sign. If even turning the great Adam Lang against Eddie can't get rid of the little bleeder, maybe it's time for me to think again. Look at things another way, p'raps. What do you think, David?"

"I think you're mad."

"You might be right." King chuckled. "Yeah, I think you might be. But the thing is, David, old son, tired though I am, mad though I may be, blocked though I always find myself when I go after your lousy, stinkin' ancestor, one fact remains: Your Eddie owes me. No matter how you cut it, he owes me a sister, and he owes me for a lifetime of misery. That's a lot to owe a chap, I hope you'll agree, David."

"I've said all I've got to say to you." David began to edge away. It was time to leave. Why had he even stayed this long? But as he turned, he saw that somehow, while the old man had kept him talking, figures had slipped into the room. In the shadows around the wide space one, two, three . . . no . . . *six* haunters had entered, silent as the ghosts they were. Six! David knew then that he'd walked into a trap. He was surrounded.

"Ah, you've seen my boys and girls at last." Thomas King wheezed with glee. "Good. Now maybe you'll listen. Your granddaddy owes me, David Utherwise, but I meant what I said — I'm ready to move on. Your granddaddy owes me, but I'm going to give *you* the chance to pay."

"Me?"

"Yeah." Thomas King settled back a little into his chair, his body sounding like gristle. He grinned at David. Then, with a new burst of whirring, he directed his chair back to Adam's mindless body.

"As you know, David, I run a special little organization, an organization that does wonderful things and that pays spectacularly well. An organization that employs people like you. And as you also know, I have a vacancy."

King's right arm reached out to the machine beside Adam's bed, his claw closing on a large red switch. He looked back at David, as if making sure he had his full attention. Before David could react, King flipped the switch. Immediately the wheezing and beeping stopped as the lights on Adam's life-support machine went dead. The artificial lung settled to the bottom of its glass tube with a final sigh.

"What are you doing?" David started forward. "He's finished as a dreamwalker — you don't have to *kill* him. Send him back to his family!"

"What, so they can sit by his bedside and watch his empty body shrivel up? Why, David, you have a cruel streak too."

"Turn it back on! He might recover."

As David watched, aghast, Adam's body began twitching, his head lolling to one side. It gave one great, final heave, then fell still again. Still as bone.

"As I was saying . . ." King rolled back to David and squinted up at him with yellow eyes. ". . . I have a vacancy."

"No way." David shook his head, staring at Adam's corpse. "No. Way."

"Hold your horses, I'm not done yet," said King. "Now, listen up. We've mentioned Eddie here today, and we've even mentioned your sister. But let's not mention them again, eh?

Let's talk, you and me, about greater things. Let's see what I can do for you and what you can do in return."

"No."

David knew that he had to get out of there, but as he moved, the six haunters around him moved too, closing into the pool of light that poured down from above. They grew spectral, boiling with a ghastly blueness that by now David should have been used to, but that still filled him with an instinctive dread. The haunters grinned. One of them was the girl with the white-blonde hair. She had a tigerish motion that suggested she could be on him in a second.

"You've met Harriet, I believe." King was clearly enjoying himself. "She won't let you go again, you can be sure of that. She's one of my best. But have you stopped to think why she works for me, David, and not those wimps at Unsleep House?"

The haunter named Harriet took a curling step, leaving the ground as she did so. She drifted toward David. She was beautiful, David had to admit, despite the fury in her eyes and the pallor of her spectral skin. And she was giving him a very calculated look.

"We got off to a bad start, David," she said. "Perhaps we could begin again?"

David clamped his mouth shut.

"Oh, think, David!" King burst out. "You're a ghost! A time-traveling, dreamwalking ghost, able to turn the whole course of human history on its head! What part of that doesn't excite you, for heaven's sake? We've already seen how capable you are. Imagine what you could do with our help. Imagine the power you could command over the poor schmucks of the past! Imagine — oh, I don't know — Napoleon! Imagine Napoleon, conqueror of Europe, crouching at your feet in terror, agreeing to bury gold, jewels, priceless works of art . . . *anything*, if only you'd just leave him alone. We could do that tonight, David, now if you like. Then tomorrow we'd dig it up and it'd be yours, all yours."

King began to cough. In his excitement a gobbet of phlegm burst from his mouth. He wiped it away with his sleeve.

"And if that don't float yer boat, Davy boy, just think of the alternative. Are you really prepared to turn your back on all the fun, on what you really are, just because some chinless professor wants you to follow the 'Dreamwalker's Code'? Do you *want* your wings clipped? Do you *want* to do history assignments for the sake of a bunch of stuck-up do-gooders? No, you don't want that. You are a dreamwalker, David, a ghost! Not a *historian*!"

King's voice gave out as he spat this final word, and he slouched back in his chair, wheezing. In time his breath settled down, but no one spoke. As the moments passed the silence in the room seemed to solidify into something menacing in its own right. All around, eyes that were filled with hate, fear, or greed — and in King's case, all three — drilled into David as they waited for some sign from him. After an achingly long pause, David gave it to them.

He slowly shook his head. The silence screamed in his ears as he did so.

When Thomas King spoke again, his face was a mask of utter contempt.

"Did you miss the part where I mentioned money?"

At a sign from King, the haunters began to circle David, rising and weaving, making it hard for him to keep track of them, completely cutting off any upward escape.

"Join us . . ." King's voice was flint hard. ". . . and I'll consider Eddie's debt to me settled. Turn your back on me, and I'll settle it by destroying you and everything you've ever dreamed of. Your answer is required immediately."

"You're a monster, Tomkin!" David cried out. "Nothing but a murdering, dribbling, shriveled-up old monkey-man! And I will never join you!"

King let out a choked roar of animal rage. "Kill him! Kill him now!"

The six haunters turned on David in a flash, streaking into the space where he stood, their arms coiled back to strike. But David wasn't there.

Beneath where he had been, in the very floor, King caught a glimpse of a dreamwalker's door as it slammed shut. David had let himself fall down through it so fast that even the haunters looked dumbfounded as they arced away, crying out in frustration. Harriet shrieked like a banshee, throwing herself at the door, but it was already fading to nothing.

Thomas King's head bobbed crazily as he craned to see the spot where David had been standing, his mouth open in astonished rage.

David Utherwise was gone.

In the moments that followed, the haunters drifted away from the center of the room, leaving the old man alone in his metal chair. Even ghosts are afraid of the King of the Haunting.

"Pack up," Thomas King said eventually to the man with the goatee, who was crouching wide-eyed behind his computer.

"We are leaving now. We have much work to do."

ACKNOWLEDGMENTS

I would like to thank the Chicken House for taking a chance on this book; Imogen Cooper, Rachel Leyshon, and the whole amazing team for taking the chance out and making it work; and Barry Cunningham, who took a chance on me once before.

Thanks to the late Rosemary Canter for sticking by me through thick and thin, and for guiding me through the maze. Thanks to Jodie Marsh for doing the same for me now.

Thanks to all those friends who have shown me their support and patience, especially Marcus, whose experience and advice have been more timely than he knows.

Thanks to my family for everything they have done, across three countries, to encourage and help me. Particular thanks go to my grandmother Nan Case, who not only shared her childhood memories of the war, but who even made a brief appearance in chapter twenty-one to check I was doing things properly.

And finally, my thanks and all my love go to Célia — who believed in me and proved it in countless ways — and to my two amazing, wonderful boys, Max and Benjy, who let me write this book between LEGO sessions. Without them, I don't think I would have written anything at all.